Infinite Dendrogram

1. The Beginning of Possibility

Sakon Kaidou
Illustrator: **Taiki**

Infinite Dendrogram: Volume 1
by Sakon Kaidou

Translated by Andrew Hodgson
Edited by Emily Sorensen

Copyright © 2016 Sakon Kaidou
Illustrations by Taiki

First published in Japan in 2016
Publication rights for this English edition arranged through Hobby Japan, Tokyo.

Find more books like this one at www.j-novel.club!

President and Publisher: Samuel Pinansky
Managing Editor: Aimee Zink

ISBN: 978-1-7183-5500-2
Printed in Korea
First Printing: September 2019
10 9 8 7 6 5 4 3 2 1

Infinite Dendrogram

1. The Beginning of Possibility

Sakon Kaidou

Illustrator: Taiki

Shu
Shu Starling
Shuichi Mukudori

Ray's real-life brother, and the person who invited him to the game in the first place. He wears a bear suit because, during character creation, he accidentally made his face look exactly the same as it was in real life.

Liliana
Liliana Grandria

The first tian (NPC) Ray ever encountered. Ray's first quest started due to her sister going missing. She is the Vice Commander of the Knights of the Royal Guard and has great popularity among the people of the country.

Babylon
Babylon

Rook's Embryo. An innocent and lovable succubus whose version of seduction doesn't go beyond shoulder massages and lap pillows, all thanks to the fact that her master is underage.

Ray
Ray Starling

Reiji Mukudori

A young man who — upon finishing his college entrance exams — began playing Infinite Dendrogram. Though generally a calm person, he has a strong will and sense of righteousness that allows him to keep struggling for as long as he needs to.

Rook
Rook Holmes

A newbie boy who Ray met out in the fields. His features are stunningly gentle and, according to him, there's little difference between his virtual looks and his real life looks. His job is Pimp and he primarily fights by using tamed monsters.

Nemesis
Nemesis

A girl that manifested as Ray's Embryo. She can change into weapons, and her first form allows her to become a greatsword. She also has quite an impressive appetite.

"Counter... Absorption!"

Nemesis spawned the barrier of light just in time to stop Gardranda's fist from hitting me directly, which greatly lowered its damage.

Contents

Chapter Zero) Infinite Dendrogram

July 15, 2043. On this date, the VRMMO *Infinite Dendrogram* was released around the world. It had been nearly half a century since man had first dreamt of a VRMMO (virtual reality massively multiplayer online) game.

In the 2000s, a variety of media, such as manga, anime, and video games, began to incorporate VRMMOs into their stories as the ultimate "dream game." From among a sea of creative entertainment, people eagerly looked forward to the release of a VRMMO, and in the 2010s, quasi-VR headsets were released, offering enhanced quality of sight and sound immersion.

Although at first a mere product of fantasy, VRMMOs were anticipated, developed, and then finally given form. In the 2030s, a small number of full-dive VRMMO games were released, allowing players to enter game worlds using all five of their senses.

The reason so few were released was due to the difficulty and enormous cost of development. This meant that only companies with leading technology and sufficient resources could even make an attempt. Or perhaps more were attempted, but never completed.

However, the few completed games that did make it out into the world were quickly met with disappointment. Unlike the VRMMOs depicted in fiction, these ones lacked in realism, they assailed the senses with discomfort, and their graphics were hardly any different from existing game systems. Also, despite guarantees of a safe design, players one after another fell ill and were taken to the hospital.

The development companies behind the initial dive VRMMOs all went bankrupt due to poor sales, bad reputations, and numerous lawsuits from afflicted players.

A reviewer from the time had the following to say about these games: "They managed to create the 'dream game,' but they weren't able to create the 'dream.'"

Dive VRMMO games continued to be developed, but none were made that could be considered a success.

That is… until *Infinite Dendrogram* was released.

The lack of information about *Infinite Dendrogram* before its release was abnormal.

It was kept secret the whole time, and on the day of release, the developers only made one announcement simultaneously across the global media networks. In it, they presented four key selling points for the game.

First: the five senses would be perfectly simulated.

Second: even if there were 100 million players, all of them would play in the same game world on a single server.

Third: players could choose how they'd view the game world, with options including realistic, 3D CG, and 2D anime.

Fourth: time within the game would flow three times faster than in the real world.

In response to the announcement, voices from around the world could be heard saying: "Is this really even possible?" "Just how much money and tech did they use to make this?" "Even for a case of misleading advertisement, isn't this going a bit far?"

Although the announcement had an impact, people found its content simply absurd. Out of everyone that saw the announcement, and this included non-gamers, 99.9998% didn't believe it and didn't buy the game.

The remaining 0.0002% of people, however, said things like, "It seems like a lie, but what if it's true…" "I'll try it," "I believe it," and they headed into stores to buy the game.

The necessary hardware cost around 10,000 yen, and was an extraordinary, some would even say reckless, pricing scheme. This helped lure in customers, with some saying, "Well, even if it's a lie, it's only 10,000 yen." So they bought it and started playing.

And once they logged into the game… they all knew it was the real thing.

Overcome with amazement at the game's realism, they would log out and look at their clocks, only to be astonished even more. The dreams they saw were all real — the "dream game" was now a reality.

The day after release, amid the clamor set off around the world by posts and comments from those who played the game, the developers released another announcement. This time, the contents of the game were detailed. A man named Lewis Carroll, the lead developer for *Infinite Dendrogram*, presented the broadcast announcement and said the following:

"The game system in *Infinite Dendrogram* has a special feature. Rather than relying on thousands of possible combinations of jobs and skills, this feature provides absolute and distinct uniqueness. This feature is the Embryo. It will offer players truly infinite possibilities and unique customization.

"Embryos will respond to personal circumstances and evolve from among an infinity of patterns. These patterns will not merely be different colors and parts, but will even include unique skills, allowing them to be truly limitless in scope. This is what *Infinite Dendrogram* is all about.

"Yes, *Infinite Dendrogram* will provide you with a new world and your very own unique possibility."

These words served as the last trigger needed to turn the game into a giant movement.

March 16, 2045, Reiji Mukudori

I, Reiji Mukudori, was sitting on my heels with the game in front of me and a nervous expression on my face.

It probably sounded like an exaggeration, but after waiting a year and a half, I was finally going to be able to play *Infinite Dendrogram*. So, of course, I was nervous.

"It's been a long road," I said.

The game had been announced and released during the summer of my junior year in high school — at the same time I had been motivating myself to do my best on my college entrance exams.

I'm sure there had been other game-loving high schoolers in their junior or senior years who had been left in despair like I had been, thinking, *why of all times did such an interesting-looking game have to come out during my entrance exam years?*

However, I had now successfully made it into a college in the city, and had taken the opportunity to start living on my own. I had finished moving yesterday, and my parents, who'd helped me, had already returned home.

I can play games as much as I want now!

I had headed to the game store this morning as soon as it opened and purchased a copy of *Infinite Dendrogram*. For about half a year after its release, it had apparently been difficult to get a hold of a copy, but a whole year and a half later, I was able to buy it without any trouble.

My older brother, by the way, was one of the ones who had bought the game on release day. This whole time, he had been calling me saying, "Hurry up and let's play *Dendro* together." I hadn't been sure if this made me feel bitter or simply jealous.

But all those feelings end today!

"...Let's do this!" I braced myself and opened the box. Inside were a helmet-type game system and a manual.

According to the manual, in order to enter the game world, all you needed to do was put on the helmet and turn on the switch. There were other explanations regarding visuals and time as well, but "amazing" would be the only way I could describe them.

Really, just how in the world did they make this game? I wondered. *It seems to be ten, maybe twenty years ahead of current technology...*

However, now wasn't the time to be scared. Following the instructions and recommendations in the manual, I put on the helmet and lay on my bed facing the ceiling. I then turned on the game.

Instantly, my vision went black.

"Hello and welcommme."

Before I knew it, I was no longer in my room, but in a space that appeared to be the study of a Western-style, wooden building. The voice had come from a cat I had never seen before, which sat in front of me on a seemingly well-made, wooden rocking chair.

…A cat?

"I'm sorry for the intrusion," I said. I was confused, but decided to respond with a greeting first.

"Yes, that's niiice," said the cat. "I like people with proper mannerrrs." The cat spoke in fluent Japanese, but with a slow drawl at the end of his sentences.

"Is this like the game's tutorial or something?" I asked.

"That's riiight. You'll be sent into the game after you finish configuring various settings herrre. Oh, I'm Cheshire, control AI No. 13 for *Infinite Dendrograaam*. Nice to meet youuu."

Control AI… I see. No wonder it's able to use fuzzy logic in its responses.

Control AIs are man-made cyber intelligences with entire modern supercomputers serving as their brains. Their primary uses, as the name suggests, are in control and management. It's said that just one of them can perfectly, and at high speeds, manage the databases and networks of a small country.

If this one is No. 13, does that mean there are twelve other control AIs of equal ability involved in managing this game?

"Nice to meet you, too," I said.

"All riiight," said the cat. "First up is selecting the graphiiics. Samples of these will alternate, so choose which one you like the best, okaaay?"

After the cat… Cheshire… said this, the surrounding scenery completely changed.

The study turned into a spacious area — a somewhat Middle Ages European townscape. There were many people walking about, and after a fixed period of time, their appearance would change. Actually, it wasn't their appearance, but rather, the way I saw them was changing. It went from a realistic appearance to CG, from CG to anime, and then back to realistic.

"...Wait, how are you doing this?" I asked.

"Imagery perceived by sight is processed by the brain, after all, so there's a waaay," replied Cheshire. "And so, the way you see can be changed like this, but which one will you go wiiith? You can change it later by using an itemmm."

"I'll leave it as-is," I said.

I thought it would be better to see normally until I got used to the game, so that's what I did. Although I *was* interested in how it would feel to touch something that looked like it was from an anime.

"Okaaay," said Cheshire, and the scenery reverted back to the study. "Next is your player naaame. What do you want your name to be in the gaaame?"

"I'll go with Ray Starling." This was a name I had often used in games before. It was simply a distorted version of my first name and the English translation of my last name, Mukudori.

"Okay, then I'll set it to thaaat," said the cat. "Next, the settings for your appearaaance."

After Cheshire said this, a featureless mannequin and a bunch of window screens appeared before me. These screens contained words such as "height," "weight," "bust," their corresponding sliders, as well as facial features.

"These are..." I said slowly.

"Use those parts and sliders to make your own avatar for the gaaame," said Cheshire. "Oh, you can also make it into an animal like me, or even change your genderrr."

No, I'm not so sure about changing my gender in a game this realistic...

"It's okay to take your time and think it overrr," said Cheshire. "We have three times the amount of time here than in the real wooorld. ...Oh yeah, there was that one time when someone repeatedly logged in and out and spent one month in Earth time making their avatarrr."

That's a tremendous amount of effort and concentration, so I don't think I'll be able to go that far.

It wasn't just because of the sheer number of sliders and parts, but the values you could set for each of them were way too exact. It was almost like they were telling me to make a real human face.

For a beginner, that's way too difficult, I thought. *In that case...*

"Can I just use my real appearance as the default and make some changes to that?" I asked.

"You can do thaaat," Cheshire said and waved his tail.

The mannequin turned into me.

"Now you just need to make some changes using this as your baaase," said the cat.

"Thanks," I said.

It was fairly simple after this. I left most of the settings the same, but changed my hair color to blond, and changed my ethnicity as well, which altered my face. While I worked on this, I wondered about what my face would look like if I set it to anime or CG. *I'd be able to see it if I played without changing any of the settings, but... no, it's better that I don't play online with my actual face.*

And like that, I finished creating my avatar after about thirty minutes or so.

"And… finished," I said.

"Okaaay. Then I'll hand over your starting itemmms." Cheshire waved a padded paw in the air and a bag fell from empty space. "This is your storage bag, also known as your inventoryyy. The storage space inside it is from a different dimensionnn. You can store items in here if they're yours, but on the flip side, you can't put any items in here that arrren't."

"I see," I said.

It's a useful bag, but I guess that means it can't be used to commit crimes.

"Well," Cheshire continued, "if it's an item that dropped from someone you PKed, or one that you stole with the Steal skill, then it'll go innn."

I fell silent. *I don't know what to say to that.*

"By the way, if a player's Steal skill is high enough in level, they can steal an item from even inside this 4D pocket-like item baaag," the cat said. "So be carefulll."

Now just how exactly am I supposed to be careful against a thief that's capable of stealing from the fourth dimension?

"This bag is for beginners, but there are also other types, such as ones that are tough to steal from, small ones, and ones with a lot of capacityyy," the cat said.

"What is the capacity of this one, by the way?" I asked.

"The size is about equal to one classroom, and the weight is maybe around one ton in Earth measuremeeents."

"It can fit quite a lot," I said. "That's plenty."

"It's apparently not enough if you're a merchant, thooough," said the cat. "They're likely to buy new onnnes. Oh, item bags will scatter their contents around if they get destroyed, so pay attention to their durabilityyy."

"I'll be careful," I said.

"Next is a set of beginner equipmeeent. Ray, what will you piiick?" Cheshire pulled a catalog from a bookshelf and showed it to me.

In it were full sets of various types of armor. There was the typical Eastern and Western style armor, but in addition to these, there were traditional outfits from China, India, the Middle East, and South America. On the opposite end, there were even outfits that seemed to be from Sci-Fi movies.

"I'll go with this, then," I said, choosing a combination that consisted of innerwear, a jacket, jeans, and a bandana. The look vaguely resembled the male protagonist from a masterpiece game of the last century.

I played retro games as well as modern games thanks to my brother, so although the look was a bit behind the times, it matched my tastes.

"Okaaay. What will you pick for your first weaponnn?" the cat asked.

I turned to a different page in the catalog. All kinds of weapons were listed, including a wooden sword, a practice sword with a dull blade, a knife, a bow, a sling, and a staff.

I should choose something that matches my outfit.

"I'll go with the knife," I said.

"Okaaay. So for your weapon and equipment... Wazaaaam." It was hard to tell if Cheshire's voice was energetic or not, but as he said that, my appearance changed. My outfit switched to the one I had just chosen, and a knife now hung from a belt at my waist. Most impressive of all, my appearance had changed to mirror the avatar I'd made earlier.

"Wow, this is something else," I said as I looked at myself in the full-length mirror Cheshire had provided. *It looks pretty good.*

"Oh yeah, that's right, here's your starting moneyyy." Cheshire handed me five coins that appeared to be made out of silver. "Five silver coins is worth 5,000 lirrr. One rice ball costs about 10 lir, by the waaay."

Then 1 lir would be about 10 yen, I thought. *In that case, 5,000 lir is a lot of money.*

"Is it okay to get this much in the beginning?" I asked.

"Yep. Be sure to learn how to make money before it runs out, thooough," he said.

In other words, I probably won't get any more after this, so I should use it wisely.

"Well then, it's finally time to transfer your Embryooo," he said.

"Oh, the thing in all the rumors!" I said.

Embryos.

I'd heard they were the greatest feature in *Infinite Dendrogram*. They offered true uniqueness and evolved in infinite ways based on the player. They were partners that exceeded the likes of items and equipment.

My brother, who was already playing the game, said, "If this hadn't been a well-made dive VRMMO, but just a regular MMO instead, I'm sure it still would've been a hit as long as it had the Embryo system."

"Do you need an explanation on Embryoooos?" asked the cat.

"Since you're offering, I guess I should listen to it," I said. *It's probably best to hear the tutorials for unique systems, after all.*

"Okaaay," said the cat. "All players receive an Embryo at the starrrt. The only time they'll look the same is while they are in this zeroth fooorm. With the first form and beyond, they'll change in completely different ways based on their ownerrr."

"Ohhh," I said. *As a gamer, I can't help but be fascinated by features that allow for something to be totally unique.*

"Although the possibilities are infinite, there are some rough categorieees," added the cat.

"Oh, I didn't know that," I said. This was because I'd done my best to block out any information before I started playing. I'd been worried that I might abandon my entrance exams if I'd found out something about the game, as it would have made it harder to resist playing it.

The only information I'd heard from my brother was that "it's fun." It might have been the case that he'd also been worried about my exams, and so he hadn't told me anything specific.

"The broad categories arrre: Type Arms — a device type that players can equip as a weapon or armorrr. Type Guardian — a monster type that protects the playerrr. Type Chariot — a vehicle type that players can riiide. Type Castle — a building type that players can reside innn. Type Territory — a barrier type that players can deployyy. That's about ittt."

"Ohhh," I said. I was starting to get excited to see how my Embryo would turn out.

"Also, besides these ones, there are rare and advanced categories that an Embryo can evolve into, tooo. There are even categories that are unique to one Embryooo. It'd be nice if you could get onnne."

"Wow!" I exclaimed. "But if that's the case, there are bound to be players who keep resetting their character until they get a rare category."

"Ahh, you can't remake your character in this gaaame," said the cat.

"Huh?"

"Even if someone bought different hardware and played the game, that person would log in as the same character as the first tiiime," Cheshire explained. "Their Embryo would also be the saaame. This is because we keep records on our side of users' brain wave dataaa."

"......" I was silent.

They record our brain wave data... I thought. *Yeah, that sounds kind of scary.*

"Even if they were able to reset, it's all based on that person anywaaay, so I think their Embryo would end up exactly the saaame," said the cat.

Is that how it works?

"Annnd... while we were talking, your Embryo finished transferrinnng," the cat added.

"Huh? ...Ah." I realized that on the back of my left hand was now embedded a faintly glowing oval gem.

"That's your Embryooo," Cheshire said. "It'll be stuck to your left hand during its zeroth form, but it'll come off after it hatches and reaches its first forrrm."

In other words, I guess it's sort of like I'm incubating an egg.

"By the way, is there any chance it can break while it's an egg?" I asked.

"That won't happennn," said the cat. "Any damage an Embryo receives while in its zeroth form will be passed on to the playerrr."

Ahh, I see. So that means the Embryo will be safe even if the player dies.

"But after they hatch, Embryos can be damaged and break like anything elllse," the cat said. "They'll self-repair over time, thooough."

It's kind of like a living creature.

"By the way, after your Embryo turns into its first form, a tattoo of a crest will appear where the egg waaas," said the cat. "It serves as a sort of identification for players in this worrrld. Without it, you wouldn't be able to tell players apart from NPCees."

"Is that so?" I asked.

But no, there's no way you would mistake an NPC for a human… right?

"Also, the crest has the ability to store your Embryooo," said the cat. "When you don't need it, you can keep your Embryo in your left hannnd. You'll be together with it as long as you play this game, so please take care of ittt."

"Got it," I said.

I'm still not sure how my Embryo will evolve, but that's fine. It all comes down to oneself anyway, so I guess it'll work out on its own.

"It's nice to meet you, partner," I said.

Needless to say, there was no response from my Embryo, but I got the feeling that it shined slightly.

"Lastly, please choose which nation to joiiin." Cheshire laid out a map on the study's desk. It was an old scroll map. After it was unfurled, however, pillars of light rose up from seven locations on the map, and from within them, I could see various towns. "The nations with pillars of light are the ones you can join in the beginninnng. What you see in the pillars is the capital of each nationnn."

Floating in letters of light around each of the pillars was the name and explanation of each nation.

Surrounded by castle walls is a Western fantasy town, with a white limestone castle at its center.

Kingdom of Altar: the land of knights.

Sakura petals dance through the air in this city made of wood. A Japanese-style castle looms high above it.

Tenchi: the land of blades.

Subtle elegance hangs in the air of these mountains. A large river flows for all eternity through its valleys.

Huang He Empire: the land of the hermits.

Black smoke rises from countless factories and forms a cloud that blocks out the sky. On the ground is a modern day city made of steel.

Dryfe Imperium: the land of machines.

Bazaars nestle up to a giant oasis, surrounded by desert as far as the eye can see.

Caldina: the commercial city-state union.

Made from connecting countless large ships together, this man-made landmass floats in the middle of the open sea.

Granvaloa: the maritime nation.

At the base of Yggdrasil deep in the forest, elves, fairies, and demi-humans live in this secluded garden of flowers.

Legendaria: the homeland of fairies.

"Ohhh…" I said.

Seeing this makes me want to visit every one of them, I thought. *Tenchi has a similar feel to the Azuchi-Momoyama Period, while Huang He gives off a sense of Chinese fantasy. Dryfe seems like they'd have robots, and just walking through the bazaars of Caldina would feel like I was sightseeing. The seas of Granvaloa call out to me to seek adventure, and as for Legendaria, there's no need to even think of a reason.*

However...

"I'll go with the Kingdom of Altar," I said.

"Okaaay," said the cat. "By the way, as a quick survey, what would your reason for choosing that beee?"

"My brother is waiting for me."

"Oh, is that so..."

I had called my brother from the store right after I'd bought the game, and he'd said, "Then I'll be waiting for you in the Kingdom of Altar's capital."

...Since he's waiting, I have no choice, I thought. *But why did he choose the Kingdom of Altar, anyway? I'm pretty sure he likes robots and warships, so why didn't he go with the Dryfe Imperium or Granvaloa? Well, I guess I'll just have to ask him in person.*

"There are events that allow you to change the nation you belong to, so don't feel so down about ittt," said the cat.

"Yeah, thanks..." I said.

I need to change gears, I thought. *The Kingdom of Altar seems kind of plain and normal, but it just might be a nice place.*

"Okay then, I'm going to send you to the Kingdom of Altar's royal capital, Alteaaa," said the cat.

"Ah, just a second. What are the goals in this game?"

In all the games I'd played since I was a kid, even online ones, they'd had established goals such as defeating the evil god or demon king. I thought this game would be the same, but when I asked this to Cheshire...

"Anythinnng," was the response I got.

"Anything?" I asked.

"That's what I meannnt. Anythinnng. You can become a hero or the demon king, a king or a slave, a good person or an evil person. You can do something, or you can do nothing. You can stay in *Infinite Dendrogram*, or leave it. It's all up to you. If it's possible, then you can do anything you want." Cheshire's way of speaking had changed. "Just like the Embryo in your left hand, what's about to begin is infinite in possibility."

His speech had morphed from the slow drawl. It was almost as if he were narrating something.

"Welcome to *Infinite Dendrogram*. We warmly welcome you," a voice said.

As soon as these words were spoken, the study disappeared from my surroundings. The desk, the bookshelf, and even Cheshire, vanished, and I was left floating in the air.

"Huh?"

Below me was a familiar-looking world. I was looking down on the same continent I'd seen on the map just moments earlier. Before long, almost as if my body was being sucked down toward one point on the continent — the Kingdom of Altar — I started to fall at a great speed.

And just like that, I set foot in the world of *Infinite Dendrogram*.

In front of the South Gate, Royal Capital Altea, Kingdom of Altar, Ray Starling

"I thought I was going to die…" My heart was pounding after being suddenly dropped from the sky, and I forced in breaths to help calm myself down.

The feeling of the fall still remained with me:

The sight of scenery changing vividly before me at high speed.

The sound of my body scraping against the air as I fell.

The chill in the air whipping around me.

The smell of wind I had never smelt before.

The taste of dirt from the ground — I had fallen over in a daze, confused at how abnormally safe my landing had been. There hadn't been any pain — it was apparently turned off by default — but all five of my other senses had perceived this world just as they would the real one.

"This… is too real," I said quietly.

A true dive VRMMO… I finally had a sense that the dream game had become a reality.

I did think the theatrics had been a bit over the top, but I had now made my way into the world of *Infinite Dendrogram*.

I looked about my surroundings and saw a large gate behind me. It was encompassed by white castle walls that stretched up as far as I could see. There were also soldiers clad in Western-style armor serving as its gatekeepers.

This gate is one of the places I saw in Cheshire's room, so it's probably safe to say this is Altea, the Kingdom of Altar's royal capital.

The gate was open leading into the town, and for a while now, carriages and people had been coming and going.

It seems I can pass through just fine.

As it was my first time, I timidly — or, more accurately, suspiciously — passed through the gate and was able to enter the town without any trouble.

"All right," I said with relief. *It looks like they don't do inspections for people entering or leaving Altea.*

Since I'd safely made it into town, all that remained was to head to where I was supposed to meet my brother.

"If I remember correctly, he said a large water fountain on the capital's central street," I said. "He did say I could reach it by heading straight from the entrance, but… hmm… I'll take a look just in case."

I recited the words "main menu" in my mind, and just like it was described in the manual, a game window appeared in front of me. The window was split into two; on the right side was my name and a simplified view of my stats, while on the left side was a list of various menu commands.

I glanced over at my stats and saw that my current level was 0. Jobs in *Infinite Dendrogram* supposedly each had their own level, and since I was currently jobless, my level was stuck at 0.

"Map… Here it is." I found what I was looking for in the menu and opened it up. A new window appeared displaying a map of the Royal Capital Altea.

Normally, a map had to be filled in by traveling around or by buying maps. However, the manual explained that a player's starting area, the capital of the nation they joined and its surroundings, got input into the map from the start.

This is useful.

"I see. I see," I murmured.

The city of Altea was circular in shape and surrounded by castle walls. These walls had a gate at each of the four cardinal points, and stretching out from each of them was a large, stone-paved road leading to the center of the city.

The roads would have intersected into a cross if they had continued; however, this was not the case. At the center of the royal capital was another ring of castle walls, and inside it was the area for nobility. Special permission was required to enter this area, and at its center was the royal castle.

Well, I probably won't have any need to go there for a while, I thought.

The central street we were supposed to meet at was the one running from the South Gate to the nobility area. The gate I had just passed through, by the way, was the South Gate.

So if I simply head straight, I should be able to reach the water fountain.

I was walking while looking at my map and thinking this, when...

"Ah?!"

"Huh?" Somehow, I had locked eyes with a woman I didn't know. She had run out from a side alley, and since I'd been engrossed in my map, I hadn't noticed until she was right upon me. I reacted late and wasn't able to avoid her, causing us to collide. As a result, I was flung more than fifteen meters away.

"Gah..." I muttered. *That felt like it caused some serious damage.*

As a matter of fact, the window screen I still had open showed that I'd lost 80% of my HP. In addition to this, I appeared to have broken some bones. The status effects "broken left arm" and "broken right leg" were now being displayed.

Just one collision with a lady, and I receive such near-fatal wounds as these... come on, just how shockingly frail am I?

"A-Are you all right?!" The woman that ran into me rushed over to my side with a pale look on her face. She had soft hair and kind facial features... and was wearing white, metal armor that looked absurdly heavy.

I wouldn't be surprised if that thing weighs a hundred kilos.

"I-I'm…" I tried to tell her, "I'm okay. It was no big deal." However, my body was still numb from the damage and I couldn't properly move my tongue.

"I'm so sorry! Force Heal!" Her hand instantly glowed white and particles of light fell from it onto my body. My HP was completely healed, and the status effects for my broken bones were also gone.

"Oh… ohhh…"

That must've been healing magic. It was a common occurrence in video games to nearly die and then get completely healed, but this was what it was like to actually experience it. …*It's kind of scary.*

"I'm terribly sorry! This is all because I wasn't paying attention to what's in front of me while running…" she said.

"N-No, I was also looking away… By the way, are you okay?" I asked. We'd collided with enough force to give me near-fatal wounds, so I was worried that she might have been injured as well, but… she was completely unharmed.

She appeared to be a really high-level player, and the equipment she was wearing looked to be of a high-grade as well. Her stats, then, would most likely be high, too.

So that's why our collision ended up the way it did.

"I'm fine," she replied. "But I caused you to get such a terrible injury…"

"Oh no, y-you were kind enough to heal me, so I'll be just fine." I couldn't help but speak politely. On top of that, I was fairly sure my voice was shaking. The damage from when we'd collided had caused me to lose my nerve.

"B-By the way, it looked like you were in quite the hurry. Is there something wrong?" When I asked her this, the woman suddenly appeared to have remembered something.

"Well actually, my little sister left the house and I was in the middle of searching for her."

"Your sister?" I asked.

"Yes. This is her in this picture. Have you seen her anywhere?" Asking this, she took out a picture and showed it to me. *Although this world has a fantasy setting, it would appear that pictures are readily available.* In the picture was a cute little girl. She looked like a younger version of the woman in front of me, but with straight hair instead of wavy.

Her sister, huh? I thought. *Like me and my brother, she must be playing this game together with her sister.*

I could only stay silent as she looked at me in desperation. I felt bad for her, but I hadn't seen her sister. "I'm sorry. I just started recently, and I just entered this town through that gate a moment ago..."

"Is that so... Then she might already be inside... Um, this is my contact information," the woman added. "If you happen to see my sister anywhere, please contact me! Also, I'm really sorry for running into you!" She took out a piece of paper, wrote something on it, and then handed it to me.

"There's no need to apologize, so please go and search for your sister," I said.

"Thank you... Well then, goodbye!" she said and darted off, leaving me with a memo in my hand. The following was written on it: "Liliana Grandria, Knights of the Royal Guard Vice Commander, Kingdom of Altar."

"Huh?"

Characters I had never seen before were being translated into Japanese in my head. More shocking than that, however, was the rest of the memo...

"The quest 'Search for Milianne Grandria, Difficulty Level 5' has started. Please see the quest screen for further details."

I was at a loss for words.

Umm... yeah.

Although she looked like a real human to me, this meant that she wasn't actually a player, but instead...

"She was an NPC?!"

And just like that, I realized again just how unbelievably realistic *Infinite Dendrogram* was.

Shortly after I met Liliana and received my first quest, I arrived at the large water fountain on the central street where I was to meet my brother. On the way there, I had a look at the help information, and apparently difficulty level 5 quests were supposed to be undertaken by a party of advanced players. So without a doubt, it wasn't something I could partake in.

Why would a quest like this be given to a beginner, anyway? I wondered. *I should just ask Bro about it for now.*

Thinking about this, I had hurried my way to the water fountain, and...

The scene that greeted me left me speechless.

There was a nearly two-meter-tall *bear costume* with a sign reading "Welcome little brother" parked in front of the water fountain.

"...What in the world is that?" I managed.

There's no way... But... No, no way... But then again...

This is where we're supposed to meet.

There likely aren't that many people out there waiting for their younger brother.

He wouldn't know my character name, and it's not like he can use my real one, so it makes sense to write "little brother" on the sign. I get that part.

But...

"Why the costume?" I asked aloud.

It's going to take some guts to talk to that thing.

For a little while now, children had been gathering around the bear. I couldn't tell if they were NPCs or players, but they seemed to be very attached to the bear. They were climbing onto its head and lap, as well as hanging from its arms.

I wasn't getting anywhere at this rate, so I steeled my nerves, and decided to talk to it. "Excuse me. I would like to ask you something..."

"Yes, yes, just bear with me for a moment."

Was that a pun...? I thought. *I get that you're a bear, but still...*

"Are you Shuichi Mukudori... Forget it, is that you, Bro?" I asked.

"Indeed it is," he said. "Hey, Reiji."

...I so wanted to be wrong.

"I'm glad we were able to meet up." The bear — I mean, my brother, Shuichi Mukudori — stood up and said, "Shall we go, then?"

He then pulled out some candy from his storage bag — or rather, a pocket attached to his stomach — and passed them out to the children gathered around him.

Is he pretending to be that famous character? I thought. *In that case, he should be a cat, or at least a raccoon.*

"Yay!"

"Thanks, Mr. Bear!"

The children received their candy and then headed off in cheerful spirits. Before long, only my brother and I were left remaining.

"I guess first up should be introductions," my brother said. "My name here is Shu Starling."

"I'm Ray Starling," I said. "So like I thought, we did end up with the same name."

Since it was so easy to use the English translation of our last name, Mukudori, whenever someone in my family made a character, eight out of ten times we'd end up with the name Starling.

"So, what should we do?" my brother asked. "It looks like your Embryo hasn't hatched yet, so should I show you around the town? While we're at it, if you want to pick up some equipment, I can lend you some money at no interest."

"Oh, well, actually..." I explained to him about the quest I had just received.

"Really... A quest from Liliana," he said. "I've never received one before."

"Really, though, why would I get a quest like this when I'm at level 0?" I asked.

"That's because this world is realistic, and a lot of quests are triggered by coincidence," he said. "Incidents don't occur in order to create a quest, but quests arise when there happens to be an incident.

There are many quests you won't be able to trigger intentionally, and there'll be a lot of cases where you end up going on one you didn't intend to. Well, consider it a good baptism... you were able to get a sense for how realistic the people of this world are, right?"

"Yeah," I said. "It was so realistic, in fact, I'm a bit suspicious as to whether I'm talking to the real you, or just an NPC pretending to be you."

"Of course it's me," he said. "You better bear-lieve it."

"Stop it with the bear stuff!" It made me feel weird because I knew the person inside and could picture him.

"Ha ha ha. By the way, Liliana is a contender for the first or second most popular person in this kingdom. She even has a fan club made up of both players and tians."

"There's a fan club... Oh, and what's a 'tian'?" I asked.

"A person that isn't a player," he said. "Well, you can just think of it as the general term for NPCs."

"Interesting... so that means even NPCs participate in fan clubs," I said.

"According to the developers, 'their personalities and ability to think are on the same level as humans.' So that kind of thing is the bear minimum of their capabilities."

Really, this game is so sophisticated, it's almost alarming.

"By the way, did it say anywhere in the quest information about where to search?" my brother asked.

"No, nothing," I said. "They're telling me to search for someone without any hints. That's why I don't know where or how I should start."

Although to be accurate, this memo would count as a hint, I figured.

"Hmm," he said. "Can you hand me that memo for a sec?"

"Here you go."

My brother took the memo, but instead of reading its contents, he flipped it over and showed its back to me.

Dear Sister,

The shops were all out of remberries, so I'm going to go get some. I'm bringing bug-repellent incense, so I'll be okay. Please look forward to it and wait for me.

From Milia.

"Isn't this…" I said slowly.

"She must have been in a real hurry," said my brother. "She wrote her contact information on the back of the memo her sister left and gave it to you."

I didn't notice it either. Since the memo had been written on parchment paper, I hadn't been able to see through it.

"What are these remberries?" I asked.

"Remberries are one of the high-grade specialties from around here," he said. "Just think of them as really delicious fruit."

"'Go get' must mean that she went to go search for them," I said. *Milianne seems to be quite the proactive kid.*

"There are two places around here where you can get remberries," said my brother. "The first is an orchard within the capital. You can harvest there if you pay the fee of 5,000 lir per basket."

Isn't that the entire amount you get at the beginning of the game? I thought. *That's expensive!*

"The other one is just outside the South Gate. It's called Old Reve Orchard."

"Old Reve Orchard?" I asked.

"Some things happened, and insect-type monsters have taken up living there. So it's an abandoned orchard," he said. "Even now, there are a lot of fruit trees growing wild there, but at the same time, it's become a nest for monsters."

"So the stuff about bug-repellent incense must mean..." I said slowly.

"Probably so."

That's way too proactive!

"Go to the safer orchard!" I shouted.

"5,000 lir is asking a bit much from a child," said my brother. "Even the market value of 50 lir for one would be tough."

"But still, that doesn't mean..."

"Old Reve Orchard, by the way, is a place players usually mistake for being beginner-friendly due to how close it is to the starting point," he said. "However, it's a dungeon where beginners enter and then get killed right off the bat. It's also known as the 'newbie killer.'"

This couldn't be any worse.

I'd just realized this now, but when I'd met Liliana, she had probably been headed toward the old orchard. When Liliana had said, "Then she might already be inside," she must have been convinced that Milianne had already entered the orchard because I hadn't seen her after passing through the South Gate.

"Well," my brother continued, "in any case, it'd be best to clear this one quickly. It's probably the type where you'll fail if time elapses."

"What?" I asked.

"I told you, right?" he said. "In this world, incidents are realistic and occur spontaneously. That's why there are no guarantees that things will be fine until the player clears the quest, unlike in older games."

"Yeah, but…"

"Let me tell you this from my experience as one of the starting players," he said. "There have been examples in the past of people dying. A sage revered as a hero, the commander of the knights, and even the king of this nation — they all died."

"……" I didn't know what to say.

"Despite that, the world of *Infinite Dendrogram* carries on without a hitch," he said. "That's because it's real."

I began to imagine…

What if the girl in the picture gets attacked by monsters and tragically dies? Imagining it gave me an unpleasant feeling. Thinking about Liliana caused those feelings to sink even further. *I know that they're NPCs, but…*

"That'd leave a bad taste in my mouth," I said.

"Wouldn't it?" my brother agreed. "So let's clear it and shoot for a happy ending."

I couldn't see my brother's face because of the bear costume, but I had the feeling that he was smiling on the inside.

Thus, my brother and my newbie self formed a party, and we set off to tackle my first quest.

The quest to clear was "Search for Milianne Grandria."

The difficulty level, 5.

The location was the trap dungeon "newbie killer," Old Reve Orchard.

The goal… was a happy ending.

Start quest.

Chapter One ⟩ Nemesis

"By the way, have you pawsed to look at your starting stats yet?" my brother asked me as we headed toward Old Reve Orchard.

Come to think of it, not yet, I realized.

"Status information… Here it is." I clicked on the option and a new window appeared displaying my stats.

My level was of course 0, and I currently had no job equipped. It seemed multiple jobs could be equipped at once, and so in addition to the level for each job, there was also a total level. My level for both was still 0.

The other stats displayed were HP, MP, SP, STR, END, DEX, AGI, and LUC. Each of them was fairly low; other than having 98 HP and 23 SP, the rest were all below 20. I didn't have anything to compare them with, but those stats were probably weak.

…But then again, I guess there's no way a newbie at level 0 would be strong, I reminded myself.

"So I'll be going into this dungeon called the 'newbie killer' at level 0, won't I?" I asked.

"You'll bearly make it past zero if you don't equip a job," said my brother. "Do you want to get one before we go?"

"…No, it doesn't look like we have the time. I'll go like this," I said.

It'd be unbearable if the girl in the picture were to die while we were doing that, I thought. *The most important thing right now is speed.*

My brother and I talked as we ran.

"Can I ask you a few things?" I asked.

"I guess I can bear that."

"I didn't see a stat for INT, so what factors into magic strength?" I asked. "There is magic in this game, right?" *Liliana did use healing magic, after all.*

"It's based on your max MP and the level of the magic skill," said my brother. "Also, the total amount of MP you pour into it. And there is no INT stat in this game, by the way. Your intelligence is the bear basics, yourself, after all."

That makes sense, I thought. *I wouldn't really get what it meant if you told me my intelligence went up.*

"Oh, and as for skills that use SP, their strength isn't based on your SP, but on various other related stats," my brother went on. "Well, those various stats will receive adjustments from your Embryo, so their variation will be infinite."

"That sounds complicated," I said.

"If you bear with it, I'm sure it'll go fine! How things turn out will be a pawsitive reflection of your individuality."

...He's really getting into those bear puns, isn't he?

"Oh, yeah. Let me give you some accessories I have." Bro Bear handed me some items from his bag.

When I looked at them, these included: ten Healing Potions that could easily heal me to max health, one Lifesaving Brooch, and four Dragonscale Ward accessories.

"The Lifesaving Brooch bears the brunt of your fatal damage, but it has a 10% chance of breaking," my brother explained. "How many times this is checked is determined by the amount of damage divided by your HP. The Dragonscale Ward will reduce incoming damage by 90%, but it'll break after one use."

I see, they appear to be throwaway accessories, but they'll definitely help.

"This game has level and stat restrictions for equipment," said my brother. "So I'll beef you up with these accessories instead since they don't have any level restrictions."

There are five slots for equipping accessories, so they'll all fit perfectly.

"Thanks, Bro… Hey that reminds me, what's the death penalty in this game?"

A death penalty: it was a feature found in many online games. To put it simply, it was some sort of demerit for a character that died. They could lose levels, for example, or have their stats lowered for a period of time.

Since he's trying to help me avoid dying, this game must have some kind of a death penalty, I thought. This was why I wanted to ask him what that penalty was, but…

"A 24 hour login ban."

The answer I received was unexpected.

"…A what?" I asked.

"If you die in this game, you won't be able to log in for 24 hours in real time, or 72 hours in the game world," he said.

…Are they out of their minds? I thought incredulously. *I can't believe there's a game that won't let you play it as a death penalty.*

"The frightening thing about this penalty isn't that you can't play the game; it's that three days will pass by in *Infinite Dendrogram* without you," he said. "So for example, if you're in the middle of a quest like we are, you'll have to abandon the quest for three days.

When you're in a world as realistic as this one... that's what's so scary."

What would happen if Bro Bear and I were to leave this quest alone for three days?

...The answer to that was obvious.

"I'll tag along and try not to die," I said. "I'm not sure how useful I'll be at level 0, though."

Or more like, I won't be of any use at all.

"By the way, like I mentioned earlier, Old Reve Orchard is a trap dungeon known as the 'newbie killer,'" said my brother. "Innocent newbs starting *Dendro* without any prior knowledge enter the dungeon saying, 'Yaay, I'm gonna go on an adventure nearby,' and then it's game over, they get their bear butts exposed and smacked to the extreme. They get insta-killed and can't log in for a whole day."

It's like a trauma-generating machine.

"However, it's strange. Why is the difficulty level 5? Based on the levels of the monsters in the dungeon... it's too high."

As I listened to my brother mutter this, we passed through the South Gate of the Royal Capital Altea.

The orchard was located about ten minutes' running distance from the South Gate. It was surrounded by a metal fence, and a worn-out sign at the entrance read, "Welcome to Reve Orchard." The place, however, seemed long-abandoned. Plants grew wild, and the color on the sign had faded.

"Well then, it's time to storm in, but..." My brother stopped in front of the entrance to Old Reve Orchard, which was now a den of insect monsters. Right after that, a new window appeared before me.

"Party request from Shu Starling.

Will you join this party? Yes / No"

"It'll be easier to cover for you if I can constantly track your status," he said.

"Okay, got it." I clicked "Yes" on the window, and as soon as I did, a screen opened up showing the status of our party. My brother's name had been added to it as well.

There's space on the party screen for four more players, so this game must have a maximum party limit of six.

Displayed along with my brother's name were also his stats. However...

"What's going on with this?" I asked.

On my brother's status screen, everything other than his name was blacked out, including even his level and HP.

"Ah. That's the concealing ability of this suit," he said. "If there's a difference in level between me and an enemy or ally, then they can't bear witness to my stats."

What kind of ability is that? I thought. *That makes it harder to help with support magic... Not that I have any... Oh, that reminds me.*

"Hey Bro, I didn't get the chance to ask this because of the quest, but why are you wearing a bear costume?" I asked.

My brother rubbed the eyes of his costume with his bear fingers. "It's a story that'll leave us both in tears."

"We're kind of busy, so hurry up and answer my question," I said.

"My little brother is looking at me so coldly..." he grumbled to himself, before gradually starting to speak. "So, you know how there's a part where you create your character, right?"

"Yeah."

"It was a pain to make it from scratch, so I tried to do it using myself as the base."

"So did I."

"Well, I made a bit of a mistake…"

"A mistake…" I began. "What did you do?"

"I accidentally confirmed it without making any changes."

"…Oh boy."

So in other words, inside the suit was my brother's actual face and appearance. Playing an online game with your actual face was a risky thing to do. This was especially true in my brother's case.

Yeah, with that you'd have no choice but to wear something like a suit.

"By the way, the reason I chose this kingdom is because I saw a store in the capital selling costumes," he said.

"Oh, so that's why you didn't go somewhere that was more along your tastes, like Dryfe or Granvaloa," I said.

"Drastic times called for drastic measures… Oh, and by the way, costume number one cost 4,980 lir."

"That's almost the entire starting amount!" I cried. *Just how exactly did he get by in the beginning?!*

"On top of that, it was a gag item with no defense," he said. "I was one of the first players, so there was no information available. Really, from that hopeless start, it's been a path full of hardship until I got a hold of this costume."

"So what abilities does this one have?" I asked.

"Take a look."

"Ultimate Suit Series: Hind Bear
Ancient Legendary Armor

DEF +903 (beary high)

Skills:

Disguise: completely hides your stats from anyone with a total level of 100 less than yours.

Built-In AC: a built-in AC designed for any environment. The perfect temperature any time, any place.

Power Assist: supports movement with muscle motors. STR +903.

Bullet-Proof Made: able to withstand even crossfire. Reduces damage from physical ranged attacks by 903.

Knife-Proof Made: feel safe on even the days with a lot of assassins. Reduces damage from physical close-ranged attacks by 903.

Utility Bear Hands: mysteriously, these hands can properly grab things, and they can be used quite skillfully. Increased damage to fish and insect monsters.

????: ∎"

What's with this overly high-spec gag item?

"What's '+903 (beary high)' supposed to mean?" I asked. "Is it actually as high as that implies, though? Wait, what level are you anyway, Bro Bear?"

I can't see his stats at all right now, so at the very least, his total level should be over 100, but…

"That's a bearied se-cr-et," he said.

Man, that's irritating.

"All right then, that's enough of our comedy skit for now. Let's go save the girl."

"…About 90% of the material came from you, Bro Bear, but I agree," I said. "Let's go."

We made our way into Old Reve Orchard. Once inside, we followed a path of weeds and broken signs. On one of the signs was written, "500 metels to remberry field."

"I take it that means 500 meters?" I asked.

"Pretty easy to understand, isn't it?" my brother agreed. "Also… have you noticed?"

"…The sound, right?" I asked. "I've been hearing it for a while now."

From the direction the sign pointed in, I could hear clashing sounds and the cries of something inhuman. I couldn't see anything due to all the plants in the way; however, Liliana, who'd entered the dungeon ahead of us, was without a doubt fighting something.

That was when I realized that the sound of battle could only be heard from the remberry field, while everywhere else was quiet.

"Are there no other players here?" I asked.

"Ahh, there are a lot of people with trauma from this dungeon," said my brother. "On top of that, the drop items and materials you can gather at these levels aren't all that great, either. Also, the insects attack in swarms, and a lot of them can cause Poison or Paralyze, so a counter for status effects is a must."

I guess it's what you'd call an unpopular hunting ground.

"Well, thanks to that, it does make it easier for me to fight…" my brother muttered. "Baldr, activate in second form."

"Ready." An electronic voice I hadn't heard before answered him.

The back of my brother's left hand began to glow through his costume, and then something suddenly flew out from it. The bear's silhouette now had the following strange additions to it: a ring of gun barrels, a motorized mechanism for quick reloading, an ammunition belt, and a giant drum-like magazine.

Right there before me was a heavy firearm known as the Gatling gun.

"...Isn't this game supposed to be primarily fantasy-based?" I asked. As I looked at my brother's Embryo, which was likely a Type Arms, I couldn't help but ask this question.

I envisioned Type Arms to be more, you know, like a demon sword or a demon spear. Is something like a Gatling gun allowed? I wondered.

"The machine Imperium Dryfe also exists in this world, so my Embryo is just fine." Bro Bear laughed as he hoisted the drum magazine on his back and lifted the barrel of the Gatling gun under his right arm.

As I stared, somewhat shocked at the surreal sight of him...

"KIKIKI..."

"CHIKI... CHIKI..."

Bee and ant-type insect monsters had begun to swarm around us.

"All right then, let's bear-eak our way through to the remberry field," Bro Bear said, as he readied his Gatling gun... and fired away. "YEAAAAAAAAAAAAAAHHHHHHHHHH!"

In the next instant, the sound of explosions roared about us. The insect monsters were smashed to pieces, and their bodily fluids were scattered all around.

The gun barrel spun, and each bullet it spit out added to the number of corpses. As soon as the monsters fell to the ground, they turned into specks of light and disappeared.

It was a one-sided killing spree. Bro Bear mowed down the monsters faster than they could appear. In under a minute, a few thousand empty cartridges had been ejected from the Gatling gun.

Normally, there would be no way he could hold and fire something that heavy-looking. However, based on what he had showed me earlier, his costume was essentially a power suit.

His STR is at least ninety times higher than mine, so that might be why it's possible, I thought. *Even so, it's bizarre for him to be shooting while walking.*

The reason he didn't run out of ammo while firing at that pace was probably because his Gatling gun was an Embryo. It was likely using some sort of mysterious power.

Seeing him carry a Gatling gun and rapidly fire like that... It's almost like that one scene from that old, famous movie, I thought. *I think it was the second film in a series about cyborgs, and the most well-known title of an actor who later became a state governor.*

Well, given that it's a bear costume doing it and not a muscle-bulging, macho man actor, it'd probably turn into a C-class movie.

"In any case, it really doesn't look like I'll be of any use..." I said. If I were to carelessly get out in front, I would probably end up like Swiss cheese in an instant.

"Oh, you can ignore the drop items. I want you to stick right behind me," said my brother. He was referring to the drop items that had remained behind after the monsters disappeared.

Parts like this are really game-like.

"Gotcha," I said. "Hm? Isn't this situation kind of like..."

It was a situation found in a lot in games. The low-level player character would get help in the beginning from a high-level character and proceed through the game. This character would be really powerful and helpful, but would usually end up dying. The death would sometimes be used to close out the opening act.

"'Uuuuuurgh,' I think it is," I said. "That brings back memories."

"…Wait, I'd be the one that dies in that scenario." My brother's voice sounded unsettled.

It was hard to tell if we were in battle, working, or doing a comedy skit, but we traversed the 500 meters and arrived at the remberry field.

"Who's there?! Y-You're…" As expected, Liliana was engaged in battle at the remberry field with a swarm of insect monsters. She was taking on a countless number of them while protecting her younger sister behind her.

"Yes, we made it!" I said, relieved.

"The bear cavalry (no horses) has arrived!" my brother agreed.

He fired his Gatling gun again in grand style. The insects that had been encircling Liliana started to fall at an incredible rate.

I was worried he might hit the two of them, but he handled his Gatling gun skillfully, and there wasn't even a ricochet. He easily wiped out the encirclement of insects, and we made it safely over to the two sisters.

"Are you all right?" I asked, repeating back the same words Liliana had said to me earlier.

"You're the one from before… Why are you here?" She looked at me in surprise.

Hm? She's reacting as if she just realized who I was, I thought. *So then when she said "Y-You're" a moment ago, was that directed at… my brother?*

"And you, as well…" Liliana said. "Really, why?"

"We came to help," said my brother. "My little brother was saying, 'I can't leave them alone! I'm going to go rescue her, no matter what!' so I figured I'd bear with him."

I didn't say that! I thought. *I don't recall saying anything that embarrassing!*

"Your little brother… so that's why," Liliana whispered to herself as if she had understood something.

The mood here… I think Liliana and my brother just might know each other.

Liliana turned to me and bowed deeply. "Thank you very much. If you two hadn't come, I wouldn't have been able to protect my sister, Milia."

"O-Oh, no," I said. "All I did was watch from behind…"

"Still, please let me thank you," she said. "Even though I caused you trouble, you brought reinforcements to come save me… I won't forget this kind deed."

Her words went beyond making me feel embarrassed; they made me feel a sense of guilt. The quest had been automatically accepted for me, and all I had done was stick safely behind my brother like a parasite.

That guilt caused me to avert my gaze from Liliana, and when I did, it landed on her sister, Milianne.

She's as cute as she was in the picture. No, even more so.

"Loli?" my brother asked. "Lolicon?"

No I'm not! I fumed.

"Sniffle, sniffle…" Milianne was crying.

Well, yeah, she would be, I thought. *She was surrounded by a bunch of insect monsters, and her life was even in danger.*

However, given that there were still about five fruits — most likely the remberries — inside the basket she was holding, she really had her stuff together.

"A-Anyway, let's get out of here," I suggested. "It'll be dangerous if more monsters come."

"Very well," replied Liliana, and a change occurred on my menu screen.

"NPCs have joined your party.
Liliana Grandria has joined.
Milianne Grandria has joined."

Ahh, NPCs can join parties, too. And their stats are...

Milianne's stats were lower than mine were at level 0. Liliana's stats, however, were very high. Her Paladin level was 60, and her total level was 210. She even had over 5,000 HP.

Well, then again, she is the Vice Commander of the Knights of the Royal Guard, which means she's ranked second out of all the knights in this kingdom, I thought. *So it shouldn't be a surprise she's this strong.*

I then noticed that Bro Bear was silent and his expression was serious. I couldn't actually see it directly, but given how long I had known him, I could tell from the mood.

"Ray, the quest still hasn't been completed, has it?" he asked.

"Um, yeah," I said. "It hasn't changed at all."

"I see." Bro Bear readied his Gatling gun and looked about our surroundings. He appeared far more serious than when he had been mowing down insects earlier.

"Bro...?"

"Ray, the difficulty levels of quests are calculated individually by the control AIs in charge of them. The control AI takes into account information about the surrounding environment and people related to the quest."

"What?" I asked.

So the difficulties are calculated with information on the environment and related people? Control AIs really are impressive to be able to do that for every quest... but what does that have to do with anything?

"So, I was thinking the difficulty for this quest was high due to a time limit." My brother started to put his thoughts into words bit by bit. "I thought we cleared it easily because I'm suited for fighting against large numbers, but..."

His gaze fell to one spot on the ground.

"...we met up with Liliana and eliminated the swarm of insects. And yet, the quest still isn't complete. In other words, this quest has a difficultly of 5 even after taking into account that Liliana's total level is 210."

Right after he said this, the ground where he was looking exploded. Something huge and long flew out from it.

"GYULUUUUUUUUUAAAAAAA!" It was a giant centipede almost thirty meters long. "Clink!"

The giant centipede had large, stag beetle-like jaws growing on its face in all four directions. Its skin was also covered in reptile-like scales. The bullet my brother had swiftly fired at it had been easily repelled.

It was completely different from the bugs my brother had been trampling over earlier. Even a beginner like me could tell.

This thing is strong.

I could hear Liliana's shocked voice beside me. "A Demi-Dragon Worm!"

"GIIIEEEEAAAAAAAA!" The ground exploded again, and another Demi-Dragon Worm appeared.

"A Demi-Dragon class monster, huh…" my brother said. "I get it now. If we need to protect this girl while facing off against several of these, then I can see why it has this difficulty rating even with some help. But even so!"

His voice sounded cheerful, almost as if his worries had disappeared. I, on the other hand, was intimidated by the two monsters and was at a loss for words.

"If you're up against me, that amount just isn't going to cut it!" My brother then lifted up both his arms and said, "It'd be fine to just smash them to pieces, but this is a good opportunity! Baldr! Activate your fourth fo—"

"GIIIEEEAAAALEAAAAAA!"

"GYULUUUUUUUUAAAAAAA!"

"GYUIIILUUUUAAAAAAAAAA!"

"GYULUUUUUUUULOOAAAAAAA!"

Just then, four more Demi-Dragon Worms appeared from the ground in each direction, trapping my brother.

"Hey, wait, I can bearly move right now!" he protested. "Really though, there are still—" The newly appeared Demi-Dragon Worms locked their jaws onto my brother and then disappeared into the ground.

"……..Huh?" I couldn't process what I had just seen.

"Ah!" gasped Liliana, as she bit her lip at the unexpected turn of events.

I checked the party status, but my brother's stats were still blacked out. I couldn't tell if he was alive or dead.

"Um, Bro, I'm sorry for triggering a flag, but… isn't this a bit sudden?" I hesitated.

With my brother missing, the remaining two Demi-Dragon Worms drew toward us.

I was terrified. In an instant, I had been cast from the safe zone behind my brother into danger.

The biggest animal I had ever seen in my life was an elephant. Now, monsters far larger than that were bearing down toward me with cold hostility. Even if I knew this was a game, my legs shook.

"…There's something I wish to ask of you," Liliana said to me.

"Wh-What is it?"

"I'll hold back one of them. Both, if possible. During that time, could you please take my sister to safety?"

"But…" I paused.

There are two of them, I thought. *Even for Liliana, by herself that'd be…*

No, I'm thinking wrong, I reminded myself. *At level 0, I won't be of any help to her. In fact, I'd just get in her way if I stayed behind. That would put not only me, but Milianne in danger as well.*

"…All right." I pulled Milianne's hand and started running. Behind us, the battle between Liliana and the Demi-Dragon Worms commenced.

The path where my brother had just recently mowed down enemies with his Gatling gun was clear of monsters.

We can make it to the exit in one go like this, I thought. *I have to say, though…* I only realized this after running desperately, but this game also incorporates the concept of fatigue.

On top of that, my legs were shaking, and the game was kind enough to display that I had the status effect Fear. *Infinite Dendrogram's* absolute realism even went so far as to convey the terror of a giant creature.

Even so, I ran, making sure that I never let go of Milianne's hand.

"Heh… Heh…" Following behind me, Milianne also ran in earnest. Her face was full of dread.

Both scared, we continued to run.

"By the way…" I said to Milianne. It was an attempt to help ease our worries, if even for a bit. I wasn't sure myself just exactly whose mind I was trying to put at ease though. "Milianne… Milia, so why did you come all the way here to get remberries?"

I asked her this half out of curiosity; the other half was for distraction.

"T-Today is Sister's birthday… She loves remberry cake, so I thought I would make it for her…" she stuttered.

"I see," I said.

"But there weren't any for sale at the shops, so I didn't know what to do," she said. "And then, a guy with glasses told me, 'If you have this incense, you can go get some from the orchard outside.'"

…*So this is that four eyes' fault,* I thought. *I don't know what he was thinking telling her that, but I'd like to punch that idiot for sending a kid to a place this dangerous.*

"Sister came to get me, but the effect of the incense wore off…" she said.

We had covered half the distance while we were talking.

Just the other half left, I thought. *At this rate, we'll make it the rest of the way.*

"…uluuuu!" Just then, I heard a roar and felt the ground tremble behind me.

I made the decision on the spur of the moment. I picked up Milianne and jumped to the side.

In the next instant, a Demi-Dragon Worm burst from the ground and chomped its jaws as it passed through the area where we had just been running.

"She couldn't have…!" An unpleasant thought compelled me to turn around, but I could still hear the sounds of battle.

Liliana was still fighting.

Could this be one of the two she was fighting, and it left to chase after us? I wondered. *Or maybe it's one of the ones that dragged my brother underground? The real issue is that, no matter which one it is, I don't have a way of fighting back.*

My stats were still at their default levels, and the Embryo on my left hand still hadn't hatched. *Even if it did hatch now, I can't imagine a newly-hatched Embryo would be able to stand up against an enemy that my brother's Gatling gun didn't work against.*

My heart pounded in terror and unease, while a cold sweat broke out on my forehead and down my back. I thought I might die just from how realistic it felt.

"GYULUUUUUUUUUEAAAAA!" The Demi-Dragon Worm exposed its long body from the ground and roared, not in an attempt to intimidate us, but rather in triumphant laughter.

"…The end of the road, huh?" I muttered.

The "newbie killer," Old Reve Orchard, I thought. *It looks like I'll also experience my first death here.*

But…

"W-Waaah…" Milianne was crying in my arms.

She's an NPC... a tian. Unlike me, if she dies, she won't come back. The thought left me unsettled. *Bro said that even the king died. I'm sure there aren't any special circumstances just for her. In this world, she'll die just like anybody else.*

"...Like I said, that'd leave a bad taste in my mouth!" I took off the Lifesaving Brooch and equipped it to Milianne. "Milia, can you run to the entrance from here by yourself?"

"...What?" She looked up at me with unease.

"I have to go and beat up this damn centipede for a bit," I said.

Right after I said this, the Demi-Dragon Worm charged at us. I pushed Milianne away, and like getting hit by a truck, I flew into the air.

"Gah... hah..."

It was a powerful impact, even worse than when I had collided with Liliana back in the town.

However, the damage had been 93. My remaining HP was 5... *I'm still alive.*

One of the four Dragonscale Wards I had equipped had broken and disappeared. I'd survived thanks to its ability to reduce the damage of the attack by 90%.

I forced my numb body to move and drank a Healing Potion from the item menu. My HP was fully restored.

I can still move.

As I turned around, I saw that Milianne was still standing there.

"Go! I'll take care of this guy!" I shouted.

It was a big lie; there was nothing I could do. However, I could at least buy some time. If she could run away during that time, that was all that mattered.

Milianne stood up and ran for the exit.

If she can get to the exit and return to the field, there should be other players and tians there. This is for the best, I thought, and was then immediately flung into the air again.

It was my second cycle of near-death, the Dragonscale breaking, healing with a potion, and then recovery.

"Hah! If you include the death penalty, I can take another three of your hits, you damn centipede!" I shouted.

The third attack came, but this time I avoided it. *Even at default stats, if I move, I can dodge it.*

However...

"What?!" I was caught by its tail and knocked aside.

The damage was nearly the same. My HP was dangerously low again, and another Dragonscale broke.

"Damn... it."

Only one more left.

Milianne still hadn't made it to the exit.

At the very least, I have to bide my time until then, I told myself. As I thought this, the Demi-Dragon Worm changed its focus of attack.

"GYUUUUEAAAA!" It twisted its large body around and laid its sights on Milianne.

"Hey, you bastard! What are you looking at?" I shouted.

It ignored me and charged after her.

"Waaaiiiitttt!"

I chased after it, but I couldn't catch up with it at my speed. The large Demi-Dragon Worm struck Milianne, sending her small body floating upward into the air like a leaf. The basket she had been holding so dearly was forced from her hands, and tumbled to the ground.

"Aaaaahhh!" I dived headfirst and caught her falling body. There was a large impact as I caught her, and the last Dragonscale shattered.

That's not the real issue right now.

I was frightened to do it, but I looked at Milianne's face. A pain different from physical pain was stinging at my heart.

She was unconscious... but unhurt. In exchange, the Lifesaving Brooch I had placed on her had shattered.

It apparently works even when equipped to Milianne, I thought, relieved. *However, now that the brooch is broken, there won't be a next time.*

My last Dragonscale was also gone. We no longer had any means to withstand the Demi-Dragon Worm's attack.

Liliana's still fighting, I thought. *Bro still hasn't come back since disappearing into the ground... I'm all out of options.*

"GYUUUUAAAAAAAA!" The monster in front of me had become irritated at its tough prey, but it now appeared to be shaking in joy at finally being able to finish things.

In a last-ditch effort, I tried drawing the knife I had received with my starting equipment. However, after removing the knife from its sheath, I discovered that its blade was broken. Before I could even use it, it seemed the repeated collisions had caused the knife to break.

The chances for us to survive were now at zero.

I looked at the unconscious girl in my arms.

Her weight, her warmth, her breathing, and the emotions she had showed me — they were no different from real life. She was alive, so realistically alive.

And like death in the real world, that life was about to be lost.

"...Damn it." I couldn't give up.

For me, this world was a game. It wasn't a problem if I died.

But even if I know this world is a game, it'd leave a bad taste in my mouth if this girl were to disappear from it forever. I clenched my fist in frustration.

On the back of that hand... was my Embryo in its egg-like zeroth form.

"Hey..."

I...

"If they say an Embryo is supposed to offer a player... If you're supposed to offer me infinite possibility..." I pleaded, "...then give me that possibility."

The monster in front of me raised its head to deliver the final blow.

"Give me the possibility for a happy ending, the possibility to save this girl!" I cried.

To my left hand I pleaded. To the incarnation of this world of possibilities known as *Infinite Dendrogram*, I pleaded from the bottom of my heart.

"Wake up already and give me even 1% of a possibility!" I cried.

The Demi-Dragon Worm launched its last attack.

"You're an unexpectedly overbearing Master, aren't you?" said a voice. "However, I am one that is born from you. I don't dislike that part about you."

In an instant, the fatal charge was blocked by someone.

"...Huh?"

Just like when my brother had disappeared into the ground, I couldn't process what was happening before my eyes.

I couldn't understand why in front of me was not the tragedy that should have taken place, but instead, a miracle that shouldn't have occurred.

The Demi-Dragon Worm that was supposed to kill us had been repelled by a wall of light and was bent over backwards.

My Embryo had vanished from the back of my left hand, and in its place was a glowing, blue crest.

Between the Demi-Dragon Worm and us now stood a girl I didn't know. Her jet black hair waved in the wind, and her skin glistened like white porcelain. She swung her gothic skirt made of black fabric and white frills as she turned to look at me. Her eyes were made of the black of night and a white that reminded me of the stars.

"Morning," was the first thing she said.

I couldn't say anything.

"Hm, you seem out of it," she said. "Good grief, aren't you something? I forced myself to wake up because you told me to, and yet..."

The way she spoke almost made the mystique she had disappear, but her words made me think of something.

"Are you my..." I began. ...*Embryo?*

"Of course," she said. "Well then, Master, that damn centipede is still in good health. To cheer things up in celebration of my birthday, what do you say we finish it off in style?"

"How?" I burst out.

Before I could even finish asking this, the girl had disappeared. She lost her human form and turned into a swarm of black, shining lights that enveloped my right arm, and then transformed into a black greatsword. It was organic and sinister looking, but in some way, still beautiful.

"I'll leave the timing to you," she said, her voice coming from the sword. "Swing down when the damn centipede comes charging at us. We're all going to die if you screw up, got it?"

It felt like she was telling me, "I gave you your chance, now the rest is up to you."

"...Got it." I was aware there were things that needed to be done before asking any questions.

The Demi-Dragon Worm seemed to be furious as it charged at us faster than it ever had before. It was a straight shot at a speed I was able to see, but not avoid.

However, I still had time to swing my sword.

"The three times Master almost died, and the one attack I absorbed... The four attacks you made with everything you had..."

Right before the jaws of the Demi-Dragon Worm could reach me...

"I'll double them and pay you back," said the girl as I swung down the black greatsword.

"Vengeance is Mine!" she shouted.

There was an impact the moment the greatsword made contact.

Then a moment of stillness.

Right after, the Demi-Dragon Worm, almost as if it had been crushed by a monster several times its size, shattered into pieces starting with its head.

Just exactly how many times today am I going to see something I struggle to understand? I wondered.

While I was thinking this, I looked at what was in front of me. The Demi-Dragon Worm's large body was gradually breaking into pieces that turned into light and vanished.

Behind me was Milianne, still unconscious, and beside me was the girl. She had changed back from the black sword.

"Success, success," she said happily. "Isn't that great, Master? You grabbed hold of the possibility you'd hoped for."

"You really are my Embryo, aren't you?" I asked.

The girl lightly lifted her frilled skirt and bowed with contrived respect. "I'm Nemesis, a Type Maiden with Arms Embryo. I was born from your heart, body, and soul." The girl — Nemesis — introduced herself like that and grinned broadly. "It's nice to meet you, Master."

Outside Old Reve Orchard, Ray Starling

After I defeated the Demi-Dragon Worm, I picked up its drop item, a Demi-Dragon Worm Treasure Coffer, and escaped from Old Reve Orchard while carrying Milianne.

I didn't think about going to aid Liliana.

On the window screen displaying our party members' status, I could see that she was doing fine. Moreover, there was no way that a miracle like what had just happened would occur a second or third time. I had the feeling that if I were to get full of myself now, then it would definitely ruin things.

"Withdrawing is the right choice." Nemesis, who was apparently my Embryo, explained the battle situation like so. "That tian girl won't die. She's the stronger of the two, so even if it takes some time, she'll win for sure against that damn centipede."

"Even though you were just born, you seem to be more informed about this world than I am," I said.

It appears she even knows about Liliana, so maybe she has memories from before she hatched.

"That's because even if I take the form of a human, I'm not one," she said. "Mysterious things like that exist. More importantly, Master, if you possess a thing called curiosity, then isn't it about time you had something to ask me?"

Nothing sprang to mind. I didn't respond.

I'm starting to get a handle on it, but Nemesis seems to be the type that likes to speak in a roundabout way, I thought. *Well, I guess I'm not one to talk, since I'm able to understand her.*

In other words, she was saying, "Hurry up and check out my abilities on the status screen."

I looked at the status screen and saw that a category for Embryo had been added. I clicked on it right away and a window appeared displaying Nemesis and her parameters. Displayed on the window was the name "Maiden of Vengeance Nemesis," and "Type Maiden with Arms."

Additionally, there were ATK and DEF stats listed, as well as modifiers for each stat. The ATK and DEF stats applied when equipping Nemesis as a weapon.

So this is the same as normal weapons and armor.

The stat modifiers, however, appeared to always be in effect just by having Nemesis around, and they apparently weren't just a set value boost to my stats. When leveling up, increases in my stats would also take these modifiers into account.

As an overall evaluation, her stats weren't that strong. The modifier for HP was a bit high, but the rest were low. The ATK stat for equipping Nemesis was only about 50.

It's strange to compare this with Bro Bear's costume, but even after taking that into account, my stats themselves don't seem like they've gone up that much, I thought. *Well, I guess that goes without saying since Nemesis was only just born as an Embryo. But in that case, how was I able to defeat the Demi-Dragon Worm?*

As I pondered this, I found the section for skills. Listed there were the two skills "Counter Absorption" and "Vengeance is Mine."

The Counter Absorption skill was the wall of light that Nemesis had used. It had a max stock of two uses, and with each use, a wall of light could be created to nullify attacks. It replenished one of its stock every 24 hours.

And then there was the skill that had defeated the Demi-Dragon Worm, Vengeance is Mine.

This skill took the total damage received from an enemy within 24 hours, doubled it, and then unleashed that damage as an attack that ignored all defense. Even damage that had been reduced by other skills and items, or nullified by Counter Absorption, was added to the total.

But once the skill is used, it looks like the damage counter is reset for that enemy, I noticed.

"Okay, I get it now," I said. "So that's how I was able to defeat that Demi-Dragon Worm."

Although the damage was reduced by the Dragonscale Wards, I did take three of its hits, I thought. *On top of that, Nemesis nullified one attack with her other skill, Counter Absorption. So that's four in total, and the damage would come out to roughly 3,600. Plus, the ability for Vengeance is Mine then doubled this to around 7,200.*

I don't know how much life that Demi-Dragon Worm had, but this must mean that it wasn't more than 7,200 HP. Or maybe its head was a weak spot, and landing a direct hit on it had some effect.

"...Even if I know how the trick worked, it's still a miracle," I thought aloud.

The one-hit killer move had only worked because I had been weak, and my opponent had been strong. What had also played a big role was that I had overcome several near deaths thanks to the items my brother had given me. But more than anything, Nemesis's skills had been a perfect match for the situation.

"The end result sure seems convenient," I said to myself.

Embryos are supposed to be unique and based on things like one's personality, biorhythm, and attributes, right? I thought. *Looking at the results this time, it almost seems like it was set up. Also, a skill that gets stronger the more damage I take... I feel as if I'm getting treated like a huge masochist.*

"A masochist, huh... I'll have you know, this is the result of my having observed you, Master. There were no mistakes," said Nemesis, seemingly offended.

Wait, can she hear my thoughts?

"But anyway, you said 'observed'?" I asked.

"The zeroth form is a time period for Embryos to observe their Masters," she said. "After observing their psychology and behavior, an Embryo's first form is then born based on this."

I see, I thought. *So in other words, my experiences since starting have more or less been factored in.*

...Now that I think about it, I collided with Liliana right after I started, and then I also fought a Demi-Dragon Worm. I feel like I've been taking a lot of near-fatal damage. So I guess these skills are the end result of all of that, huh?

"Well," continued Nemesis, "even if the experiences and behaviors are the same, there will be differences in an Embryo's form and skills based on each Master. Also... I think Counter Absorption was derived from your personality."

"Hm?" I asked. *I wonder what she means by that.*

"Oh, and another thing," she went on. "I'll go ahead and say this myself, but a Type Maiden Embryo is quite rare, you know? You should be grateful to me and reflect upon how blessed you are."

Oh yeah, that's right, I realized. *Maiden wasn't one of the normal categories Cheshire mentioned. She seems to be a rare type, and it's a big help that she's explaining various things to me, but it's still somewhat of an iffy feeling having a girl come out of an Embryo that's based on me.*

"Iffy? Did you say 'iffy?'" she asked huffily.

Ah, that's right. She can hear my thoughts.

"I *can* hear them!" she shouted. "Iffy? What do you mean by 'iffy?' You hit the jackpot with me! This beauty! This rarity! What could there be to complain about?"

"No I didn't mean that you were iffy, Nemesis, but the fact that you emerged from me, you see…"

As we went back and forth, Liliana appeared from the exit of Old Reve Orchard. The armor she was clad in was dirty with mud and dust, but Liliana herself seemed to be unharmed.

"Milia!" Finding us, Liliana quickly ran to our side, and after looking at her sister's sleeping face, she let out a sigh of relief.

"Thank you very much… for protecting my sister… Truly, thank you!" Liliana burst out as tears fell from her eyes.

"Um, yeah…" I said. *This is troubling. I don't know how to respond.*

"That's right," said Nemesis. "You should be grateful to my Master, and even more so to me."

And that's Nemesis for you…

"Is she your…?" asked Liliana.

"Yeah, umm… my Embryo."

Liliana looked at Nemesis, slightly surprised. "I see. So, after all, as his brother, you're also a Master chosen by an Embryo. But a Maiden, it's almost like that…"

Just as she was about to say something…

"All right! I've escaped from the bearied underground world!" Bro Bear jumped out from the ground together with a loud sound effect.

"…Ummm," I said. *You were still alive, Bro? Well, his stats were displayed the whole time, just blackened out so I couldn't tell, but still…*

For some reason, Bro Bear wasn't carrying his Gatling gun, but instead had a shovel in his right hand.

That can't be how he moved through the ground, can it? I wondered.

"The underground tunnel is now open!" he proclaimed.

Right after he said this, the ground shook slightly, and the sound of something caving in could be heard. The hole Bro Bear had come out of then closed.

"And it caved in right away!"

Oh, shut up.

"You were all right, Bro?" I asked.

"Oh yeah! Me and Baldr's fourth form tore them to shreds!"

"Fourth? Not the Gatling gun from earlier?" I asked.

"That's the second form."

I guess that means there are various forms.

"For some Embryos, you can use their previous forms at will," Nemesis chimed in. "Brother Bear's Embryo must've been one of those types."

…Is "Brother Bear" referring to my brother? I wondered.

"Ray, is that blali your Embryo?" he asked me.

He meant "black loli," shortened to "blali"… *Neither of those terms are all that great.*

"It's a pleasure to meet you," she said. "I'm Nemesis, Ray Starling's Maiden with Arms Embryo. I hope we get along, Brother Bear."

It appears Nemesis is determined to push through with calling him "Brother Bear."

"Setting that aside… Bro, if you were alive, I wish you'd come out sooner," I said. "I was this close to dying."

A total of about four times, actually.

"That would've been difficult," he said. "Because the whole time, I was locked in battle underground with all the Demi-Drags."

All the Demi-Drags?

"There were swarms of Demi-Drags bearied in an underground cave," he continued. "I don't hate bugs, but that really sent shivers down my spine."

I stayed silent.

That thing?! Swarms of them…

Good thing I didn't stick around for long.

"An outbreak of those centipedes… the 'newbie killer' is way too scary," I said. *I guess that's just what you'd expect from a trauma-generating machine.*

"Normally there shouldn't have been even one Demi-Drag living there…" said my brother.

"Huh?" I asked.

"Oh, well. I took care of every one that I found, so they shouldn't multiply anymore," he said. "More importantly, let's head home."

"You're right," I agreed. "Let's head back."

And so like that, Nemesis, Bro Bear, Liliana, Milianne, and I all started on our way back.

Due to our close proximity to the royal capital, we arrived in no time. After we passed through the gate, we then parted ways with Liliana and Milianne.

Before leaving, Liliana said, "I'll be sure to repay this debt of gratitude."

Milianne, who had woken up, gave each of us a remberry from the basket she had held onto so dearly, and said, "Thank you."

As I watched the two sisters walk home hand-in-hand…

The message, "Quest 'Search for Milianne Grandria' has been completed," was displayed, and I finally felt like the quest had ended.

"It's over…" I said, exhausted. *I feel like I've gone through some crazy danger and chaos right off the bat.*

"The reward is one remberry, huh?" asked Nemesis. "A tad shabby considering what we went through, I'd say."

If I recall, it's a fruit worth about 500 yen.

However, I felt that it had more value than that.

I wiped the remberry on my clothes and took a bite. It had the taste of a strawberry and the texture of an apple, but that one bite was more delicious than either one.

It was the taste of accomplishment.

"All righty then, it's time to party," said my brother. "It's dinnertime. Since today is Ray's first day playing, I prepared a feast."

"You did?" I asked.

"I have heaps of meats and vegetables ready. Not that bear-bones stuff, either! Top-grade stuff."

"Ohh, that sounds fascinating," chimed in Nemesis.

That does sound tasty, I thought. *Nemesis seems to agree, as well… Wait, Embryos eat food too?*

"And for dessert I've got remberries."

"Ohhh…" I said. "Wait, what?"

"For dinner, I bought up all the remberries available at the market this morning. It's all-you-can-eat."

"………You."

If I remember correctly, the reason Milianne went to Old Reve Orchard was because all the remberries were sold out, right? I thought. *Which means…*

"Damn it, Bro Bear, you were the start of this whole mess!" I couldn't stop myself from shouting, and it echoed about the royal capital as the sun began to set.

After chewing my brother out for a while, we made our way to the restaurant he had made reservations at. It was run by a player, and not only did they serve their own food, they also allowed customers to bring their own ingredients that chefs from the restaurant would then cook. My brother had apparently already handed over a mountain of ingredients.

"All right, in celebration of Ray's first day and completing his first quest, cheers! Thank you beary much!"

"Cheers!" said Nemesis and I, as we all clinked our drinks together. My brother had a rem liqueur (made from remberry), while Nemesis and I had a drink that was similar to orange juice.

Infinite Dendrogram checked age restrictions based on each player's citizenship, so I apparently wouldn't be able to drink alcohol until I turned twenty. If I were to go into further detail, sexual material was R 18, while alcohol and tobacco was R 20.

Since these things exist in the game, I'm not sure if I should call this wholesome or indecent.

"Hmph. Thanks to my kiddy Master, I can't drink any alcohol, either," Nemesis griped. "Six years in our time... that's long."

"Based on appearances, when it comes to who shouldn't be drinking, you're number two," I pointed out.

Number one would be my brother... for various reasons, I thought. *...Don't drink alcohol from a glass while in a bear costume.*

"Chomp, chomp," grunted my brother. "Go on now, eat up. Meat. Eat some meat. Chomp, chomp, chomp, chomp." My brother ate the food laid out on the table and encouraged us to do the same.

Really, you can eat and drink while wearing that costume? I thought. *It's high-spec, even in weird ways.*

"Okay, okay... What is this? It's delicious!" I cried. I was surprised at the taste after trying the unknown food I had been recommended. It had been made using ingredients and cooking methods I didn't know, and yet it had all come together in a tastiness I could comprehend. On top of everything, it was incredibly delicious.

"The owner of this place is a Star Chef," said my brother. "It's the top class fur the Cook Job. His cooking skills would be about a three star in our world."

"That's amazing," I said. "But after eating a feast like this, it'll be tough to deal with the difference between this and what I eat in the real world."

It should be about dinnertime for me back home, and I should be getting hungry.

"By the way, my body back in the real world should still be lying down, right?" I asked.

"Yes. But you'll get a notice if something happens in the real world. Like fur bathroom breaks or hunger, for example."

Right after he said this, a window appeared at the edge of my sight.

"Notice: urge to urinate.
Notice: hunger."

Oh, I see. "Okay, then I'm going to log off for a bit," I said.

"All right. Try to come back as soon as you can."

"Do return quickly, Master," said my Embryo. "I can't help myself to the food until you come back."

"Yeah, yeah," I said, and then selected the Logout option from the Main Menu.

"Logging out. Should your next log in point be your save point or current location?"

"Current location," I replied.

"Understood. We await your return."

And like that, my avatar disappeared from the world, and as if waking from a dream, my consciousness receded from *Infinite Dendrogram*.

"...Ohh." The first thing I did after logging out of *Infinite Dendrogram* was check the clock. The time was about three hours later than when I had started the game. I was impressed to see that time really had only advanced by a third of what I had spent in the game world.

I then went to the bathroom. After that, I ate a balanced nutrition bar and drank some mineral water to replenish my body's nutrients. Although I had eaten inside the game, my actual stomach hadn't been filled.

I checked my cellphone in case I had any missed calls or messages, but there were none. I also looked at the news on my computer, but there wasn't anything that stood out.

After about ten or so minutes, I logged back in.

"Welcome back."

"…You," I said.

Upon arriving back, I saw that the food on the table was all different. It appeared that he'd eaten everything that had been there initially.

…For him to eat all that food by himself… is my brother really a bear? I wondered.

"Waahh?! The a la carte I was looking forward to is gone!" As I logged in, Nemesis materialized and let out a scream.

"Don't worry," said my brother. "There's still plenty of food left. What you've seen so far is only about 10% of it."

"That's too much! Just how many people is this for?" I exclaimed.

If Nemesis hadn't been born, then it would've been just the two of us. Why did he prepare so much?!

"…Oh well," I said finally. "By the way, Bro, I still have a few things I want to ask you."

"How I got this costume?"

"No… well, I am a bit interested, but no."

There were two system-related things and one thing about Liliana that I was curious about. *I guess I'll start with the easier questions.*

"Embryos change form as they evolve, don't they?" I asked.

"That's right. My Baldr increased its weapon-y-ness. It also got beary much bigger."

I thought that Gatling gun was quite large, but… that was only its second form, right? Anything bigger than that and I don't think you'd be able to carry it.

"By the way, I wasn't able to show it to you, but the fourth form I used today is a tank," he said.

"A tank?!" *Is that even allowed?* "So Nemesis will also eventually turn into something different from her current human form... like maybe even a tank."

Nemesis, who was eating beside me, became scared and said, "Th-That's so ominous."

"How they evolve depends on their Master, but in your case, Nemesis will probably always be a Maiden," said my brother. "Although the 'with Arms' part might change to a different type."

"Speaking of that, Nemesis turned into a sword. What would she be regarded as?" I asked.

"Like I was saying, she's a Maiden Embryo that turns into an Arms. Maidens are generally hybrids... A mix of various types."

"Really?" I asked. *That seems like kind of a bargain.*

After I thought this though, Nemesis complained, "What do you mean, I'm a cheap girl?!"

"There's one person I know that has a Maiden Embryo," my brother explained. "She stayed as a Maiden while the 'with' part changed into various things. It's even become a Superior Embryo now."

A Superior Embryo?

"The first to third forms of an Embryo are called low-rank, while the fourth to sixth forms are called high-rank," explained my brother. "And then the current highest level that can be reached, the seventh form, is called a Superior Embryo. It's called this because it surpasses the limits of the high-rank forms."

"The final form... Superior Embryo," I murmured. *I wonder if Nemesis will reach that one day. She's still in her first form, though, so I don't know how long it'll take to reach that.*

"By the way, out of all the players, there are fewer than a hundred that have reached this form," my brother added.

The game has over 100,000 active players, and yet there are less than a hundred?! I thought. *Just how difficult of a path is it?*

"Those people are way too hardcore," I said.

"It's not like they all achieved it solely through their play time," my brother said. "There are a lot of players who started on release day and still haven't reached it, while there are those who were able to do it in half a year."

Does that mean it requires some special conditions?

"Oh yeah, Bro, you started playing on release day," I said. "So how far has your Embryo evolved? What form is it up to?"

"That's a bearied se-cr-et."

That's annoying.

Also, Bro Bear mostly spoke normally when he was explaining things, but used bear puns when he was teasing me. It was irritating, now that I had caught on to this.

While Bro Bear and I had been talking, Nemesis had cleaned off all the food on her plate before I had even realized it.

...We were talking about you, you know.

"Okay, on to my next question," I said. "It's about our standing in this world."

"And by that you mean?"

I was thinking over how Liliana had spoken and acted. "Liliana called me something like 'a Master chosen by an Embryo,' and not a player. I don't really get what the circumstances are regarding that... or what the status for us as players is within the setting."

Somehow, I didn't get the feeling she was thinking of me as a player in a game.

"Hmm," said my brother. "You can find out about that by reading the background setting on the official site, but... you'll lose several hours of time if you do, so I'll give you the short explanation." My brother then began his lecture on the world's setting.

"In this world there are Masters and tians. All of us players are called Masters here. The meaning is something like, 'One chosen by an Embryo.' So a Master is someone who raises and uses an Embryo that possesses infinite possibilities. Due to this, a Master's power is enormous, but in exchange, they are burdened with one condition."

"Condition?" I asked.

"Their bodies are frequently spirited away to a different world."

...Hm?

"A Master may vanish from this world for as little as a few minutes, or for as long as several months," said my brother. "Also, there are times when they return to the place where they vanished, as well as times when they are flung to a special location called a save point."

Wait, isn't that...

"At the moment before death, a Master can also use the power of an Embryo to send their body to another world and survive," said my brother. "However, if this happens, they will not return for at least three days."

"So what that means is that logging out and the death penalty for players have been incorporated into the foundation of this world?" I asked.

"That's right," he said.

"...Wow."

As far as I can tell from interacting with Liliana and Milianne, the way tians think is at the same level as real humans, I thought. *So in order to allow those tians to go about without realizing this world is a game, they've defined how players return to the real world and their immortality as truths of this world.*

I see. There's a lot more to it than I thought.

"By the way," my brother continued, "sometimes there are players that go around saying, 'this world is a game,' but the tians view them as 'pitiable Masters that have gone mad from being sent to different worlds.'"

"...Ahh," I said.

"Also, since Masters disappear so irregularly, for the most part they don't take on important positions in the kingdom," he added. "Even if you join the knights in order to get the job Knight, you won't be given regular work. Instead you'll get tasks specific to Masters."

In other words, you're given jobs where it'd be fine even if you disappeared during it.

"Well," said my brother, "in terms of strength, we're stronger because of our Embryos, so the jobs that get sent our way usually pay higher rewards than the ones for tians."

I wonder if I'll be asked to go slay a monster by myself, I thought. *Well, okay then, that resolved the bigger questions I had regarding the game's system. Which just leaves...*

"Bro, did something happen between you and Liliana?" I asked.

"I don't know what you're talking about."

"Don't try to dodge the question. Liliana clearly knew who you were." *And if I were to add to that, it didn't feel like it was a good impression she had, either.* "What did you do?"

Surely he didn't make a move on her, right? For example, saying something like, "Yaay! It's a real female knight! I just can't get enough!" and then hugging her?

"I didn't do anything." Contrary to my expectations, my brother answered in a serious tone. "It's because I didn't do anything... that she probably resents me."

"What do you mean?" I asked.

"It'll be another long story," he said. "And unlike before, it's not going to be a fun one."

"I don't mind."

After I said this, my brother let out a sigh and then began to talk. "Two months ago in real time, half a year ago in *Dendro* time, there was a war. The machine Imperium Dryfe invaded the Kingdom of Altar."

The machine Imperium Dryfe: it was one of the nations a player could choose when first starting. It was at odds with this fantasy world as it had an advanced mechanical civilization.

...Although I don't have the right to talk about being at odds, given that I have a tank-riding bear in my family.

"The reason given by their nation was to obtain the Kingdom of Altar's fertile land," my brother said. "As for the game's side... it was a war event."

The manual had mentioned war events. They were large-scale battles between nations, and big quests with the fate of each nation on the line.

"It was a large battle involving Masters and tians," said my brother. "Well, it was a type of event that doesn't happen very often and one of the game's bigger features, but..." he sighed. "The result was a crushing defeat for the Kingdom of Altar. A third of our territory was lost, and among tians, the court magician Arch Wiseman, half of the knights, and the king died. Put simply, many of the key people running this kingdom perished in battle."

"...Why did they lose so badly? Is Dryfe that powerful?" I asked.

No, that's hard to believe, I thought. *It'd be different in real life, but since this is a game, I'm sure they've taken measures to balance this.*

81

"The strength of both countries was essentially even," he answered. "This includes the nations' power, the soldiers' levels, and the fighting ability of important tians. However, the strength of Masters on top of that is a different story."

"So you're saying they lost to Dryfe because of the difference in the number of players?" I asked.

Dryfe certainly seems like a nation where those who like it would really like it, so maybe a bunch of players joined it, I thought. *...No, that can't be it. If that were the case, this kingdom would also...*

"The reason they lost is because out of all the Masters that were eligible to join the war, most didn't participate," he said.

"What?" It was an answer I didn't expect.

The fate of the kingdom was at stake, and it was a big-time event, yet they didn't participate?

"The king of Altar was, how to put it, an old-fashioned person," my brother said. "He said, 'This is a crisis for our kingdom. Warriors of this nation, now is the time to rise up!' It was great that he gave this speech and joined the front-lines, but that was it."

"That was it?" I asked.

"There were no rewards. Essentially, he felt that if you belong to this nation, then it's a given that you should rise up during its crisis."

...I get that the fate of the kingdom was at stake, but I still feel that's being a bit cheap, I thought. *Is that how it's normally done?*

"Of course, for Masters... for players, they're enjoying this world but they aren't staking their lives on this game," my brother said. "If they die, they just can't log back in for 24 hours. That's why even if the kingdom was in a crisis, there were many who thought that if there wasn't anything to gain, then there wasn't any meaning in participating."

I would be just the opposite, I thought. *If the login restriction was the only negative that came from dying, then I would consider joining the war, but I guess everyone thinks differently. There is the cost of the healing items you use during battle, and it'd be a huge minus if you fought some strong enemy and your equipment got destroyed.*

"Regarding this issue, the fact that Dryfe on the other side clearly stated their rewards was a big factor," he explained, and went on to describe them.

Apparently they had been quite exceptional.

They had offered 5,000 lir for every Kingdom of Altar soldier defeated. For each Embryo holder — in other words, each Master — the reward had been 50,000 lir. In addition to this, they had offered various rewards for defeating key people, such as rare items and a privileged status within the nation.

As a result, the morale of Dryfe's players had risen, while the motivation of players in the Kingdom of Altar had dropped considerably.

"There were even some players saying things like, 'I want to fight on Dryfe's side,' and 'There might be a rare event if this kingdom gets destroyed,'" my brother said.

I wasn't sure what to say. *As a gamer, I can't say I don't understand how they feel. I can understand them, but...*

"And the real decisive blow for the crushing loss was that the Kingdom of Altar's Big Three — the top players for the kill rankings, duel rankings, and clan rankings — all passed on participating."

"Rankings?" I asked. "They have those?"

"That over there," he said and pointed outside the window.

This restaurant faced the square with the water fountain where I had met up with my brother. He pointed at a splendid-looking notice board in front of the water fountain.

"That's the Kingdom of Altar's ranking board. It's updated every three months in game time. There are the kill rankings where you compete with your accomplishments defeating monsters. Then there are the duel rankings for PvP achievements, and the clan rankings that compare the size of clans. The top thirty ranking players for each of these is listed there."

"Hmm," I said.

"And this part is important: the only players that can participate in wars are the ones in those rankings. As for the clan rankings, if you're a member of a clan within the top thirty, then you can participate. So you could temporarily join a clan as a mercenary and fight in a war."

So in any case, that means a player can't fight in wars unless they make it into those rankings.

And at the time of the last war, the top-ranking players for each category, known as the Big Three, had supposedly said the following when the kingdom sought their participation:

The top of the kill rankings, King of Destruction (name unknown), had said, "I don't want to participate in a big event and carelessly expose my face."

The top of the duel rankings, Over Gladiator Figaro, had said, "I'm not interested in sloppy fights."

The leader of the top clan on the clan rankings, High Priestess Tsukuyo Fuso of The Lunar Society, had said, "We were unable to reach an agreement with the Kingdom of Altar."

As a result, the other ranking players' already low motivation had been brought down even further.

I'm sure they could see it'd be a losing battle, I thought. And like that, the war had started without many of the ranking players.

The ones that had participated had included some of the ranking clans, players that had temporarily joined them, such as members of fan clubs for popular tians like Liliana, as well as naive players.

The result had been a terrible sight.

The scene on the battlefield could only have been described as a massacre. The overall number of players had been disparate, and most devastating of all was that the top-ranking players on Dryfe's side had all participated.

Top of the Dryfe Imperium's kill rankings, King of Beasts.

Top of the Dryfe Imperium's duel rankings, Hell General Logan Goddhart.

Top of the Dryfe Imperium's clan rankings, Giga Professor Mr. Franklin, leader of the clan, Triangle of Wisdom.

Two out of the three had Superior Embryos, and their fighting power had been enormous. The Knights of the Royal Guard Commander and the Arch Wiseman had died at the hands of these three. Even the king had been killed.

"If things had kept going as they were, without a doubt, this kingdom would've been on a straight shot to ruin," said my brother. "But after being forced to give up a third of our territory, the nation of Caldina began their invasion into Dryfe. Except for some troops they left behind in the territory they took, the rest of Dryfe's forces retreated back to their homeland, and so the Kingdom of Altar managed to survive by a hair."

However, my brother continued to explain, since Caldina had already pulled out of Dryfe, Dryfe would likely attack again in a few months.

...He was right, I thought. *This wasn't a fun story.*

"So what's this about you saying that Liliana resents you?" I asked.

"That's because I was one of the ranking players listed there that didn't participate," he said. "Moreover, the former commander of the knights that died in battle was Liliana and Milia's father."

"...Man," I said. *This really isn't a fun story.*

"And so, having heard this not-so-fun story, what do you plan to do, Master?" Nemesis, who had been engrossed in her food this whole time and hadn't joined our conversation, asked.

"There's nothing I can do, right?" I asked.

What will I do when Dryfe attacks again... well, for now, I've already made my decision.

"Even if there's no reward, I'm not too keen on refusing to participate," I said. "Even if there's a cost, I would think there's some value in taking part." *Even if you were to just view it as a game event.*

"Yeah, well, you're right about that, but the players' mood at the time was more of a boycott against the cheap nation," said my brother. "I even get the feeling that Dryfe might've prepared their crazy rewards as a way to create this mood."

If that's the case, then the Kingdom of Altar probably lost to Dryfe strategically before the battle even began.

"Why didn't you join, Bro?" I asked. "Was it because of the lack of reward for you, too?"

"...In my case, it was because having my equipment break would equal exposing my real face."

"...Ahh, yeah."

Well yeah, that would be a huge problem, but still...

"Well, I've changed my equipment since then, so I'll be joining next time," he said.

That costume's DEF stat and physical damage reduction are certainly impressive, I thought. *Although it's still a gag item, no matter how you look at it.*

"The next time we do fight, though," he continued, "the strength of their nation will have increased, while ours will have weakened. So it'll be tough."

"Weakened?" I asked.

"Since losing the war, there have been a lot of players switching to different nations. There are even tians leaving the kingdom. People on online chat boards have been saying things like, 'The Kingdom of Altar is past its prime,' and 'It's game over.'"

I remained silent.

Defections, refugees, and rampant resignation... That's the path of a country headed towards collapse in the real world.

"With the latest update to the rankings, about 70% have been replaced," he said.

"Hmm..." I said. *Put another way, now might be the chance to get on the ranking boards.*

"In that case, I guess I'll start from there," I said.

Listening to all this has helped me solidify my plans... no, my plans are still the same, but my goals have increased.

"Have you decided on a new objective?" asked Nemesis.

I nodded. "As things stand, there aren't a lot of things I can do, and I can't take part in the war."

Which is why...

"First I'll raise my level," I said, "and then I guess I'll aim to get onto the rankings."

Earth, Undisclosed Chat Room

Members: Professor

General has joined.

Beast King has joined.

Members: Professor, General, Beast King

Professor: Good evening.

General: good evening

Beast King: eve

Professor: Gentlemen...

Professor: Did you both watch the video I sent you through Infinite Dendrogram?

Beast King: saw it

General: thats why we're here, obviously

Professor: That's true.

Professor: Now then, regarding our plan to eliminate an important tian. To put it simply...

Professor: It failed.

General: ya, fail

Professor: Those things I released in the dungeon...

Professor: The horde of Demi-Dragon Worms got wiped out, didn't they?

General: werent there holes in this plan from the start?

General: giving the targets sister bug repellant incense and directing her to the orchard

General: and then springing a trap on the target there

Professor: Originally, I had a different set of steps planned.

Professor: But for some reason all the remberries had disappeared from the market.

Professor: Even the portion I intended to use for my plan was gone. lol.

Professor: Tis a real shame.

Professor: The plan was to give a poisoned remberry to the little sister...

Professor: and use that to kill the older sister.

Professor: Lil Sis, "Big Sis, congratulations."

Professor: Big Sis, "Thanks. Guhah!"

Professor: Lil Sis, "Big Siiisss!"

Professor: This was how it was supposed to go, so what a shame, riiiiiight?! boo hoo, lol.

General: what u think is a shame isnt important

General: the issue is that the new plan got thwarted

Professor: Wasn't that bear scary? To go up against almost 100 Demi-Dragon Worms by himself...

Professor: and even more, to win unscathed.

Professor: Just one of those things should be a match for a player with a high-rank job. lol.

General: thats not that big a deal

General: its possible if ur leveled up and strong...i could do that too

General: but...defeating a demi dragon worm at lvl 0 with no job

General: i dont remember anyone being able to do something that absurd

Professor: My, my. So does that mean his Excellency the General is more concerned by that newbie than the bear?

General: pfft...i look forward to crushing him

Professor: As usual, way to play the stereotypical evil top brass character.

Professor: Me too though! lol.

General: whatever. this is how i am

Professor: lol.

General: but i cant deny it if u call me evil

General: the destruction of a nation…its this games first big event

General: i look forward to the chance when dryfe, no, when WE get to accomplish that

Professor: Well, last time ended with us just taking out some key people and gaining a portion of their territory, so that was a bit hard to stomach.

General: i had fun fighting with the knight commander

Professor: The king was boring.

Professor: It would've been better to fight a bunch of soldiers instead.

General: the arch wiseman…was it beast king that took him out?

Professor: That was pretty awesome. Just what I'd expect from our strongest player.

General: hey

Professor: Oh, okay, okay. His Excellency the General and Beast King are both the strongest. lol.

General: ya whatever. i'll prove it to u in the next war

General: this time i'll put an end to the kingdom of Altar

Professor: Yes, please do let me see that. lol.

General: btw, beast kings been silent the whole time, but dont u have something u want to say?

Beast King: the bear, was really, cute

General: ……………

Professor: …………… lol.

General: …i dont understand ur taste, beast king

Chapter Three 〉 Starting Point

Heaven's Three Star Restaurant, Royal Capital Altea, Ray Starling

Last night, after I had talked about various things with my brother, the dinner had turned into a normal banquet.

My brother and Nemesis, who had eaten more than double what I had, had given up partway and had left more than half the food untouched. So we'd passed out the remaining food and drinks to the other customers in the restaurant, and the entire scene had morphed into a party.

If an observer were to look about the restaurant, they wouldn't be able to tell who among those partying was a player (Master), and who was an NPC (tian).

The one saying to my brother "Hey big spender" is probably a player, I thought. *That was a joke from a retro game. The one with a glass of wine in one hand and an exaggerated way of speaking is probably a tian.*

Other than the distinction of who had an Embryo crest, these were the only sorts of vague differences... *They all look human to me.*

The whole scene made me appreciate again just how amazing *Infinite Dendrogram* was, and along with this, I felt there was something I needed to think about.

I felt this, however...

"My head hurts…" I groaned. The headache made it impossible in my current state to think about anything philosophical.

"Is this a hangover?" groaned Nemesis from beside me, holding her head like I was. I looked about the restaurant and saw that every person at the party who had consumed that drink was in the same state as us.

A hangover… I thought. Yeah, this must be a hangover.

Normally, underage players couldn't drink any alcohol. However, among those who had joined the party yesterday, there had been a Master with a skill that could change water into "an alcohol-like drink." To which I'd just like to ask, "Why would there be a skill like that?"

"This isn't alcohol, okaaay?" the person who'd offered me the drink had said. "It's just juice, okaaay? Drink it and you'll just feel as light as air, okaaay?"

It had tasted great, so I had drunk several cups. And so when the sun had risen, I found myself in this state.

"Ugh… Why does it have to show up here, too?" I muttered.

"Hangover" was also displayed on my status, and even though the pain setting should had been turned off, my head was throbbing.

"That drink, it was similar to alcohol but it was probably actually poison," said Nemesis.

"Ahh, a poison disguised as alcohol that gives you status effects, huh?" I responded.

In that case, it made sense that a skill like that existed, as well as why I had been able to drink it while ignoring the underage restrictions.

There was a folk tale about something like that in Japan, so there might've been an Embryo based on that.

The person who made the drinks was just fine after drinking it, though.

"Why would you drug someone like this…?" I wondered aloud.

"It's Lei-Lei's beary special way of welcoming you." Bro Bear, who had been passing out water to those suffering with a hangover, said this with a strained laugh.

"Welcoming?" I asked.

"She makes sure to get every newbie to drink that Divine Oni Poison Sake (light)."

"Why would anyone do such a thing…?"

"She's teaching you the lesson, 'Surprise attacks like this exist, so you need to be careful, okaaay,' by letting you experience it."

Oh, I see, I thought. *No wonder I thought the people who didn't drink her alcohol seemed like they were grinning or looking on with nostalgia. I'm sure they received the same welcome earlier.*

"…I learned a good lesson, then," I said.

"By the way, she's one of the Masters I mentioned yesterday who bears a Superior Embryo," said my brother. "She's also known as the Prodigal of Feasts Lei-Lei."

"Prodigal of Feasts…" I murmured.

She seems like an extraordinary person, but I wonder how she got a second name like that?

"Oh, also by the way, she wasn't able to participate in the previous war due to a schedule conflict in real life, it seems," said my brother.

I guess it goes without saying, but there are people who're too busy to participate in the game's events.

In the end, I wasn't able to move during the morning until my hangover had passed.

...The item someone from the restaurant gave me to cure the Hangover effect didn't work, I thought unhappily. *That's some pretty nasty poison for you not to be able to cure its status effect...*

Putting that aside, we were back to normal, so we had decided to go shopping in town.

"Hey, Bro, I want to sell the drop item I got from the Demi-Drag and buy some beginner equipment, Dragonscales, and brooches. Do you know where they sell those?" I asked.

"What? You're going to stock up on those?" Bro Bear's expression looked troubled.

Nemesis's skill requires that I take damage, so I was thinking that the Lifesaving Brooch and Dragonscale Ward were a must, but...

"Is there some sort of problem?" I asked.

"Those accessories are beary expensive," he said. "The Dragonscale Ward is the top ward-type accessory and costs about 300,000 lir for one. The Lifesaving Brooch goes for about 5,000,000 lir."

"Say what?" I burst out.

That's 3,000,000 and 50,000,000 in yen. Those items were that expensive? I was taken aback. *However, thinking about it, I guess that's reasonable. It is on the level of determining life or death for you. I would've died several times if it hadn't been for them.*

"...I'll hold off for now," I said. *Also, sorry for breaking them all yesterday...*

"That'd be for the beary best," my brother said. "As for beginner equipment, I know a player-run shop that's fair. By the way, did you already open the Demi-Drag's drop item?"

"Open it?" I asked.

"For boss monsters like the Demi-Drag, the items they drop are usually crates. Inside should be one item derived from the boss you defeated, and then one to five random items based on the boss's level."

"Oh, really?" I asked.

Come to think of it, the item it dropped was a Demi-Dragon Worm Treasure Coffer, I remembered. *I'm pretty sure "coffer" is another word for "chest."*

I selected it from the item list and the message "Will you open this item?" was displayed.

"Would it be better to open this?" I asked.

"Hmm… There's a chance it'll be a miss, so you could just sell it as-is," said my brother. "But if it's from a Demi-Drag, then it might have something quite good in it. So I think it's okay to open it."

"Okay, then 'yes' it is."

Acquired Natural Demi-Dragon Worm Full-body Armor.
Acquired Ementerium.

"It says I got natural full-body armor and Ementerium," I said.

"Full-body armor is beary nice," he said. "It should have a skill that reduces physical damage by 150."

Wow, that's really good… I think, but I'm not sure anymore after having seen Bro Bear's costume.

"What does 'natural' mean?" I asked.

"Oh, it means that it's a naturally-made full-body armor."

…What does "a naturally-made full-body armor" mean?

"All right, then I'll equip it right away…" I said. "Huh? I can't."

I looked closer and saw that the following messages were displayed: "You do not meet the level requirement," and "You must have a total level of 150 and a job level of 51 in order to equip this item."

"…I guess I can't use this for a while," I said in disappointment.

"It looks like it'll be some time before you can equip it, so I think it'd be fine if you sold it," said my brother. "It'll fetch you at least 400,000 lir. Also, Ementerium is an item you sell. It's worth about 20,000 lir."

Ohh, those are pretty good prices, I thought. *Although they don't even come close to reaching the brooch.*

"Ementerium though… For the Demi-Drag's drop item that you're supposed to sell, it only goes for 20,000?" I said to myself.

If, for example, the full-body armor that he said was a winner hadn't been in the crate, and instead it had been an item based on the Demi-Drag with the same value as Ementerium, then that'd be a total of 40,000, I thought. *I'm finally starting to understand how extraordinary Dryfe's rewards were that I heard about yesterday. I'm sure it'd be much easier to defeat eight soldiers than one Demi-Drag. I bet it was a* profitable *battlefield for those that took part.*

…In any case, I've acquired some war funds, so I guess I'll go buy some equipment.

At the shop my brother had recommended, I had them choose a few items for me that I could equip even at level 0.

The equipment was supposedly part of something called the Riot series, and they were widely used by lower level players. It was a set consisting of light armor, bracers, pants, and boots.

The equipment I had bought happened to be the quality product of an armor craftsmen. Due to this, the Riot light armor had received the following bonus effects: Increased HP, HP +200; and Reduced Damage, which reduced physical damage by 10.

This will probably be a big help while my level is still low.

"Nemesis will do fine for my weapon, so I should be good to go grind levels now," I said.

"Not 'Nemesis will do fine!' You should be saying, 'Nemesis is the greatest!'" my Embryo shouted.

"Ne-me-sis is the grea-test," I intoned.

"Don't say it so monotone!"

I had also sold the drop items to this shop for the market value of 420,000 lir. Buying the set of equipment and some healing items, by the way, had cost me only about 20,000 lir. I still had the complete amount I had received for selling the full-body armor, but as there was no need to use it, I decided to just keep it.

At any rate, I was now prepared to go grind levels.

"Ah, hold on a sec," said my brother. "Before you go grind levels, you should equip a job. You'll be at level 0 forever if you don't."

"...Ohh," I said. *I forgot. I'm still jobless.*

"Should I explain a bit about jobs?" asked my brother.

"Please do," I replied.

My brother explained the following things to me.

Jobs in *Infinite Dendrogram* were divided into three large categories: low-rank jobs, high-rank jobs, and Superior jobs.

Low-rank jobs were ones that jobless players acquired first. They were easy to get, and had a level cap of 50. High-rank jobs had set conditions for acquiring them, and they were capped at 100. Six low-rank and two high-rank jobs could be equipped at once, giving a player a total level cap of 500.

So then what about Superior jobs?

Superior jobs were extremely difficult to acquire, and on top of that, only the first player that acquired the job would be allowed to equip it. Also, the greatest feature of Superior jobs was that they had no level cap.

That's right. With Superior jobs, your level, that was normally maxed out at 500, could be increased as much as you liked.

There was no balance whatsoever to this. But of course, as your level rose, so did the amount of experience needed for each new level. That was why even without a cap, there apparently weren't many people with ridiculously high levels.

...Which is to say, there are *a few players with ridiculously high levels,* I thought. *Given how there were also those Superior Embryos that came up last night, I feel like the development team is deliberately setting up different levels of strength.*

Also, it appeared that there were even cases where tians had Superior jobs.

This is somewhat of a digression, but the terms "low-rank job" and "high-rank job" used their translated versions in each player's language. The term "Superior job," however, was unified across all countries and cultural regions.

Given how this overlaps with Superior Embryos, I wonder if the development team is trying to give some deeper meaning to the term "Superior," I thought.

By the way, when using just the word "Superior," this apparently referred to a Superior Embryo and its Master.

...Like I thought, it's confusing.

"What'll happen if I choose a job that doesn't mesh well with my Embryo?" I asked.

"If you're at a save point, you can reset your job whenever you like," replied my brother. "And even if you reset your job, your Embryo's growth won't change."

So that was why there were apparently some players that would repeatedly reset their jobs in order to try various ones. You could repeat this process until you found a job that suited you. After finding it, your Embryo would have developed due to the time spent up until then, so you'd then be able to level up even easier than before.

"Speaking of jobs… what are the jobs of the ranking players you talked about yesterday?" I asked.

"If they came up in yesterday's conversation, then they all have Superior jobs," said my brother.

"I thought as much," I said. *Titles like "King" and "High Priest" certainly seemed like ones only one person could acquire.* "Do you know what kind of requirements they had?"

"Oh… The requirements for King of Destruction were: surpassing 100 million total damage dealt, defeating a certain number of high-rank boss monsters solo, and also completing a special quest," said my brother. "The rest probably had something similar."

100 million damage… I could use the same skill I used against the Demi-Drag, Vengeance is Mine, 10,000 times and it still wouldn't be enough, I thought. *The jobs for ranking players are as impressive as I'd expect.*

"By the way, the stat modifiers stack for all the jobs you have equipped, but you won't be able to use some skills if the grouping of your main job changes," said my brother. "So that means you won't be able to use Gunner skills while you're a Cook."

"Oh, really?" I asked. "Being something like a Cook and Soldier seems like it'd work out, though." *Like in that one movie.*

"Well, you can also change your main job at save points, and you can still use skills if they're within the same grouping," said my brother.

It's probably best to keep that in mind when choosing which jobs to equip.

"Okay, then what jobs can I equip now?" I asked.

"Ta-daa! The Suitable Job Diagnostics Catalog," he said in a voice as if he were going to take out some sort of secret tool. What he did pull out, though, was a thick book. "If you read this catalog, you can find the job that best fits you out of all the ones you can equip right now."

"That's useful," I said.

"Since the format is a questionnaire, I don't know if it'll really be the best fit, but this'll work just fine when you're not sure what to do," he said. "Because at any rate, there are over a hundred low-rank jobs that you can equip in this town from the beginning."

"That's way too many!" I cried.

"Well, you'll probably be using this going forward, so I'll give this to you." He handed me the book.

"Thanks," I said. *At any rate, let's give it a try.*

And so, after five or so minutes the results came in...

"A Paladin?" I thought aloud. *It's certainly a staple in games, but I'm not so sure it fits me.*

"Ahh," said my brother, "Paladins get a boost to their HP, STR, and END. Also, they can learn damage-reducing skills and healing magic."

I see, I thought. *In that case, it's perfect. As long as I'm using Nemesis, then it'll probably be a great match.*

"That's strange, though," he continued. "Paladin isn't a job you can get from the start. I mean, it's a high-rank job."

"A high-rank job?" I asked.

"Yeah," he said. "You can't get it unless you meet certain conditions."

"What kind of conditions?" I asked.

"First, you need to defeat a boss of a certain strength… a Demi-Dragon class monster, while also doing more than half the damage to it."

"I did that," I said. *I cleared that in the battle with the Demi-Drag.*

"Next, you need to donate 200,000 lir to the church."

"I can do that," I said. *Right now I have around 400,000 lir.*

"And last, you need the recommendation of a key person related to the knights," he finished.

"A recommendation… that I don't have," I said. *I just started playing* Dendro, *so I don't think I'll be able to get a recommendation.*

"Wait, wait. Didn't something along those lines happen just yesterday?" Nemesis, who had been quietly listening the whole time, suddenly cut in.

"I see," said my brother. "So that was the real reward from yesterday's quest. Well, of course they wouldn't display such a tactless message as, 'Your relationship with so-and-so has deepened.'"

"Huh?" I asked. *Somehow, the two of them seem to have gotten something I didn't.*

"Master… have you forgotten just who it was you helped yesterday?" asked Nemesis.

"…Ah."

We then made our way over to Liliana's house. Liliana was the Vice Commander of the Knights of the Royal Guard, and likely because of what had happened yesterday, she was at home with Milianne.

We received a warm welcome and thanks for the day before. After we chatted with the two, I mentioned to Liliana that I wanted to become a Paladin. She readily agreed and wrote a recommendation letter for me right away.

I took care of the donation at the church as well, and within the day, I had become a Paladin.

And with this, I was finally prepared to go grind levels.

"All right, then this is where I'll take my leave," Bro Bear struck up his hand and said.

"What? You're not going to help us grind levels, Brother Bear?" asked Nemesis.

"I had planned from the start to go separate ways after the welcome party was over," he said.

"Why's that?" I asked.

"If you do power leveling, then a gap will develop between your status and actual playing skill," he said. "A player's skills and ingenuity are beary important in *Dendro*, so you need to set out on your own to develop these as well."

"I'm here too, though, so it'll be the two of us," said Nemesis.

Power leveling was a method of easily grinding levels by getting help from a stronger player. An example of this would be letting the stronger player take all the hits from a strong monster, during which you would chip away at its health, defeat it, and then instantly gain levels.

Yeah, I guess if I did that, my level would go up, but my skills wouldn't improve.

"Also, *Dendro* has the Embryo system," said my brother. "If you constantly ask fur others to help you, your Embryo won't develop in a good way."

"Is that how it works?" I asked.

"It's possible," answered Nemesis.

Since Nemesis was born this way as a result of my play style since starting, I guess it is possible.

"And so, I'll say adios to you here-," said my brother. "But if you get into any serious trouble, contact me."

"Yeah, if I get into serious trouble," I agreed.

"That's all right, but for starters, try to do your best on your own," he added.

"Got it," I said. "And, um, thanks for all your help since yesterday."

"Don't worry about it. I bearlieve it's only fair to help you out a bit. Oh, and also…" Bro Bear brought the head of his costume closer to me. "If anything happens with a ranking player, make sure you contact me right away." His voice had taken on a more serious tone again.

"Bro?" I asked.

"Well, that thing from yesterday might've been just an anomaly. But crazy things shouldn't happen that often, so just relax and enjoy *Dendro*." Bro Bear said this and left, leaving just me and Nemesis behind.

At the same time, a message was displayed saying, "The party has been disbanded." My brother's status, which had been showing the whole time, also disappeared.

"Well then, Master," said Nemesis. "It's finally time for you — no, for us — to stand on our own feet, but have you decided on where to go?"

"Bro told me about some low-level hunting grounds, so I think I'll go check those out," I said.

"I'm looking forward to grinding levels," said Nemesis. "Heh heh heh! Tonight I starve for blood."

"It's still noon, you know?" I said.

$$\Diamond$$

The first hunting ground we headed to was Easter Plains, right outside of Altea's East Gate. It had a very clear view, and I could see monsters leaping about here and there, as well as the players fighting them.

That reminds me, this is the first time I've seen other players fight.

"All right, then let's get started too, shall we?" I asked.

"Yeah," said Nemesis, and she then changed into the same black greatsword as yesterday.

I swung the greatsword up and down as I held it in my right hand — or rather, it was wrapped around my whole arm.

"This really isn't as heavy as it looks," I commented.

Even at my STR level, I can swing it with no trouble, I thought. *It's about the same weight as that fake sword I bought as a souvenir a long time ago on my school field trip. Or maybe about the same as a metal pipe.*

"Isn't it rude to mention a lady's weight?" asked Nemesis.

"But this is clearly lighter than when you're in your human form," I said. *What happened to the law of conservation of mass?*

"...You're concerned about the law of conservation of mass in a world with magic and where time flows differently?" she asked.

Well, yeah, that's true, but...

"And besides, it shouldn't feel light to anybody else," she said. "It'll only feel light for you."

"Is that how it is?" I asked.

"That's how it is."

Okay, then I guess I'll leave it at that, I thought. *My level isn't going to get any higher if I spend all my time asking questions.*

"All right then, time to start grinding levels," I said.

"I'm itching to get started."

Two hours later.

My level had gone up by 3, and I hadn't taken any damage yet.

"...How come I'm not taking any damage even though I've been getting pummeled?" I wondered.

Since I had arrived here, I had been fighting monsters like Little Goblins and Pashi Rabbits. They were the type you could take one glance at and say, "Ah, these are the small fry monsters you find in the beginning." However, no matter how many times they had attacked me, I hadn't taken any damage.

"You shouldn't be surprised," replied Nemesis. "You have fairly good equipment for your level. Also, wasn't there a Reduced Damage skill? Isn't all the damage below 10 becoming 0 because of that?"

So that means the monsters here can't do more than 10 damage to me.

My initial HP had been a little under 100. Taking into account that this was a hunting ground for beginners, it was possible they had only placed monsters here with low enough strength that they wouldn't kill a player with that amount of HP.

Incidentally, my HP was now over 700 at level 4. Liliana's HP had been in the 5,000s with a Paladin level of 60 and a total level of 210, but at this rate, by the time I reached Paladin level 60, my HP would probably be well over 6,000.

"This may get crazy down the road," I said.

"It might be because it's a high-rank job, but its stat boosts are nice," said Nemesis. "Also, HP is the highest out of all my stat modifiers."

So the large growth in my HP was apparently the result of the total modifiers from the Paladin Job and my Embryo. *The modifier for Embryos is pretty big,* I realized.

Although it wasn't as much as my HP, my other stats had of course gone up, as well. In addition, I also learned the healing magic skill First Heal.

With this, I can heal myself to some degree now.

"Hmm… I guess I'll change spots, then," I said. *As things stand, I should be okay somewhere with enemies that are a little stronger.*

"Yeah, I agree," said Nemesis. "I also felt things were a bit underwhelming."

Well, yeah, that's because it only takes us one hit to slice the goblins and rabbits in half, I thought. *Even though I was the one doing it, it was still kind of scary. The monsters' corpses don't remain behind, but if they did, it'd be one extremely gory sight.*

"Let's see," I said, "the next suitable hunting ground would be Noz Forest, just past the North Gate."

"Then shall we first return to the royal capital?" asked Nemesis. "It's almost time for sweets, after all."

Time for sweets…

"I'm okay with paying for some drinks," I said, "but…"

What will I do if she eats as much as dinner last night? I wondered. *I would like to keep the remaining money I got from selling those items to get my next set of equipment.*

At any rate, we headed back toward the royal capital. On the way, I watched the other players as they fought. There were a lot of players with outfits that were in the catalog from the tutorial, so they were probably beginners like me. However, even if they had the beginner outfits, they all had at least one thing other players didn't.

One player had a sickle and chain. The player would hurl it in the air and the chain would extend on its own to attack the monster — or so I had thought, but for some reason, it was the sickle that would travel underground and then attack the monster instead.

Another player had a baby carriage. Inside the carriage was an egg-like object, and for some reason, the player was pushing the carriage with their left hand, while desperately swinging a sword in their right hand to fight off monsters.

Another player had a stone hut. There was an opening at one section in the wall, and the player was attacking monsters from there with a slingshot. Monsters that bit onto the hut stopped moving as if they were stunned.

Another player had a red barrier. Monsters that entered the barrier would blow up as if they had stepped on a mine.

Ah, the player got blown away as well, I noticed. *I wonder if all of those are Embryos like Nemesis.*

"...There are a lot of different types," I said, amazed.

"The sickle and chain is an Arms, the hut is a Castle, and the mine field is a Territory," explained Nemesis. "The baby carriage is... what exactly? A tool that's an Arms? Or maybe a Chariot?"

So those are the non-Maiden base category Embryos... they look really interesting.

"Are you cheating on me?! Are you thinking about cheating while you're embracing me with your right hand?!" cried Nemesis.

...Does this count as embracing?

"I'm not thinking about cheating or anything, I just thought it was interesting how they all have their own abilities and personalities," I said. "It's really fantasy-like."

Bro Bear's Embryo was such a heavy firearm, the issue went way beyond whether or not it was fantasy-like, I added silently.

"Well, having something solely unique to each Master is the fundamental principle of Embryos, after all," said Nemesis.

"Also, compared to the others, your first form is fairly rugged, Nemesis."

"Rugged?!" she exclaimed.

Yeah, your greatsword mode, that is.

As we continued to walk like that, we came across another player engaged in battle with monsters. Unlike before, however, I could see the silhouettes of two people.

One of them wore a coat that appeared to be starting equipment. He was a player of about middle or high school age. He was dirty with mud and blood from battle, but even still, he was an attractive young boy that you could get away with calling either cool or cute.

As for appearances, the other person was quite unique, as well. She had a demon tail and bat wings, and was a beautiful, imp-like young girl.

"Haaa!"

"Take that!"

The two of them were fighting with all they had, but they were surrounded by four Little Goblins, and the odds were slightly stacked against them.

Now, I'd like to help, but it wouldn't be good to just cut into their battle.

"First Heal," I said, and healed both of their HP. I did it partly as a way to test the new healing magic I had just learned but hadn't yet used. It was what you might describe as a drive-by heal. I couldn't see their HP since we weren't in the same party, but their wounds noticeably disappeared.

"Ah! That helps a lot!" one of them cried.

"Thank youuu!"

The two regrouped and resumed fighting.

After about five minutes, the two managed to wipe out the Little Goblins.

"Good work out there," I said. "First Heal." I cast the healing magic one more time on the two after they had finished fighting.

"Thank you very much for healing us! That really helps," one of them said.

"Thanks," the other added gratefully.

"I just wanted to try out my healing magic, so no need to worry about it," I said. *If anything, it feels awkward to be thanked.*

"Well, you have been getting thanked non-stop since yesterday..." said Nemesis. Her weight then unexpectedly disappeared from my right hand, and she was standing next to me in her human form.

"Huh? What?!" one of them gasped.

"Oh? Are you..." asked the other.

The two of them appeared to be surprised, but Nemesis paid no mind to that and just stared at the imp girl.

"I see, I see," said Nemesis. "A fellow Maiden... no, a Guardian, huh? However, it's rare for a Guardian to look this close to a human."

"Hey, stop staring at her, Nemesis," I said. "That's rude."

"My apologies," she said. "I was just curious about something."

Just what that something was... well, I was curious about it, too.

"I'm sorry, my Embryo was being rude," I said.

"Please don't worry about it," said the other player. "That's amazing, though. There are even Embryos that transform!"

"That's right. I'm Nemesis, a Type Maiden with Arms Embryo!" Nemesis introduced herself with such vigor it seemed like a sound effect should've accompanied her.

...This is embarrassing.

"Oh, sorry for the late introduction, but I'm Ray Starling," I said. "I started playing *Infinite Dendrogram* yesterday."

"Ah, I'm Rook," said the other player. "I also just started playing yesterday."

"I'm Babylon! A Type Guardian Embryo! Call me Babi, okay?" the girl announced.

"Rook and Babi," I repeated back their names. "I have to say, though, weren't Guardians supposed to be a type of monster?"

Other than her tail and wings, Babi looks exactly like a human. You could even say that there's no difference, since I'm pretty sure tails and wings can be added when creating a character. If I had to say which she looked more like, between a monster and a human, I would say a human.

"That's because I'm a succubus!" she declared. "I'm sexy and cute and everyone falls head over heels for me!"

Succubus......... a succubus?

"Babi, I told you not to be so open about that in front of people...!" Rook wailed.

"Whaaat? But I'm an Embryo that takes pride in being a succubus, so it's not embarrassing at all."

"It's embarrassing for me!" he cried.

"…Rook, you're embarrassed by me?" Babi looked at him with puppy dog eyes.

Even as someone on the sidelines, I thought that looking up at him with teary eyes was just unfair.

Rook became flustered in an instant. "You see, umm, I'm not embarrassed by you, Babi. It's just that it'd be embarrassing if people were to start prying into my inner thoughts since you were born from me, you see…"

What is this sense of deja vu? I thought. *Also, I feel like I could get along with Rook.*

"Now, now, you shouldn't cause too much trouble for your Master, Babi," Nemesis scolded.

"You're one to talk," I muttered.

Rook and Babi were done with their hunting, so we decided to band up and make our way back to the capital as one group. And, since we had no reason not to, Nemesis and I invited them to our little sweets party.

They gladly accepted, but…

"Peaches sure are delicious this time of year." Despite it being her first time eating peach tarts, Nemesis spoke as though she knew everything about it and hastily sank her teeth into her seventeenth serving.

"No sweet thing is complete without *this*." Babi poured chili sauce all over her strawberry parfait.

"…No, chili sauce shouldn't even be an option," I said.

"I think so, too…" Rook agreed. "But the speed at which Nemesis eats is also quite…"

"Yeah, I know exactly what you mean..." I said.

The scene before us was strange in many ways. For example, despite not being older than a day, Nemesis and Babi were familiar with the concept of seasonal fruit, they had their own tastes, and they expressed awareness of flavoring.

Yesterday Nemesis had told me that, despite being humanoid in form, she wasn't really like us. But that didn't stop the sight before me from seriously throwing me off.

"When born, we Embryos make use of our Master's memories," she had explained after reading my mind. "Our knowledge of this world came from the world's system, but our knowledge of worldly affairs came from our Masters."

Oh, so that's how she knows about peach seasons and the like.

"Basically, we Embryos know *everything* about our Masters," she added.

"What kind of girls do I prefer, then?" I asked.

"Ones like me, of course!"

"Wrong."

"Why?!" she howled.

So, to sum it up, they didn't know *everything*, but merely came equipped with common sense.

"Still, what kind of common sense would make Babi eat something so... blasphemous?" I couldn't help but ask.

"Perhaps she does it *because* it's blasphemous, no?" Nemesis answered. "After all, her name is Babylon, right?"

The Whore of Babylon was a figure from the Book of Revelation, often portrayed riding a seven-headed beast as she spread depravity, adultery, and defilement, making her a sworn enemy of the martyr. I had no idea if any of that applied to Babi, but Nemesis had the name of the Greek goddess of vengeance or divine punishment, and befittingly, her ability was a counterattack. There was reason to believe that Embryo names were related to their powers.

"That aside, Babi, being a succubus, you must know many ways to express your sexuality and make men go crazy about you," Nemesis commented.

What the hell are you saying, you damn goth loli?

"Of course I do," said Babi.

D-Does she really?

Babi's words actually made Rook choke on his food a bit.

"Ho ho..." Nemesis said gleefully. "Care to share?"

"Umm, there's the shoulder massage, the massage where you lightly step on the lower back, and the best one — the lap-pillow and ear-cleaning combo! Sexy, right?!" Babi exclaimed.

"...Hm?" Nemesis asked.

Sexy? I thought. *None of that goes beyond normal massage. I wouldn't even call it "lewd."*

"That's not what I wanted to hear. Don't you have anything befitting the name 'Whore of Babylon?'" Nemesis asked.

"Like?" Babi looked puzzled.

"W-Well, I-I'm not one to know..."

Don't give her a question that flusters yourself, you damn goth loli.

"Umm... I'm underage, so I think that Babi is just acting accordingly..." Rook stopped choking on his food and gave us a highly agreeable reason.

"Ahh, age restrictions, huh." I expressed my understanding. Just like they affected alcohol and tobacco, age restrictions reduced the sexiness of succubi to the point of making it equivalent to girls giving massages to their dads.

Man is it hard to tell if Infinite Dendrogram *is wholesome or indecent.*

Before parting ways, Rook and I — both being newbies — made a little promise to party up and go adventuring sometime.

Also, Rook didn't have a job yet. In fact, he'd started playing without having read anything about the game, so he didn't even know how to get one.

I let him take a look at the Suitable Job Diagnostics Catalog my brother had given me, and he quickly found a job he was interested in. To make it into a little surprise for the next time we partied up, I chose not to ask what it was.

Anyway, after Rook and I went our own ways, I walked to the northern Noz Forest.

"Shall we?" I asked Nemesis.

"Yes, let's raise your level."

With Nemesis already in her greatsword form, I entered the second easiest hunting ground in the capital's surroundings.

Unlike Easter Plains, this place had a number of trees that took a toll on visibility. The forest was so dense that it was hard to see twenty meters ahead. However, I could hear the sounds of battle coming from the distance, so it clearly wasn't *completely* inaccessible to us players. The sounds were probably being made by beginners like myself, who were no longer satisfied by the Easter Plains.

About two minutes after we began searching for monsters, we found some wolf-like beasts. Right when they entered my vision, the name "Teal Wolf" was displayed above them. There were three in total.

"Man, this is sudden," I said. As in most RPGs, fighting multiple enemies right after entering a higher level hunting ground wasn't the best idea, but I had no choice.

Quick and nimble as they were, the wolves made the first move as the one closest to us jumped and bit into me. The hit dealt 22 points of damage, and it was the first time I'd felt pain that day.

Since I would be able to take about thirty such attacks, I decided to go on the offensive.

As the Teal Wolves surrounded me, I targeted only the one straight ahead. They all began attacking, slightly out of sync with each other. I ignored the two coming from behind and intercepted the one right ahead.

The hit from my black greatsword made the wolf whine in pain. Unlike Little Goblins and Pashi Rabbits, it didn't get split in half, but the damage I gave was great enough to make its movements more dull.

"Yeah, this isn't anything I can't handle," I said.

I continued the grind.

Several minutes later, with my health at 50% and a level higher than I'd had before, I stood surrounded by drops from three monsters.

"All right, so we can take on three of these at once," I said.

"Indeed we can," Nemesis agreed.

In preparation for the next battle, I restored my health with First Heal. Possessing both high HP and an ability to self-heal, Paladins were simply ideal for leveling.

"All right, I'm healed." I said.

"So, now you're just level 5 and already have over 800 HP," Nemesis commented. "Your defense has increased, too, so you might even be able to bear a Demi-Drag's attack without any accessories. Don't you think so?"

"...Even if I can, I'd like to avoid boss battles for now," I replied. Endlessly repeating events *that* intense would simply drain my life away. "I'll hunt standard monsters until I reach level 20."

"That's a good idea." said Nemesis. "I might've evolved into my second form by that point."

"What will happen when you evolve, anyway?" I asked. "My brother said that Embryos don't change *too* much."

"I imagine it won't go beyond new skills and changes to the weapon," she answered. "Though, I do not know if the same can be said for the evolution between the third and fourth form."

"High-rank evolution, was it?" I asked.

"Yes," Nemesis confirmed. "First to third forms are low-rank, while fourth and above are high-rank. As far as I understand it, high-rank forms display a whole different level of uniqueness. There are even cases where the focus on certain skills leads to Embryos entering their own, unique categories."

The fourth form of my brother's Baldr was a tank, which was categorized as a "Chariot." However, it had originally been an Arms-type gun, meaning that it had evolved into a different category.

"If high-rank forms display a lot of uniqueness, what about the seventh — Superior — form?" I asked.

"There are no details on that in the knowledge I was granted with my birth," she replied. "We're simply not given this kind of information, it seems."

"I think I see how it is," I said. It was top secret knowledge not meant to be seen by the average person. Not surprising that there were fewer than a hundred people who got there.

"However, I *do* know that Embryos of fourth or higher forms get called 'high-rank' not just for classification, but for power, as well," Nemesis said, giving more details. "That's why you must hurry and uplift me into the fourth form… and beyond, if you can."

"Well, that's the plan, anyway."

The rankings were probably full of people with high-rank Embryos, so if I wanted to get there, I had no choice but to get on their level.

"For now, I have no choice but to do some honest leveling," I said. "I'm gonna reach level 13 and move on to another hunting ground while it's still today."

The orange patches of sky I saw between the trees clearly showed that it was getting late, but I had no intention of ending the hunt just yet.

Hell, more monsters spawn at night, so it actually makes me excited.

"That's the spirit," said Nemesis.

"All right, then, let's g—"

Suddenly, my vision slanted.

No — it wasn't just my vision, but myself.

The numbness — the remnant of an impact — on my forehead was a sign that something had just hit my temporal region. My status display showed me that it had taken away a whole 80% of my HP.

"…The hell?" I'd been struck by sudden critical damage with no rhyme or reason behind it. Since it'd hit my head, I was left dizzy and unable to properly move my limbs.

"Master!" Nemesis raised her voice.

117

I thought she was simply worried about me, but I was wrong. It was a warning.

"Hh! Counter Absorption!" she cried. Twenty-four hours had passed since she'd used it yesterday, so Nemesis could use Counter Absorption again. Right as she did that, the newly-created wall of light was hit by something.

"Gyaghg, ghgee!"

It was a small monster that combined the aerodynamic shape of a bullet with the dreadful visage of a preta. It writhed — to no avail — as it tried to break through the wall of light. More likely than not, the damage I'd taken a second ago had been dealt by this thing.

"Is this a monster?" I asked.

...*No way,* I thought in disbelief. *This monster's offensive ability is way too great compared to the Teal Wolves I've been fighting. However, it didn't seem like it was a boss monster like the Demi-Dragon Worm, either. I mean, it doesn't even have the name pop-up that appears over every monster in sight. Could it be...*

"Kh!" Counter Absorption's wall of light vanished, and so did the monster that had hit it.

"A suicidal-type monster that dies right after its first attack," Nemesis explained. "It's both a monster and not at the same time... Master! This is a...!"

"...Guardian!" I completed her sentence.

Type Guardian... A monster-type Embryo. Unlike Babi, who was of the same type, this one was a *real* monster.

"Master, retreat! Someone is targeting you!" Nemesis exclaimed.

"Don't have to tell me twice!" I cried.

With my dizziness gone, I dashed towards the North Gate while healing myself.

Soon enough, I became fully aware of the situation. Screams of players were echoing all over Noz Forest. It wasn't just one or two people, either, but dozens of them. Since that monster was an Embryo, the one responsible was another player.

PK — Player Killing. Just as the name implied, it was the act of killing other players — a concept that had existed since the dawn of MMOs. The person who had attacked me was attacking other players, too, increasing his number of victims with every passing second.

With Nemesis's buff and stat increase due to the high-rank job, my HP was significantly larger than that of most people close to my level, and yet a single attack had been enough to bring me to the verge of death. No player without similar circumstances could survive it.

It was no longer a "newbies' hunting ground"… but a "*newbie-hunting ground.*" We had become the hunted.

"That Guardian died right then and there, so why are the victims increasing?!" I cried.

"They're probably part of a high-rank Guardian categorization. Type Legion," Nemesis answered. "It's an Embryo that's basically a colony. As far as I know, the quantity comes at a great cost to quality!"

"You're saying that the attack that almost killed me was 'low quality?' Nice joke," I said.

Wait, if the Embryo is a high-rank, the Master must be high-rank, too, I realized.

"We're at a disadvantage!" cried Nemesis.

We have to hurry back to the capital, I agreed. *This player-killing asshole shouldn't follow us there.*

However, before I could act out my thoughts…

"Gyaghghghghghghgh!" I heard it behind me — a monster flying towards me like a meteor.

"Mast—!"

It's going to kill m—

"Like hell!" Turning around, I swung my black greatsword at the bullet monster.

"Ghh...ghghghgh." The impact made the bullet monster blast away into the trees, ending its life and role.

"...I did it!"

"Well done, Master!" Nemesis cried. "Now, you just have to—"

—run to the city. Nemesis didn't get to finish her sentence. In her greatsword form, Nemesis didn't have a face. However, I could easily tell what she was looking at.

Someone was standing there beyond the trees, lightly veiled by a dark haze. I couldn't tell whether it was a man or a woman, young or old, or even if it was actually human or not. Though light, the haze distorted the silhouette to the point of making me unable to see such basic things. All I could tell was that the figure held a gun-like object in its right hand...

...and that an Embryo crest was shining on its left.

At that point, it couldn't have been more obvious.

It was this person. This person was the one trying to kill me.

"Run away! Master!" Nemesis exclaimed.

Before I could even respond, I began dashing with all I had. The distance was twenty meters. It was much smaller than the distance I had to run when escaping the orchard, and the city was right beyond it.

I kept on running.

However, I suddenly heard a gunshot. At the same moment, I felt a dreadful, daunting sensation.

I had to keep running.

But the terrible chills running down my spine made me turn around. The sight that awaited my eyes was beyond anything I could expect.

Nemesis and I had been able to fend off a mere two of those bullet monsters, and still only barely. And, upon turning around, I was greeted by a hellish *swarm* of the very same creatures, numbering so many that they blocked out the view behind them.

A moment later, before I could even blink, the monsters charged at me and pulverized my body.

[Fatal Damage]

[Party Eliminated]

[Resurrection Period Expired]

[Death Penalty: 24 Hour Login Ban]

Reiji Mukudori

"...Ghh!"

Right after they destroyed me, my consciousness was ejected to reality as if I had been only dreaming. Unlike how people felt when waking up after a good night's sleep, my mind was completely clear. However, I wasn't sure if I could properly process and accept what had just happened.

Sure, I'd heard the final message loud and clear. And I was fully aware that the penalty for dying was now in effect. But I still couldn't wrap my head around what had actually happened back there.

"Let's just test it and..." Sure enough, I wasn't able to log in to *Infinite Dendrogram*.

As I made my attempt, I noticed the message on the display fixed to the side of the device. It said "Penalty Active. 23h:55m:16s remaining."

"...Well, damn," I said.

I looked outside and realized that dawn had yet to break. The clock said that it wasn't even five in the morning. There wasn't much I could do at this time of day.

"...Guess I'll sleep for now." I spread myself out on the bed and tried to pass out. However, when I closed my eyes, I couldn't help but picture the moment I'd been killed. That led to me trying to imagine what I could've done to survive.

It was a case of Tetris Syndrome. Just like people would imagine what block placement would get them to a higher score, I ran my head through various survival strategies.

As such thoughts dominated my head, I realized just how shoddy my movements had been. With the regrets and considerations of what I could've, should've, and would've done spinning in my mind, I eventually fell asleep.

I woke up at about eight in the morning and had my breakfast while watching the morning news. They were discussing something about the entertainment industry and the world tour of that famous singer — Rachel Raymuse. It wasn't anything I could bring myself to care for.

"...Man, this is dull." I was referring to the taste of the food I was eating.

Since I had all the time in the world right now, I'd decided to make something myself, but the result had been far below the fancy meals I'd had in the game. I had a feeling that continuing to live like this would quickly drain away my excitement for real food.

After I finished eating and took care of the dishes, I went to an online message board and looked for info. It didn't take long for me to find something on the incident I'd been involved in.

The tragedy at Noz Forest was actually big news in the message board dedicated to *Infinite Dendrogram*.

Normally, simple player killing would never get this much attention, but this was a special case. That was because players were still being hunted in all the beginners' hunting grounds. However, this was only happening in the Kingdom of Altar.

Simultaneously and continuously, the kingdom's newbies were being killed off. It was clear that it was an operation executed by multiple members of an organized force. The only question left was: Who was behind it?

Most people on the message board suspected the Dryfe Imperium, which was rumored to be planning to attack Altar soon. The reasoning behind the suspicion was the idea that Dryfe was trying to keep Altar's war potential low for when they decided to make their move. Since it was only happening in the kingdom, the possibility of that being true was high.

As one would expect, the kingdom's players were responding to this. Some volunteered to act as vigilantes and hunt down the player killers. A number of bigger battles had happened between the two sides. However, the vigilantes had failed to get even a single victory. That made it quite obvious that the player killers were made up of highly proficient players. Just like the others, the one who had killed me at Noz Forest remained undefeated, but there was a slight difference. The vigilantes weren't even able to find the player killer.

The beginner hunt showed no sign of stopping, but no one could even find the person responsible, let alone defeat them.

"...It had to be that person, right?" I said. Back then, I'd seen both the bullet monster Embryo and its Master. Due to the strange mist surrounding them, I hadn't been able to tell if they were male or female, young or old. That might've had something to do with the vigilantes' inability to find them.

I ran my eyes through the comments, which were many and varied. Some said, "Welp, the Kingdom is screwed," others went "Dryfe players are such scumbags," and some saw this as an opportunity and said, "If you're thinking of deserting, I recommend Caldina. Noobs welcome."

Among them, I saw complaints from unrelated people.

One said, "Man, I got killed while I was just passing by. My Embryo was *this* close to evolving and the death penalty messed it all up."

Another replied with "Same here, and I was about to start living the high-rank dream..."

Were there more death penalties than the login ban? It got me curious, so I typed up and posted a message saying "Noob here. Just started and died for the first time. What's this about death penalties?"

Replies came quickly.

One simply went "Get lost, noob."

Another was fooling around and said, "Let me teach you my ways. Step one: You get naked..." but there were those who properly explained it to me.

Apparently, there were rumors that a high number of death penalties decreased the speed at which Embryos evolved. Most players believed this information and treated it as truth.

It was hard to gauge, considering that Embryos were unique to each player, but rough comparisons showed that Embryos belonging to players with many death penalties evolved slower than those with less. This demerit might've been one of the reasons why the kingdom's players weren't enthusiastic about participating in the war.

After giving my thanks for the info, I switched to another board.

I thought I'd be seeing grim posts about war and player killing everywhere I went, but Tenchi and Huang He were full of people talking about the tame events going on there.

Cherries were blooming in Tenchi, so people were talking about the cherry blossom viewing sponsored by the tian "Conquest General."

In Huang He, panda-like monsters were breeding so much that a whole mountain had become black and white. It was possible to use a camera item to take photos or films and send the output to external media. Someone had posted a screenshot of the panda event, and the heartwarming sight made me smile.

The only battle-related event I found was in Legendaria. There was a great battle royale to compete for tickets to the concert where "everyone's idol" — Fairy Queen Titania — was the main event. Though it was clearly PVP, everyone seemed to be having tons of fun.

"...Why is the Kingdom of Altar the only place that's getting terrorized and reaching the verge of death?" I began to understand why some players would want to defect.

Reading it all was a real buzzkill, so I just turned the PC off.

All right, what now? I thought. *My death penalty ends before dawn tomorrow. I guess it's a good time to take care of some stuff.*

I had to stock up on household supplies and food, not to mention that I'd yet to unpack all the things I had brought here upon moving. Plus I had to start getting ready for college, which would begin in just a month.

There were lots of things I had to do in reality.

By the time I was done shopping, unpacking my stuff, and finishing up dinner, it was already past ten o'clock. I checked the message boards, and sure enough, the player killers weren't taken care of even after two days of in-game time. If the rumors were true and Dryfe Imperium players were really the ones responsible, they would likely try to keep the situation like this until right before the war started. That put me in a bit of a pickle, since I wouldn't be able to use any of the standard places for leveling. All the hunting grounds close to the four gates of the capital were occupied by player killers. That meant that I couldn't even leave the capital.

Even if I somehow broke through their blockade and got to another town, the only hunting grounds that fit my level were around the capital.

If there's one place I can go to...

"Guess I have no other choice," I said aloud.

...it's that special beginner's hunting ground that my brother told me about.

All of the hunting grounds he'd told me about were beyond the four gates of the capital, but there was one exception. I'd been told it was a place that the player killers couldn't reach, and since I hadn't seen anyone posting that it was affected, it was probably true. However, that hunting ground had problems of its own.

My brother had told me what those problems were, and I'd become averse to the idea of going there. However, since I couldn't use the standard hunting grounds, that place was my only real option.

I went to sleep early, woke up at dawn, confirmed that the penalty was gone, and hastily logged in.

$$\diamond$$

Three days had passed in the game. The time of day was evening — just like when I'd died.

The place I'd spawned at wasn't Noz Forest, but the large fountain where my brother had waited for me on the first day. While we had been walking around the town and shopping, he had told me that it was one of the capital's save points, so I'd set it as the place where I'd revive.

All is as it should be, I thought. *The death penalty ends and you automatically revive at your save point.*

"...I see you're back, Master." Before I realized it, Nemesis was standing next to me in her human form. She'd left the crest without me noticing it.

"Yeah. I'm back," I said.

She said nothing.

"...Hmm."

Man, this is awkward. The fact that I had gotten the death penalty made our reunion really unpleasant. I'd gotten killed because of my own ineptitude, so I had to apologize to her...

"Sor—"

"No need." She stopped me before I could finish.

Oh, yeah, she knows exactly what I'm thinking.

"Stop thinking such ludicrous things," she said. "I'm the one who feels awkward and needs to apologize."

127

"Eh?"

Why?

"...Before the incident, I went on and on about how I was the greatest and nothing could ever match me, but the very first time we fought against an enemy Embryo, I could do nothing to protect you from dying. I am infuriated by my own lack of worth and power." Nemesis expressed her frustration by biting into her lip so hard that I could see a small trail of blood go down her chin. *That* was just how guilty she felt.

But...

"But you're wrong." I said. "If you hadn't protected me against the second attack, we would've been defeated way earlier. Seriously, it's my fault for being bad at the game. It makes me look pretty pathetic when you consider that I want to join the rankings."

"No! It's my fault because my skill wasn't strong enough to protect you from the final attack!" Nemesis exclaimed.

"Don't be stupid! It's my fault because I couldn't operate in a manner appropriate for our ability!"

Nemesis hit me in the chest. The punch was very weak. And the words that left her mouth...

"It was my lack of power. If you hadn't been a Master — a player — I... you and me both... would now be gone forever... and that scares me beyond belief..."

The words that left her mouth displayed a fragility far greater than the fist on my chest. The same girl that hadn't stopped talking about the extent of her greatness was now showing her weak side.

"Nemesis..." I said.

She only sniffled in response. Nemesis was crying. Her permeable tears were a sure sign of fragility and transience. When she cried, Nemesis didn't seem like a mere game character.

"…you might be right."

My words made her shoulders shiver. As if to calm them down, I placed my hands on them.

"However, Nemesis, I really don't think that this failure is only your fault," I continued. She was one or two heads shorter than me, so I bent down a little bit and looked her straight in the eyes. "And… just as you said, it wasn't only my own powerlessness, either."

"Master…?" Nemesis asked.

Nemesis wasn't the only one who was inept. Nor was my powerlessness the only thing to blame for this.

"This failure… is *our* fault," I concluded. That was the only correct answer. "My level was low. You haven't matured as an Embryo. And most important of all — we both lacked experience. That's why we were killed by him."

That defeat was in the past, and the past wasn't something you could change.

This death penalty might leave a stain on our record.

"Even so, both of us are alive," I said.

I had gotten killed, but since I was a player — a Master — my life continued as normal. And, if you ignored the possibility of her evolution slowing, Nemesis was okay, too.

"Which means it's all fine, isn't it?" I said. "We can still go on and become stronger than before."

We Masters and Embryos can get back on our feet countless times, I thought. *Who cares about a stain on our record, anyway? I don't want the path I travel to be a bed of roses. Even if we're slightly hurt, we're still standing on our own two feet, aren't we?*

"Let's become strong and have our revenge on that scumbag," I said.

In fact, we have a new goal now, I thought. *We'll level up, evolve, become better at the game, and eventually grind him into paste, fair and square.*

"...You are an unexpectedly demanding man." My words made Nemesis adopt a wry smile. "However, you couldn't be more right," she went on. "Indeed, not letting go of the past when it hinders your march to the future is the height of folly. We still have a road in front of us."

She wiped away her tears. All that was left on her face was a familiar, indomitable grin.

"I don't know his name, but that Master will get what's coming to him." Nemesis raised her right hand. "Let's go, Master! Let's become strong — no, the strongest! No one will be able to harm us then!"

"Hell yeah!" I cried. "Let's do this, Nemesis!"

And so, we linked our arms together. I didn't get any inelegant messages saying something along the lines of "Your bond with Nemesis has deepened," but I could feel it having happened. Nemesis and I were closer than ever before.

That moment was our true starting point.

By the way, I didn't care about it while talking to Nemesis, but since the fountain was a save point, we were surrounded by many other players. They could see and hear our exchange with no problem, and when Nemesis and I joined hands, we were greeted by a round of applause.

With our faces red from embarrassment, we chose to leave the place, giving our conversation an unsatisfying ending.

Chapter Four   Tomb Labyrinth

Royal Capital Altea, Paladin Ray Starling

After running away from the fountain plaza, we went out on a large road surrounded by shops on both sides.

"All right, so we both want to become strong," I said. "Our best option would have been to level in the hunting grounds surrounding the capital, but the current situation doesn't allow that."

"The player killers are still active, after all," Nemesis agreed.

If we wanted to have our revenge on the player killers, we'd have to level in Noz Forest, but with them still being there, we'd end up getting PK'd the moment we left the capital.

"That's why we'll go to the last available hunting ground that my brother told us about," I said.

"The Tomb Labyrinth, correct?" she asked.

"Yeah," I said.

Tomb Labyrinth. Out of all the hunting grounds surrounding the capital, it was the only one that was *inside* it. It was a great, maze-like dungeon that extended below the capital's graveyard.

While my death penalty had been active, I'd taken a look at the walkthrough wiki and found out some important things about it.

First, it was an underground dungeon with a theme and set of monsters that changed every five floors down.

Second, the deeper you went, the stronger the monsters became.

Third, the lower floors were swarming with monsters so powerful that they put Demi-Dragon Worms to shame.

Fourth, the monsters in the upper floors were weak — about as strong as those appearing around the capital.

Fifth, the walkthrough wiki's volunteers had confirmed 415 floors so far.

The most important point was the fourth one. In the upper floors, we newbies could level without worrying about getting killed by players.

"Normally, the other beginners would completely flood it, but that won't happen here, right?" Nemesis spoke.

"Yeah, most of the other beginners should be unable to get in," I replied.

"...Tough world, isn't it?" she asked.

"Seriously."

Once we remembered the reason why the other beginners couldn't enter, Nemesis and I heaved a long sigh.

After dinner, we arrived at the graveyard where we could find the Tomb Labyrinth.

As obvious as it might've been, the graves here were Western-style, not Japanese. We were surrounded by countless tombstones, displaying the names of the deceased and the years they had been born in and died. It was a large graveyard, so there was a map at the entrance. It showed that the Tomb Labyrinth was quite a distance inside. There was even a guardroom for the soldiers stationed there.

Making our way to our destination, we walked through the graveyard.

I've gotta say... this unfamiliar sight of a Western graveyard at night is pretty creepy, I thought. *Though I guess thoughts like that will only get Nemesis to make fun of me and... hm?*

"Nemesis?" I asked.

She didn't respond. There was no expression on her face. In fact, she was making an active effort to not display any emotions.

It's gonna be our first battle since coming back from the death penalty, so she might be a bit on-edge, I thought.

"Nemesis," I said.

"What… is… it…?" Nemesis spoke so clumsily that I could almost hear her voice creak like the mouth of some rusty old doll.

"…It's nothing."

"I… see…"

I wondered, *Is she on-edge or just tense? I can't tell. Well, I don't mind if she's on-edge. We just recently revived, after all. But man, this graveyard is really grim.*

Well, nighttime graveyards weren't lit up by anything, so it was only natural for them to be grim. It was the perfect place for one of those generic horror movie scenes in which zombies crawled out of their graves, banded up into an army, and closed in while losing parts of their bodies.

"…Hm?" I asked.

Right after I pictured a horror scenario, Nemesis took hold of my hand. I could feel it shaking, and when I looked at her face, I saw nothing but anxiety.

…Oh, I see how it is.

"Are you… afraid of ghosts and stuff?" I asked.

She didn't respond. Instead, she simply looked away.

I guess she is and doesn't want to say it, I thought.

Nemesis always spoke in a proud manner, ate a lot, and was slightly arrogant. Yet, she was afraid of ghosts. Despite us becoming closer, I still didn't have a good grasp of her character.

"If you're afraid, why not just change your form right now?" I suggested.

"...Okay." Still holding on to my hand, Nemesis transformed into a greatsword. For some reason, I could feel her becoming more composed.

I guess her form has an effect on her mental strength, I thought. *Keeping her psyche safe comes at the cost of making me look like a weirdo who hangs around graveyards with an unsheathed greatsword in hand, but whatever. I'll just go to the entrance before anyone notices.*

I finally arrived at the entrance to the Tomb Labyrinth. It took me about ten minutes, which spoke volumes about just how large the graveyard was.

Well, there's a large labyrinth underground, so it's only to be expected, I thought. And since I was near the entrance to a dungeon now, no one would tell me off for holding a weapon.

The gate to the Tomb Labyrinth was made of stone and looked really sturdy. There was a soldier stationed right next to it. He quickly noticed us.

"Master, are you wishing to explore the Tomb Labyrinth? You need to have a 'Tomb Labyrinth Exploration Permit' to do that," he said.

A Tomb Labyrinth Exploration Permit. This item was the very reason why no beginners were exploring the Tomb Labyrinth.

It was a possible reward for quests of difficulty level three or a random drop from boss monsters. They were being sold on the player market, too, but one went for an average of 100,000 lir. It wasn't an amount an average beginner could easily procure. Basically, this was a harsh beginner's hunting ground that required the players to pay a kind of toll.

Luckily for me, I'd had the leftover money I'd gotten from selling the Demi-Dragon Worm's drops. So, before going to this graveyard, I had bought my permit. I'd even finished filling it in and actually making it effective, so I was good to go.

When I reached for my items and dug for the Permit with my left hand...

"Oh? You're a Paladin, aren't you?" the soldier asked. "Then there's no need for that. Please go inside."

He moved away from the gate without me having to show my permit.

...Excuse me? I thought.

"...What about the Tomb Labyrinth Exploration Permit?" I asked.

"Paladins don't need one," he answered.

...Are you for real?

"Oh dear, what a waste of 100,000 lir," Nemesis chimed in.

"Oohhh..." Groaning, I fell to my knees.

Not even the death penalty could do it, but this loss of money had made me collapse in an instant.

The shock was huge. If I had to gauge it, it was about three times worse than playing one of those retro RPGs, spending tons of time getting enough money to buy an iron sword, only to get it from the next treasure chest you found.

Goddammit, that money is the equivalent of 1,000,000 yen... I thought. *I filled it in, too, so it's exclusive to me and I can't even resell it now...*

Why didn't my brother tell me about this...? Well, I guess he wouldn't know, not being a Paladin and all.

As I kneeled on the ground due to the shock, the soldier called out to me in a worried tone. "A-Are you okay, sir?"

Nemesis chimed in, "I know you're shocked, but nothing will come out of moping about it."

"...Y-Yeah, you're right," I said.

Time to get a grip, I told myself. *I simply have to raid this dungeon with the intention of making up for the lost money.*

"So, can I go inside?" I asked.

"Y-Yes. Be careful, sir." The soldier spoke a spell that opened the gate. Beyond it, I saw a gloomy darkness and a staircase leading down.

"Let's go, then," I said.

"Onward," Nemesis agreed.

We made our first step into the Tomb Labyrinth.

My brother told me about the Tomb Labyrinth during a little break we had while we were buying my gear.

"Here's something to bear in mind: the largest dungeon in this country is *inside* the capital," he'd said.

He had just finished telling me about the beginner's hunting grounds surrounding the city, so this info was like a little bonus.

"*Inside* the capital? What do you mean?" I'd asked.

"Bear-ly a few dozen meters below us, there's a dungeon called the 'Tomb Labyrinth,' and it's the largest one in the Kingdom of Altar — no, this whole continent," he'd explained.

Nemesis and I had stared darkly at the ground we were standing on.

"It doesn't seem like Dryfe even needs to do anything for this country to be destroyed," said Nemesis.

"Just bear with me here. The Tomb Labyrinth is a created dungeon," my brother had continued. "The monsters inside will never crawl out — you can be paw-sitive about that."

"'Created dungeon?'" I repeated the unfamiliar term, and my brother instantly began explaining it.

"*Dendro* has two bear-ly similar types of dungeons," he began.

You really like giving explanations, don't you, bro? I thought.

"The first type is a 'natural dungeon,'" he continued. "It's used fur places that weren't dungeons before, but that got the function due to various circumstances. The Old Orchard is the bear-fect example."

He went on to add that natural dungeons also included dens created by intelligent creatures and fortresses felled by monsters.

"The other type is a 'created dungeon,'" he went on. "Just as the name implies, these are places that were created fur the sole purpose of being dungeons. Bear with me if I sound a bit meta here, but they're basically dungeons made by the devs."

"Oh?" I asked, expressing my desire to know more.

"There are three main differences between natural and created dungeons that you must always bear in mind," he answered. "First of all, monsters in created dungeons never go outside."

That makes sense, I thought. *Living in the capital would be too dangerous otherwise.*

"The second difference is that monsters automatically respawn regardless of any ecosystems and reasonable causes," he continued.

The people of this world had realistic personalities and lives, and monsters normally weren't different in that regard, since they adhered to proper ecosystems. They wouldn't simply appear with no rhyme or reason. Just as dead tians wouldn't come back to life, entire species of monsters could be made extinct.

However, that didn't apply to created dungeons, where monsters respawned without limit. It was perfectly natural for there to be undead-type monsters despite the lack of corpses.

"The third difference is that every few floors you run into a boss monster that — along with its standard drops — gives you additional rewards," he added.

Unlimited monsters meant unlimited treasure. The grade of the drops increased the lower you went, and — in the deeper levels — items that could be sold for 1,000,000 lir weren't uncommon.

This dungeon was a real cornucopia.

"There are other created dungeons, but the one with the most bear-able entry requirements is the Tomb Labyrinth," my brother added. "When you look at *Dendro* as a game, this is obviously the best reason to choose the Kingdom of Altar. After all, to get in, you only need to have a permit and be aligned with the kingdom."

He paused for a moment, then continued.

"Just like the fertile land around these parts, it's one of the reasons why Dryfe wants to conquer this country. They can't enter the Tomb Labyrinth until they do that, you know?"

So, to Dryfe, the Kingdom of Altar is like a treasury with an endless supply of commodities, eh? I thought.

"Did you stay with the kingdom so you could raid the Tomb Labyrinth?" I asked. "Is this the reason why you didn't switch to the country you like once you got your suit?"

"I've bear-ly been there," he answered.

Not the reply I'd been expecting.

"Why?" I asked.

"...Baldr's fifth and higher forms are too large to use in the dungeon," he admitted.

I had no words. The saying "less is more" crossed my mind. I didn't know if it fit his case, but it was a clear example that there were pros and cons to everything.

And holy crap, what kind of Embryo is larger than a tank? I thought.

And now, Nemesis and I were exploring the very same Tomb Labyrinth my brother and I had talked about. Since it was underground, I expected it to be pitch black inside, but it was actually relatively well-lit. This was because the walls and ceiling were covered in luminescent minerals.

The labyrinth's hallways were quite wide — enough to let about ten people walk side by side. The ceiling, however, wasn't too high. Just as my brother had said — it would get in the way of anything particularly big.

I thought that simply breaking the ceiling would solve that problem, but my attacks couldn't even put a scratch on it. This dungeon was clearly indestructible.

"Despite having the eerie word 'tomb' in its name, it's quite a clean dungeon," Nemesis commented.

"It's probably being cleaned automatically," I said. I could only assume that, instead of realism, the main force at work in this dungeon was the will of the developers.

"I wasn't sure if I could handle a tomb, but if all of it is like this, then there's nothing to worry about," Nemesis said. She was getting increasingly motivated. "I'll split apart all the monsters this dungeon sends our way!"

"Hate to rain on your parade, but the only monster type that spawns in this floor is undead," I said.

"...Eh?" She let out an expression of shock and confusion.

I pointed further into the hallway. *Speak of the devil.*

Clad in tattered clothing, there was a person — or, rather, a monster that looked like a person's bones. The fact that it was a monster was proven by the name above it — Civilian Skeleton.

Just as the name said, it was clearly the skeleton of a civilian, rather than that of a soldier or knight. It had no weapon, so it merely extended its empty hands and closed in on me while making a rattling sound.

Due to *Infinite Dendrogram* having such realistic graphics, the skeleton was quite a scary sight. The hints of red and yellow on the bones — likely left behind by dried bodily fluids — made the sight a bit too vivid and slightly unpleasant.

Things like this make me wish I had chosen anime or CG as my visual setting, I thought.

Despite the gross presence, Nemesis wasn't saying a word.

"Nemesis?" I called out to her.

More silence. She didn't respond at all.

I guess she's trying not to think about anything, I thought. After all, I was about to use her to attack it.

"Let's do this," I said and brandished my greatsword. I had my reservations about attacking a person's bones, but since I had to, I charged at the monster.

My attack made the skeleton's arm and shoulder shatter into many pieces. I then swung towards its head with the flat of the greatsword.

The skeleton's skull got easily pulverized, turning the monster into shining dust that vanished.

"Can't you do it without making me touch it so much?" Nemesis complained.

"Are you saying we have some means of fighting besides slashing and smashing?" I asked. I had no offensive magic, and Nemesis's only skills were the defensive Counter Absorption and the counterattack Vengeance is Mine. Though I'd bought some consumable magic items, they were limited.

Physical melee attacks are my only option with these enemies, I thought.

"That is true, but… it's hard on my mental health," Nemesis complained.

"Well, at least we're fighting skeletons here, not anywhere else," I said.

By "here," I was referring to the fact that we were in a created dungeon. The Civilian Skeletons here weren't actual remains of people, but monsters made just for the sake of being monsters. Even though they were eerie, they weren't haunted or anything.

When you think about it, these monsters are strangely sanitary, I thought. *They even come out dry and fresh.*

"Hmm… that makes it a bit easier to bear," Nemesis agreed.

"Good to know," I said. "Ah, there's another monst—"

I cut my sentence short and could hear Nemesis gasp. The creature that had come from the corner of the hallway made us both lose our words.

Just like the skeleton, it was an undead-type monster. However, unlike the bare, bony frame from before, this one was… fatter. That was because its bones were covered in rotten, maggot-infested flesh.

However, the covering wasn't complete, and you could see yellow and dark red liquids dripping out of the places where its flesh was missing. Since my five senses in the game were about as strong as they were in reality, I could even smell the indescribably bad stench it was emitting.

Above its head, I could see its name — Wounded Zombie.

And so, the sight of the otherworldly, revolting creature made the explorer cast a D6 for a sanity check and...

"...Whoa! This thing is so grotesque it made my mind drift away into another game!" I exclaimed.

This is a bit much, honestly, I thought. *Though I guess it's natural for an undead lair to have zombies right next to its skeletons.*

Unlike the skeleton from before — which had been silent except for the rattling — this zombie was closing in on us while groaning and splashing its fluids on the ground.

"Looks like we have another fight on our hands," I said.

"Huh?! W-Wait! Are you seriously going to use me to cut *that*?!" Nemesis yelped.

"...Like I said, that's not a dead person," I said. "It's just a monster made for this dungeon."

"No no no no! I don't care how it was born, I simply *do not* want to cut that!" she insisted.

"Nemesis..." I began. *It looks like she really doesn't want to do this, so...* "I'll polish you when we get back, so just bite the bullet for now."

"Nooooooo!"

I raised Nemesis as high as the pitch of her scream and charged towards the zombie.

Silent sniffling resounded through the hallways. Its source was none other than Nemesis. Still in my hand, she was weeping like some cursed weapon as I continued walking through the Tomb Labyrinth.

Since we'd entered, we had defeated twelve zombies, thirty skeletons, and five monsters known as "Haunted Spirits." That had gotten me two level-ups, making me level 7. My total HP was now above 1,000.

"Th-The rotten flesh... the maggots..." Nemesis continued weeping. The battles with the zombies had taken a toll on her sanity.

If there was a silver lining to this cloud of hers, it was the fact that the monster corpses completely disappeared, leaving nothing but the drops. Otherwise, both Nemesis and I would look terrible due to all the flesh and fluids covering us.

"Ohh... I never expected you to be such a sadist..." Nemesis moaned.

"Hey, I didn't do it because I wanted to," I responded. "It was necessary."

"...I feel like you performed a strangely high number of full swings, though," she snapped suspiciously.

"It's just your imagination," I said. Though doing them had made me look like the villain from some splatter flick, full swings with my greatsword had been extremely effective at shattering the fragile undead around here. It had made me feel like I was in a Western action game.

Also, although unrelated, the groans of the zombies had all been drowned out by Nemesis's screaming whenever she had their scattered flesh on her. I eventually got used to it, making it much like background music.

"Damn, the last battle cost me half of my Gems," I said. A Gem was an item type I had prepared for battles against spirits.

As the name implied, spirits were ghost-like monsters that had the annoying property of being immune to physical attacks. Not only that, they also drained MP or SP instead of HP and had attacks that applied debuffs to their targets.

I had no offensive magic, so I couldn't do much against them. And though Vengeance is Mine could harm spirits, it could only counter based on the HP I'd lost — not MP or SP. I was woefully underequipped to battle them.

However, I'd read the wiki info on the Tomb Labyrinth, and I'd known I'd run into spirits here. So I'd been aware that I'd need a countermeasure against them, and bought the Gems for this very purpose.

When used, a White Lance Gem would release a shining spear of holy magic, making it really effective against spirits.

However, they could only be used once, and each cost a whole 1,000 lir. I'd bought a total of ten, but the encounters so far had already cost me half of them.

But there's a little problem... I thought.

"I wonder how much we will get for the drops we've gathered so far," Nemesis said.

She'd finished the thought in my stead. For one, it was clear as day that I'd yet to gather even 10% of the money I'd spent on the Gems. To be able to continuously hunt in this dungeon, I wanted to make up for the lir I'd lost, but the returns here were far too small.

Zombies and skeletons dropped items such as Tattered Clothing or Bone Pieces, and I wasn't even sure if they could be exchanged for money. Spirits were even worse, since they didn't drop anything at all.

If, at the very least, the monsters here had been animal-type, I could have made some nice money selling their pelts or fangs. But as things actually were, my wallet was in serious trouble.

"Let's try going a bit further," I said. "We didn't even find the stairs to the next floor, after all."

Maybe we'll find a treasure chest if we keep it up, I thought. Despite being in a dungeon, we'd yet to see a single one of those.

"Understood," Nemesis agreed. "...By the way, Master?"

"What?" I asked.

"Once we're back, I will hold you to your word, and you *will* polish me," she said.

"Well yeah, sure," I replied.

I guess the fact that the fluids and pieces of flesh disappeared didn't do much to better her mood.

A few minutes later, we came across a set of stairs of the same design as the ones we had used at the entrance.

"Well, this seems like the end of this floor," I said.

"No boss to be seen here," Nemesis added. "I was told that you encounter them every five floors."

The floors in the Tomb Labyrinth came in sets of five. The first five floors were the haunt of undead monsters, and the fifth had an undead boss.

Defeating it would open the entrance to the sixth floor, which was infested by an entirely different monster type until floor ten, and from there, the pattern repeated seemingly endlessly.

The walkthrough site described floors until 415, which was in the domain of dragons. The boss on that floor was too strong for anyone to defeat, so anything beyond was simply called uncharted territory.

That term wasn't appropriate, though, since it actually referred to the fact that no one among those managing the walkthrough site or contributing to the wiki had ever made it past that floor. It was entirely possible that someone knew what was beyond floor 415, but kept it secret to have a little advantage.

Man, I have absolutely no business pondering places I can't even get to, I thought. *I'll just leave for now. But man, what should I do about this dungeon's high cost and low returns...?*

As I got lost in thought, Nemesis called out to me. "Master!"

Her quiet voice was a signal for me to be cautious.

"What's wrong?" I asked.

"Someone is coming up the stairs," she answered.

I instantly shifted my attention to the staircase.

I strained my ears and could faintly hear the echoes of someone's footsteps as they went up the stairs.

Monsters couldn't go between floors, so it was clearly a player. Done with their business here, someone was taking their leave by using the stairs.

Strangely enough, however, there was only one set of footsteps. If someone had come here to explore the dungeon instead of — like myself — grinding levels in the low-level floors, they would surely come with a party.

As I considered that, the footsteps suddenly stopped.

A moment later, from the darkness below, something extended towards me. It was almost too fast for me to perceive.

There was some distance between me and its source, so I could sense it coming. However, right when I came to realize what it was, it was already right in front of me.

The thing coming straight towards my face was an attack against me.

"Counter Absorption!" Nemesis and I shouted, and something slammed against the newly-created barrier of light.

That something... was a chain.

Its end had the shape of a pyramid. Though blocked by the Counter Absorption barrier, it continued applying an immeasurable amount of pressure to it, making me fully aware that it could have pulverized my head in a single hit.

"Th-This power...!" Nemesis's voice made it obvious that it was hard to bear. She hadn't reacted like that when defending against the Demi-Dragon Worm's attacks, or the bullet monster's.

That means that this attack is far greater than those two! I thought in disbelief.

"I... I can't take it...!" Nemesis groaned. The barrier of light that had defended me against such powerful attacks began to crack, and...

A sudden turn of events. Right before the barrier shattered, the chain returned to its source.

We got a moment of reprieve.

However, such an action from this opponent could only mean one thing.

"They're going to attack again! Prepare yourself!" Nemesis shouted.

Just as she'd said, they were preparing for a second attack.

I hastily jumped back, creating some distance between us.

"...What do we do now?" I asked both Nemesis and myself.

We had one more Counter Absorption use, but that was the extent of it. We couldn't handle anything beyond the next attack.

I got into a battle-ready posture and waited for the chain to come at us again.

Some time passed, and I grew confused. The next attack showed no sign of happening.

I couldn't sense the chain coming, but I could hear the footsteps as the attacker resumed going up the stairs.

"Master... which do you choose?"

I instantly understood what Nemesis had in mind.

There were only two options for me: to turn back and run away, or to face whoever was coming up.

If the first attack was anything to go by, the power difference between us was so great that I couldn't ever hope to win. I had a feeling that this person was stronger than the player killer we'd sworn to get revenge on.

If it was possible, I didn't want to fight them, but the possibility of having that chain attack me from behind crossed my mind, rendering me unable to move from my battle-ready posture.

If I can't move, running isn't even an option, I thought.

Hesitant as I was, I couldn't expect either choice to bring me much success, so I could only go with a certain gamble.

When he comes up, I'll nullify his next attack, multiply all the damage he was supposed to give me, and launch a counterattack, I laid out the plan in my head. *I have no idea if I'll land the hit or if it'll be enough to kill him, but it's my only chance.*

Knowing my thoughts, Nemesis readied herself and aligned her attitude with mine.

The footsteps became louder, and — sooner than later — the person was in sight.

It was a young man who looked several years older than me. Though he had a nice face, he looked as though he was glaring at something. I would have even gone as far as to call him slit-eyed.

His apparel was simply bizarre. Though the metal armor on his upper body was from the Riot set — the same as mine — for some reason or another, his lower body was covered in a hakama. Then there were his metal greaves, six familiar chains — three in each hand — rings on all of his fingers, and a feathered hat on his head.

But the most extreme article of clothing he wore was the blue long coat hanging on his shoulders.

None of his clothes were strange by design, but the coordination between them resulted in something truly bizarre.

It seemed like a generic case of "I equipped only the highest quality items and ended up looking weird" that every gamer was familiar with.

The reason I assumed the gear was high quality was simply because it all *looked* masterfully made, even to my inexperienced eye.

The man in strange clothing threw me a glance…

"…So it *was* a person."

…and spoke up with a sigh.

A moment later…

"I attacked you because I thought you were a monster! I'm so sorry! My bad!" He bowed before me and apologized.

"…Huh?" I said.

Still in the room with the staircase, the strangely-dressed man and I began having a little chat.

Nemesis had returned to her human form.

The room we were in was protected by a barrier item — placed by the man — that kept monsters at bay, so we were safe.

The first thing I found out upon speaking to him was that he wasn't a PKer. Also, his mannerisms and the way he spoke gave me the impression that he was a… reasonably good person.

As for why such a man would attack me…

"So, you confused me with a monster, huh?" I repeated his excuse.

"Yep… I'm really sorry," he said.

As he'd been making his way up here, he had felt someone examining the hints of his presence. The light shining behind me had made my silhouette look inhuman, so, just to be on the safe side, he had attacked me.

…I couldn't really blame him. After all, in her black greatsword form, Nemesis would reach right up to my shoulder. My silhouette could easily look monstrous.

"Monstr—?!" Nemesis yelled.

My observation seemed to have been quite a shock to Nemesis, but I chose to ignore it.

"So tell me, why are you going solo in such a shallow floor?" The strange man asked.

"Oh, I'm just leveling," I replied.

"Leveling? Why here, of all places?" He seemed puzzled. "Your total level is… 7, huh? Shouldn't someone your level be leveling outside? It's both easier and more profitable. I know you're a Paladin and didn't have to buy a permit, but still."

...I did buy one, though, I thought and lamented the wasted money once more. I also couldn't help but notice that he'd been able to see my level.

"Didn't you know? No one can use the beginner's hunting grounds due to the terrorism there," I explained.

"Terrorism?" he asked.

"Yes, player killers are terrorizing the beginner's hunting grounds around the capital. It's been going on for three in-game days now."

"...I've been in this dungeon for five, so I had no idea." He added that he didn't even check the Internet for game-related news.

I couldn't hold back my surprise. "You've been in the Tomb Labyrinth for five whole days?! What were you doing here?!"

"Just a little marathon," he said. "I wanted to see how far down I could go while playing solo, and then I simply came back up."

A bit of a tryhard, isn't he? I thought. His gear and the power behind his attack were proof that his level was really high.

"How deep did you get this time?" I asked, just out of curiosity.

"I got to floor 418," he said. "That's one more than my previous record."

The young man had spoken a number that was nigh impossible to believe.

"...What." That was about the only way I could react. Even while in a party, the tough guys from the walkthrough site could only reach floor 415.

It was quite hard to accept that he had been able to go beyond where they'd gone and reach the uncharted ground while going solo.

"You are...?" Nemesis asked for his name.

"Oh, my name is Figaro," he replied. "Nice to meet you."

"I'm Ray Starling," I said. "This is my Embryo — Nemesis — and... ah!"

As I introduced myself, I finally realized where I'd heard his name before.

Figaro — Over Gladiator Figaro.

That was the name of the one sitting at the top of the Kingdom of Altar's duel rankings.

"Are you *that* Figaro? From the rankings?" I asked.

"Yep, that's me," he answered. "I go through lots of matches in the arena."

"Arena? Matches?" His words slightly confused me.

"Yep. The arena," he said. "In the kingdom, it's in Gideon, city of duels. When dueling in the arena, you don't die, even when you're killed, and you can even win money depending on the audience you pull. It's fun."

"'Don't die, even if you're killed?'" I raised an eyebrow.

"There's a magical field that makes it work that way," he explained. "It's like a recreational activity with some betting on the side. There are some other tourist attractions, and the town is always lively, so I recommend you visit it someday."

I guess people's tendency to cling to their desires is fully functional even when their country is on the verge of ruin, I thought.

"Gideon is not too far after you pass the mountain in the south, and... oh, right." He suddenly stopped. "If the terrorists are preventing the use of beginners' hunting spots, then the Sauda Mountain Pass is blocked, as well. The idea of there being less traffic there is... troubling."

Figaro fell silent, pondering something...

"All right, then. I'll do something about it."

…and said that.

"I also have to make up for the attack I did, after all," he added. "I'll take care of the player killers in Sauda Mountain Pass."

"Take care? How?" asked Nemesis. "…Negotiation?"

The question mark behind that word was almost audible.

"You should be able to use the pass by tomorrow, so you just get some levels and come over to Gideon," said Figaro. "Most of the time, you can find me there or in this dungeon."

"Ah, okay," I nodded.

"All right, I'll be going, then," he said, getting ready to leave. "Oh, have this."

Figaro reached into his bag and took out a small stone. It was a Gem — just like the ones I'd used — but this one was of a different color and carried a different kind of magic.

"It's imbued with 'Escape Gate' — a spell that lets you leave created dungeons," Figaro explained. "Get all the levels you can and use it to leave this place."

"Are you sure I can have this?" I asked.

"Sure am," he said. "It's another thing I'm doing to make up for the attack I did. After all, it would've been really bad if I'd given a death penalty to a newbie like yourself."

"Thank you so much," I said. I was sincerely grateful. With this item, I could continue the hunt without having to think about the dangers I'd face on the way back.

Figaro really is a good guy.

"But man, you two are pretty good," he added.

I raised an eyebrow.

"You were able to withstand my attack, weren't you?" he asked.

"Well, yeah, but that's what our skill is," I said.

"I wasn't talking about the damage," he said. "You didn't break when I came up the stairs."

Didn't break? I thought. *What does he mean by that?*

"I'm fond of people who don't break," he continued. "I like you. Hope we get to fight in the arena someday."

"That'd be nice," I said. If — as Figaro had said — there was no death penalty there, I could act on my curiosity and fight him just to find out how strong the top of the rankings really was.

"Yep. I'm looking forward to it," said Figaro. "I'll dedicate this cleaning to the pleasures of the future."

"Cleaning?" I asked.

Figaro stood up.

"See ya later, then," he said, instead of elaborating on the strange term.

"See you, too. Thank you for the Gem," I said, choosing not to push it.

With a bright smile on his face, Figaro waved us goodbye and left the room.

"Over Gladiator Figaro, huh?" Nemesis spoke. "Not the kind of person I expected him to be."

"Same here," I agreed. "Based on what my brother said, I expected him to be more rebellious."

He'd told me that the reason Figaro hadn't joined the war was because he "wasn't interested in sloppy fights." That had made him sound really obstinate and rebellious, but upon meeting the guy, I could only assume that he'd had his reasons.

"All right, let's get started, then," I said. "We've got a Gem that lets us leave this place with no problem, so let's go all out."

"Yeah, let's do it," Nemesis agreed. "No undead can be as scary as that attack from before."

Apparently, that event had made her sense of fear go numb.

Perfect, I thought. *We'll be able to progress at a faster pace.* Up until that point, a part of me had been holding back — for Nemesis' sake. *Now I can turn this little adventure into a real splatter flick.*

"Let's resume the hunt!" I roared.

"Bring it on!" she joined me.

A few hours later, I was polishing Nemesis — still in her sword form — as she silently wept.

This continued until the break of dawn.

It was ten in the morning, the day after we'd explored the Tomb Labyrinth.

It was time to check out, so I walked out of the inn while drowsily rubbing my eyes.

The reason for my drowsiness was the fact that I had stayed up until dawn polishing Nemesis, who had still been asleep.

Instead of being in her human or sword form, she was currently inside the crest on my left hand. Nemesis was outside of it most of the time, but for most people, Embryos were something to keep in their crests.

That was obvious, of course. Otherwise, my brother would have to walk around with a Gatling gun in his hands or ride around in a tank.

And that's something that'd have him taken away by the police for questioning, I thought.

Nemesis's personality kept her outside most of the time, but now, she was focused on sleeping inside the crest.

Seems like the R-18 zombie fest took quite a toll on her mind, I thought.

However, thanks to that, I'd gotten to level 12 and gained two new skills. They were "Paladin's Aegis" and "Instant Equip."

Paladin's Aegis was an always-active defensive skill. It was pretty good, too, since it reduced all incoming damage — magic or physical — by a whole 10%. A Paladin simply wasn't complete without it. Since it cost absolutely no MP, it was possible to just activate it and treat it as a passive skill.

The other skill — Instant Equip — allowed the user to quickly switch to wielding another weapon from their inventory. There was no need to dig through the items in the 4D bag to find it. The skill wasn't unique to Paladins — everyone who used any sort of weapon would get it sooner or later.

There were downsides to both skills, though. For example, Paladin's Aegis could only be used by jobs in the knight grouping, while Instant Equip had a cooldown of five minutes.

...Well, it's not like I have a weapon I could switch to using Instant Equip, I thought. Nemesis wouldn't shut up about it if I did.

"I won't let you... cheat on me... with another weapon..." Nemesis murmured in between her breaths.

...Is she talking in her sleep? I wondered.

The first thing I did once I went outside was search for info regarding the player killings in the beginners' hunting grounds.

Figaro had said that Sauda Mountain Pass would be open by now, but I had to confirm it for myself. And, sure enough, the player killing terror in that area was over. In fact, it was disappearing in the other areas, too.

"I can understand the south, but the others...?" I whispered. It even included the place I had died at — Noz Forest.

If the timing was anything to go by, the south had been taken care of by Figaro, but what about the others? As such questions went through my mind...

"Ah, Ray!" someone called out to me. "Hey there!"

"Hm?" I turned to the familiar voice's source. It was coming from the front of a store next to the street.

In a mere moment, I realized that it was Rook — the guy I'd met in one of the beginners' hunting grounds. Unlike last time, his graceful face wasn't covered in dirt, and he was smiling at me while — for one reason or another — wearing the uniform of a shop run by tians.

"Hello," I greeted him. "Why are you wearing that?"

"Getting skills while working part-time," he answered.

Apparently, the suitable job Rook had been diagnosed with and had chosen was close to the merchant grouping. Due to that, he'd been able to learn various mercantile skills by working at shops. Just like me, he'd gained skills without having to rely on the hunting grounds.

"So, what job did you pick?" I asked.

"Pimp!" he answered with excitement.

Pimp... as in... Pimp? I wondered. *Why does that job even exist? And why is an underage boy able to take it? In fact, why is that his "suitable job" in the first place?*

"...My guess is that it's because he has a succubus with him," Nemesis said sleepily, still in the crest.

Well, that makes sense, I thought. *Look at those bright eyes of his, though. Does Rook even know what the word "Pimp" means?*

"...What kind of skills do you Pimps have, anyway?" I asked.

"I've got these ones so far!" Rook said eagerly and showed me his skill summary.

Wordlessly, both Nemesis and I ran our eyes through it.

In conclusion — he was a true pimp.

There was Male Temptation — a skill that Charmed females and had a chance to tame monsters. Then there were Female Monster Strengthening and Female Slave Strengthening, which did exactly what the names said. I couldn't ignore Influence, either, which increased the rewards from doing work and made the whole picture look very... "master"-oriented.

The only normal skill among those was "Insightful Eye," which seemed to have come as an extra.

But man, "Charm" is quite a scary debuff, I thought.

According to the game's help files, it was a stronger form of the "Confuse" debuff. Charmed creatures would protect the one who Charmed them and attack their enemies. Basically, it made them guard the enemy and fight their allies. Players weren't excluded from its effects, either — their bodies would simply start moving on their own.

"There's a theme here, isn't there?" said Rook. "I guess Pimp is a monster-taming kind of job?"

"...Something like that, I guess," I replied. Women were a strange kind of monster, after all.

In exchange for him showing me his skills, I showed mine, too.

Upon seeing my Paladin's Aegis and Instant Equip, Rook's eyes lit up. He yelled out, "That's so cool!"

...Why must such an earnest, good young boy be a Pimp? I wondered.

Rook quit his part-time position at the shop, so I waited for him to take care of whatever he needed to, and then joined him for lunch. He had only been working there because of the player killings, so no one had had any problems with him quitting now that they were over.

In fact, the owner thanked him. That was because — during the three days Rook had spent standing in front of the shop — they'd gotten five times more customers than usual. One thing to note was that all the new customers were women — Master and tian alike.

As we walked through the streets, I could feel a lot of people staring at us. To be specific, the women around us were staring at Rook.

"Just look at that pretty boy... he's so cute, I might faint," one of them said.

"That's some amazing character creation skill. Wait, how do you even make a boy *that* pretty?!" another joined in.

"He seems a bit too natural for it to be character creation," a third one added.

Hearing their comments made me throw a glance at Rook.

"...Hmm," I pondered. When I'd first met him, he'd just seemed like a pretty boy covered in dirt from battle, but now that he was clean, it was obvious that he was among the most handsome men in the world. It felt as though he'd been the result of some miracle that had happened in his ongoing transition from "boy" to "young man." The silver hair covering his head made him look like a fairy representing the ephemeral nature of snow.

"…Master," Nemesis said, having read my mind. "Is it just me, or is your description of his appearance better than the one you gave me when we first met?"

No comment.

"By the way, Rook," I said, "how much did you work on your character's appearance when starting the game?"

"I changed my hair color," he answered.

"…That's it?"

"Yes."

So a guy *this* handsome actually existed in reality, meaning that his Embryo being Babi and job being Pimp could all be attributed to him being handsome.

I can only assume that the Pimp industry is limited to handsome people, I thought.

"What do you think his relationship is with the blond guy next to him?" the girls continued their chatter.

"Well, I'd say that they're *doing it*," one of them concluded.

"Which one takes it?" a third one asked.

"The blond one," the other two replied in unison.

"I think so, too!" the third squealed. "The pretty boy's smile is that of a sadistic top!"

The exchange made a chill go down my spine, but I pretended to not hear it.

"Now that I think about it, I haven't seen Babi yet. Where is she?" I asked. *Is she in the crest? Like Nemesis?*

"Babi is working part-time, too," Rook answered. "She's in a massage parlor nearby."

"Massage parlor...?" The implications of a succubus doing such services made me imagine only the most indecent of things.

However, once I got there, I became aware that it was a wholesome place that didn't even need to operate from a back alley.

"...Yep, it's a massage parlor, all right," I said.

"Yes," Rook confirmed. "What about it?"

"Rook! I'm done with my job here!" With perfect timing, Babi ran out of the massage parlor and stood right next to Rook.

"Ah, hello there, Ray! Hey there, Nemesis!" she added, noticing us.

"Hello." I returned the greeting.

"It has been a while." Nemesis, who was no longer in the crest on my left hand, now stood beside me in her human form.

With all of us back together, it was time for lunch.

My brother had told me about a nearby shop, so I chose it simply because I had no reason not to. His recommendations rarely disappointed, after all.

As we dug into our meals, we continued exchanging information and chatting.

Rook and Babi spoke about their time working, while I told them about the hunting grounds and the Tomb Labyrinth.

"I got a new skill today!" Babi announced.

She'd gotten a skill despite being away from Rook. Humanoid Guardian type Embryos were able to gain new skills by working, training, and learning while separated from their Masters.

Babi's current setup had a skill called Lilim Temptation, which could Charm males. It was the opposite of Rook's Male Temptation, which was effective against women. When together, they could Charm both sexes, giving them a great advantage in countless situations. Another interesting skill she had was Lilim Drain, which allowed her to drain HP, MP and SP from Charmed enemies.

As for the skill she'd gained in the massage parlor, it was Angelic Massage, which could take away the effects of Exhaustion.

"By the way, Nemesis's skills got me curious. Can she use Counter Absorption and Vengeance is Mine when she's all by herself?" Rook asked.

That was a good question. I could recall her having used Counter Absorption on her own volition, but what about Vengeance?

"I cannot use Vengeance is Mine by myself," she answered. "It can only be used when I become a weapon and get equipped."

"Oh, I see," I said, understanding. According to Nemesis, Counter Absorption was closer to a Guardian type skill, while Vengeance is Mine was more of an Arms type ability. Guardians had autonomy, but Arms and Chariots had a lot of skills which could only work when they were equipped.

"It just hit me that I asked to see your skills, but didn't ask for your level. What is it now?" I asked Rook, looking at him. *He hasn't been able to grind much these past few days, so if our last meeting was anything to go by, he should be at about level 5.*

"I'm level 25," he said.

"25?!" I couldn't hold my shock. *That's more than double my level!* "How?! Where did you raise your level? The hunting grounds weren't an option, so—"

Hell, I don't think he could get that many levels even if he could use the hunting grounds! I thought.

"Yeah," he agreed. "I couldn't go hunting, but I got lots of XP for completing a Pimp guild quest."

"A Pimp guild quest?" I repeated, dumbfounded.

I hadn't been aware of it, but taking a job unlocked quests from the guild of that particular job grouping, and clearing them rewarded the player with experience. However, with the exception of those given to non-battle jobs, most of the quests in guilds required the player to defeat or defend something, so newbies like myself couldn't do much there.

Hell, I'm a Paladin — a high-rank job — so it's probably even worse for me, I thought.

"I see… but…" There was something I was curious about. "…A job that only a Pimp can do?" I asked.

Is there anything in that vein that isn't R-18?

"The one I cleared was a quest to find a model for a painting," Rook explained. "Here's a copy."

"Let's see here…" I said and looked at it.

Maestro Grantzian Valleno is looking for a model, difficulty level 6.

One of the Kingdom of Altar's greatest artists — Grantzian — is looking for a model for a new painting.

Please bring someone that he would be satisfied with.

Depending on the model, they might be asked to pose nude.

Be advised that Grantzian is a fastidious sort and that his standards are sky-high.

I had no words. The difficulty of this quest was actually a level higher than the one where I'd had to help Milianne.

"So, you went and cleared it by showing Babi to him, right?" I asked.

"No. Well, that was my original intention, but…"

"Pardon the intrusion. I am Rook from the Pimp guild, and I came here with a model."

"Hmph, another one of you useless cretins who are only good at handling your crotches. All you wretches ever bring to me are atrocious hags. So, where is the…"

"Umm, is anything the matter?"

"You're hired!"

"For some reason, *I* had to be the model," said Rook. "Well, it got me some levels and it made Mr. Grantzian happy, so I didn't mind it at all."

"…I see. Good for you," I said.

Man, this world is really kind to handsome people…

By the time we'd finished our lunch, my exchange with Rook was nearing its end.

I'd thought *I'd* had some strange experiences since I'd started the game, but his adventures had been quite something, too. I had no idea if we were unique in that regard or if getting entangled in unusual events was the norm in this world.

"By the way, Ray," Rook addressed me.

"Hm? What?" I responded.

"We just talked about the player killers, and there's something that I can't get out of my head," he said.

...It's probably the same thing that I'm interested in, I thought.

"When you met Figaro, he said he would do something about the player killers in the south, right?" he asked.

"Yeah, he said something about the hunting ground there being the passage to the city of duels," I answered.

"But the player killing is over in all the hunting grounds, isn't it?" he asked.

Exactly, I thought. That had been the question on my mind before I'd met up with Rook.

There would've been no surprise if Figaro — the top of the duel rankings — had ended the player killing in the hunting grounds. In fact, if he'd simply given them all the death penalty, the player killing wouldn't be happening for a whole three days. However, Figaro had only mentioned the Sauda Mountain Pass in the south. Therefore, it was strange that the player killings in the other places were over, too.

"I have three possible scenarios in mind," I said.

"Do tell," Rook said, looking interested.

"Scenario number one: Figaro did something about the other three, as well," I said.

This scenario is quite unlikely, though, I thought. He'd probably taken care of the southern player killers to secure the means of travel between the capital and the city of duels — his main haunt. However, he'd had no reason to take care of the problems in the other areas.

"Scenario number two: upon finding out that someone took care of the player killers in the south, the others ceased their activity, as well."

This one seems a bit questionable, I thought. Sure, getting killed would disable the player killers' activity for a whole three days here, but this particular event was organized terrorism meant to prevent Kingdom of Altar's players from growing stronger.

From the way they'd sealed all four sides of the kingdom, it was obvious that they were acting as one. Due to that, it was hard to believe that they'd stop just because one side got neutralized. In fact, I would expect them to make up for the loss by sending over some of their killers from the other areas.

Suddenly, another possibility came to mind.

What if the countermeasures Figaro took aren't as small-scale and haphazard as I think they are? I thought. *What if he actually negotiated with the player killers?*

If that was the case, it was no surprise that all the player killing had stopped.

However, that's quite a questionable assumption, too, I thought. *Figaro was a good guy, but he didn't seem like the type to act like that. I didn't talk to him for long, but the impression he gave me didn't seem to fit that scenario. After all, he almost killed me just because he couldn't see what I was. That brings him closer to "musclehead" territory... or just makes him seem like a person who is rough in the way he operates.*

"Umm, Ray," Rook said, "what's the third scenario?"

Whoa, I got lost in thought, I realized.

After a short process of elimination, I voiced the third possibility.

"Scenario number three: at the same time as Figaro was doing his thing in the south, the other places were taken care of by other people," I said.

If Figaro wasn't the one who'd taken care of them all and if the others hadn't just backed down, it could only mean that someone else had gone to the other hunting grounds at the same time as him. After all, they were player killers, so there must've been many people who wanted them gone. Therefore, it was fair to assume that someone had gone to take care of them at about the same time as Figaro.

I felt it reasonable to believe that the single cause led to a coincidence in timing — a synchronicity, of sorts.

"And you are completely right!" an unfamiliar voice broke in.

It was way too sudden. Before I realized it, a woman I didn't know was sitting down at our round table — on a chair between myself and Rook.

Despite her being right next to me, I hadn't noticed her at all until she began speaking. Which was odd, because her appearance was strange and unique, making it nigh impossible to ignore her presence.

Her hair was black and long enough to cover her neck, while her face was that of someone around my age, but neither of those points were what made her seem strange. All of her oddity was in her apparel. However, the reasons were completely different from Figaro's.

That guy had had clothes befitting a fantasy setting, but there had been no uniformity in his overall appearance. This woman's clothing, however, was completely uniform. It just happened to be a men's business suit that didn't fit the fantasy setting at all.

Not only that, but her eyes were covered by a pair of sunglasses. I wouldn't have found her appearance the least bit weird if we'd been in reality, instead of the game. Though, even in reality, it would be pretty strange to wear sunglasses indoors.

"Umm... You are...?" Rook asked as I examined the woman.

"Oh, do forgive me," she said. "I found your conversation so interesting that I couldn't help but join in. This is who I am."

As I noticed that she was talking in a slightly tomboy-ish way, she took out a business card… which was actually just a status window with her name, job, et cetera, but whatever.

Name: Marie Adler.
Job: Journalist belonging to the company known as "DIN."

The existence of the job "Pimp" is surprising enough, and now I run into a Journalist, I thought. *This game sure has great job variety.*

"What's DIN?" I asked.

"Short for *Dendrogram* Information Network," Marie answered. "Some call us newspaper reporters. However, when we want to sound cool, we like to go for 'intelligence agency without borders.' We gather information from countries all over and sell it to other countries."

"…Is that a safe thing to do in the current environment?" I asked. The kingdom was at war with a neighboring country. People who could leak info to the enemy seemed like prime candidates for arrest.

"Well, we have many DIN fans in the upper echelons of every country," she answered. "Though I'm just an underling, so I specialize in info for citizens and Masters."

"Any examples?" I asked.

"For the citizens, we recently took photos of and wrote about the pandas that were breeding so much they covered an entire mountain in Huang He."

…Oh yeah, I saw that in the message boards, I thought.

"As for Masters, we recently gathered info about the player killers that were terrorizing the Kingdom of Altar's surroundings," she continued.

"…Hmm," I pondered. If she handled info like that, she might know how it all played out and ended.

"You said that he was completely right. Do you know the truth behind the event?" asked Nemesis.

"Do you want to know? 600 lir per area, please," Marie said. "You can also buy the info on all four of the places at once for 2,000."

I see. So she only appeared before us to sell some info, I thought. *As much as I hate to admit it, I'm interested in what happened, so…*

"…I'll pay," I said.

"Ah! Ray, let me pay half of the money!" Rook joined in.

We both gave 1,000 lir each.

"Thank you for your business," she said. "I'll start with the conclusion: the player killers who occupied the hunting grounds around the capital city of Altea have been completely annihilated."

Now that's a rough word, I thought.

"Annihilated?" I asked.

"Almost all the player killers in the hunting grounds are on their death penalty now," she answered. "With something so extreme happening, I don't think they're gonna do this dirty work again. Some of the relevant clans might even split up."

Work? Clan?

"Umm…" I expressed my confusion.

"Oh, forgive me," she said. "The player killer group responsible for this event was actually a union between several player killer clans."

"A union…?" I raised an eyebrow. *I was told it wasn't a solo effort, but an actual union between player killer clans? I thought. … Wait, our country actually has enough player killer clans to create a union?*

"Yes," she answered. "Easter Plains at the east was occupied by K&R. Sauda Mountain Pass to the south was occupied by Mad Castle. Wez Sea Route to the west was occupied by Goblin Street. These three clans were responsible for the recent player killing."

Two of those clan names sound really villainous, I thought. *They'd probably chosen them on purpose. What about the north, though? That one's the most important to me.*

"As for their motives… Apparently, they did it because someone hired them to do the player killing," Marie added.

"Was it Dryfe?" Rook asked.

The question made her slightly raise her arms and shake her head. "That's the rumor, but we at DIN don't have any conclusive proof of that, so I can only say that I don't know," she answered.

Well, as things are now, the only one who could be happy about Altar being damaged in such a way are Dryfe — the country we're at war with — so it's quite likely, I thought. *Though it does seem a bit too direct.*

"From their perspective, it was probably just an attractive scenario where they could get some extra rewards for their player killing by merely switching their hunting grounds, but the world wasn't too kind to them," she continued. "They were annihilated by a certain four Masters."

"Four…" I repeated the number. Just four Masters had destroyed the player killers in all four areas.

Is that even possible? I wondered. *Well, I guess the south made sense, considering Figaro was involved.*

With that in mind, the other hunting grounds had been…

"Yes, it was made possible by the work of the four Superiors loyal to the Kingdom of Altar," she said. "They were the ones who exterminated all the player killer clans."

Superior.

That was the term used to describe the ones who had made their Embryos evolve to the final — seventh — form. They were the elite of the elite among players, and the total number of them didn't even cross a hundred yet.

"King of Destruction the Unknown, Figaro the Endless Chain, Tsukuyo Fuso of the Lunar World, and Lei-Lei, the Prodigal of Feasts," she said, naming the four. "They all went to a separate hunting ground and exterminated all the player killer clans occupying them. Oh, but Tsukuyo Fuso had her clan with her."

"Oho…" I said, interested.

So Figaro's nickname is "Endless Chain," huh? Is it because he uses chains? I pondered. Also, is the King of Destruction's nickname seriously just "Unknown?" What the hell? We don't even know his name, so he could be a serious weirdo.

"Now, take a look here." Marie took out a crystal ball and placed it on the table.

"What's this?" I asked.

"Well, it's basically an item to display visual media," she explained. "It shows what you record on magical cameras."

Magical cameras? I raised an eyebrow. Well, it's obviously a camera that works magically, but I can't help but wonder if the devs think anything goes as long as you put "magic" next to it.

"Due to all the recent happenings here in the Kingdom of Altar, we at DIN increased the numbers of secret cam… I mean, information-gathering equipment we place here," she said.

…Illegal spying, eh? I thought.

"Some of them happened to film the end of these terror events," Marie continued as if it wasn't a big deal. "This thing has it all in full detail."

She activated the crystal ball.

"Since you two were talking about it, let's begin with a look at the south, where Figaro the Endless Chain went..."

Chapter Five ⟩ Superior

Clan Leader of Mad Castle, Full Armor Giant Barbaroy Bad Burn

In *Dendro,* there were two ways for players to fight amongst themselves.

The first one was dueling.

Players would gather in an arena, agree on a set of conditions and rules, decide what items the victor would get and begin fighting. Since no one would die even if their HP hit 0 and all the damage done would be reverted the moment the battle ended, duels were much like a casual pastime.

The other means was player killing.

Players would attack other players outside of an arena and give them the death penalty. Players who died this way would drop money and items at random… just like monsters.

One of the differences between losing a duel and dying from player killing was that the former allowed you to choose what items you lost, while the latter randomized it. The other difference was in whether the defeated side died or not.

That was the reason why there were those who specialized in dueling…

…and those like us, who specialized in player killing.

I, leader of the clan 'Mad Castle' — Barbaroy Bad Burn — love player killing.

In fact, my clan and I are enjoying some wholesome player killing right at this very moment, I thought.

"Uaahhh! Waaahhh!" A newbie player who looked like — and probably was — an elementary schooler was crying as he attacked me with his starting gear. However, no matter how many times he tried, the damage he did was always 0.

"Khahah! Come on! Damage me for at least 1 HP and I'll let ya go!" I laughed.

Not that that could ever happen. Mine was a high-rank job focused on endurance — Full Armor Giant.

Not only that, but I had Damage Decrease, which decreased all incoming damage by 20%, and Damage Reduction, which took away 500 damage from all attacks, so a newbie like him couldn't damage me even if he landed a critical hit.

"Uohh! Uohhh!" Still crying, the newbie attacked me while making an attempt to run away. However, I quickly stood in his path before he could complete his escape.

Despite having a heavy, non-agile job, I was still much faster than a newbie, not to mention that I had my Embryo's ability. I also made sure to prevent him from logging out.

To log out in this game, a player needed about thirty seconds of free time. No one could do it unless they were able to spend those thirty seconds without being touched or attacked by someone else. It was a fact of the game that was meant to prevent crime, but it could easily be used *for* crime.

Well, player killing wasn't actually forbidden, so it wasn't really a "crime" in any sense of the word.

Also, for one reason or another — likely as a means against harassment — players were able to commit suicide. Even if players were rendered unable to move even a single finger, they could give themselves the death penalty at will. However, by doing that, players dropped way more money and items than when killed by a player killer, so there weren't many who used that function.

"All right, time's up," I said.

"Ah!" the newbie gasped. As he continued his fruitless struggle, I held my large shield in both hands and swung it down on him.

My shield — which was one meter in diameter — became a giant stamp and left a mark on the ground. The ink was the player. Of course, since he'd died, what was left of the newbie quickly disappeared.

Good thing I'd set my visuals to CG. The sight would've been pretty damn grotesque if I'd set it to realistic.

There's something seriously wrong with those who pick realistic visuals, I thought. *Battles with undead monsters get really grim from that perspective.*

"Eheehee! You sure are a scumbag, boss! You even made me feel bad for the kid!" laughed one of my clan members.

"Khahah! Holy shit, I sure won't be eating any tomatoes today," another joined in.

"What do you say to cheeseburgers for dinner, then?" I grinned. "As you can see, I can get the mincemeat as if it's no big deal."

"I think I'll pass, LOL." The clan members working with me began their usual banter, and I joined in, making sure to sound as scummy as possible.

Roleplaying as a bad guy sure is fun, I thought. *Probably has something to do with being able to show off a side of you that you can't show anywhere else.*

For example, in reality, Ban-blu — the one grinning at my side — was a public service worker with a husband and kids, but that couldn't have mattered less here.

Mad Castle's motto was thus: "Forget reality, get hyped up, and kill some players."

It wasn't the least bit enjoyable to the ones getting killed, mind you. However, in this game — where everyone was competing for more power — it was the weaklings' own fault for being weak.

"I've heard of people who got so traumatized by player killers that they stopped playing," said one of my people.

"Like I care," I said. Seriously, I couldn't have cared less if I'd tried. "Killing" and "getting killed" were both part of the game.

"So, boss, including this brat, how many have we killed by now?" asked a clan member.

"Well, I stopped counting the ones I'd killed when I hit fifty," I replied.

My Mad Castle clan was occupying the Sauda Mountain Pass south of the capital, and had been killing any players who happened to pass by. We only went for those we were able to handle, but so far, everyone had been weak enough for me to do it solo.

There had been a group that had come here to stop us, but me and my clan had had no problem taking care of them, too.

"But man, this is a good deal we've got," said one of my people. "All we do is kill some players, and the money comes a-flowing like a fountain."

"Yeah, it's great," I replied.

Deal. That's the word for it, I thought. We were player killing here because we had a deal going on. For every death penalty we gave, we received a flat 10,000 lir reward. And this deal would last for a whole month, game time.

We couldn't ask for better conditions. And that was without mentioning that — being a newbie hunting ground — this place was full of scrubs we could crush like insects.

178

The first day we'd started had been so damn good that it'd gotten us more than 1,000,000 lir. It'd been hilarious.

What was just as funny was the fact that it had become big news.

Unlike the clan in the north, we didn't hide our identities. That led people to find out who we were, but to us villain roleplayers, that was only a blessing.

"Though, man, we sure don't get as many players now as we did at the start," one of my people said. "Guess they're all scared shitless now. Oh, yeah. Last night, at the tavern, I heard that the guys in the east don't have much to do, either."

The other three hunting grounds surrounding the capital were occupied by other player killers. Just like our clan, the ones in the east and west were full of delinquents who didn't give a damn about what people thought and just wanted to kill some players.

"Though I've heard that Goblin Street — the guys in the west — are getting some serious extra cash," another one added.

"Well, that's because they go after NPCs, too," I said.

"Ain't that just scary?" he said.

"Maybe," I said.

Player killing wasn't a crime. *Dendro*'s laws ignored all conflicts between Masters. However, killing NPCs was a serious offense.

Ending an NPC's life without a valid reason — such as self-defense, them being criminals, or taking part in a war event — would cause them to recognize the offending player as a criminal and put them on a wanted list.

Getting on a country's wanted list made the player unable to use the country's save points.

If that had been all there was to it, simply switching to another country's save points would solve the problem, but overdoing it with the killing would get the player on the wanted list of *every* country.

When on all the seven lists, the player would be simply *done*. They wouldn't be able to use any countries' save points.

Considering that getting the death penalty in such a situation would send you to *that place*, the risks were way too high.

The guys at Goblin Street probably had save points at Caldina or something, but we had no intention of going through those lengths just so we could kill NPCs.

In fact, killing NPCs didn't make me feel good.

Once, I'd killed a criminal NPC, and it'd made me feel like crap — as if I'd broken an expensive vase. That was why we chose to not touch any NPCs trying to pass through this hunting ground.

Well, we're too scared to try, anyway, I thought.

"Yeah, I'll stick to player killing. It's both comfortable and fun," one of my clan members spoke up again.

"True," another replied. "Something's seriously wrong with the guys in the west. Even if we're all player killers, I wouldn't want to get involved with that lot."

I simply listened to them. *In all honesty, I'm more afraid of the one in the north than the ones in the west,* I thought.

The person in Noz Forest was bad news.

Unlike in the other places, it wasn't a clan there, but a single player killer. I didn't know his name. All I knew about him was that he was a trickster good at hiding himself, and that what he was doing was his day job.

There was no better term for it — day job.

He'd been playing as a hit man for as long as he'd been known in *Dendro*.

Players who were killed by other players or received some sort of harassment would sometimes grow vengeful and develop grudges. Killing players based on the requests of such people was part of his daily life. I'd even heard that he'd once gotten a request to assassinate a Superior that was on wanted lists.

"Superiors" were players that had made their Embryos evolve to their seventh forms — the elite of the elite. No one in their right mind would even think of fighting someone like that. I was no exception.

However, though he'd received serious amounts of damage, that player had been able to give the Superior a death penalty and send him to *that place*. Due to that, he'd gotten the title of "Superior Killer."

Though we were business partners right now, I didn't really want to meet him.

I didn't think I'd lose to him, but hit men like him — elusive as they were — just seemed far worse than both player and NPC killers. Not getting involved with them was the right idea.

"Boss, we've got another one," one of my clan members called me.

He was contacting me by using an item that allowed communication between members of the same clan.

We had six parties consisting of six people each. Every member of every party had split up and formed groups of six with members of other parties before positioning themselves in different places all across the area.

With this setup, if one group got destroyed in some sort of surprise attack, the actual party members would be able to tell that something was wrong by looking at their party status. It was a large-scale battle tactic that we were all accustomed to using.

"Whoa, damn. This sucker has some good-looking gear on him," he spoke through the long-distance contact item.

"Well then, if he's not a newbie, he's here to hunt us down, huh?" I asked.

"Seems like it," he answered. "He's alone, though."

"Alone? Then there's no problem," I said. "Just attack, threaten him into taking his gear off, and kill him."

"Hee hee hee, sounds good, boss," he laughed. "Today, we'll sell that gear and have a wild part—"

[Party Member "Jordan α" Has Died]

[Resurrection Period Expired]

[Due to the Death Penalty, "Jordan α" was Logged Out]

Huh? was all I could think. "H-Hey! Stop with the jokes! Shit like this freaks me out when it's so sudde—"

[Party Member "Lowered Beltmars" Has Died]

[Resurrection Period Expired]

[Due to the Death Penalty, "Lowered Beltmars" was Logged Out]

Another party member I'd been in contact with had died.

The "resurrection period" was the time in which resurrection items and magic could have an effect. If someone successfully resurrected the player before the period ended, the player would avoid the death penalty. However, the time given was dependent on the state of the corpse.

The two deaths had been instant and had left basically no resurrection period. I could only assume that they'd been turned into mincemeat in but a single moment.

Upon looking at the clan members at my side, I noticed that they had all turned pale.

Once I asked what was up, they said their party members who'd been in the same places as Jordan α and Lowered Beltmars were also dead.

Basically, the twelve clan members positioned at those two places had all met a nearly simultaneous and swift death.

Did they all get ganked by a group of players? I thought. *There's no way.*

After all, each place had had a person with a great "Enemy Detect" skill. It should've been impossible for a group of players to prepare such an attack without getting noticed.

But if the one who did it was already spotted... and if it's really just one, then...

"I-It's a player! A player from Altar!" one of my party members from another position contacted me. "I saw a chain! It took Marlo and—"

[Party Member "Ma-mdoh" Has Died]
[Resurrection Period Expired]
[Due to the Death Penalty, "Ma-mdoh" was Logged Out]

The screams coming from the other side before getting cut out were a sign that the third group had been eliminated.

However, before dying, the party member had left me some valuable information. He'd mentioned that the player used a chain. There was little doubt that it was the same well-equipped "sucker" they'd seen before dying.

Well, now this "sucker" is massacring our members as if it's nothing, I thought. *This one clearly isn't your average Joe.*

The Kingdom of Altar happened to have a famous player who used chains. His name was...

"I-It's Figarooooo!" shouted another party member. "Why is the Over Gladiator here?! He—"

[Party Member "Mohawk X" Has Died]
[Resurrection Period Expired]
[Due to the Death Penalty, "Mohawk X" was Logged Out]

…Over Gladiator Figaro.

"The Endless Chain," "One of Altar's Big Three," "The King of Hanging Around the City of Duels," et cetera… He had many names and was one of the strongest players in not just the Kingdom of Altar, but in the whole game itself.

He was a Superior, and there were even rumors that that weirdo raided created dungeons *solo*.

That lunatic was now with us, on this mountain…

…and he clearly had it in for us.

It wasn't an unexpected scenario.

Since we were committing acts of terror against the kingdom's players, it was only natural for the ones sitting at the top of the kingdom's rankings to come take care of us.

However, the rumors had suggested that Figaro wasn't the type to get involved in such events. I'd heard he spent most of his playing time either raiding the dungeon or dueling in the Colosseum.

After all, he hadn't even participated in the war, and yet…

[Party Member "Goro Mushoku" Has Died]

[Resurrection Period Expired]

[Due to the Death Penalty, "Goro Mushoku" was Logged Out]

Suddenly, I heard some rattling. A frustrated grunt escaped my mouth. Right after I got the message that the members in the fifth position were eliminated — meaning that we were the last — my "Killing Intent Perception" skill went off and warned me about the attack coming my way.

I didn't know the direction it was coming from. Still, I only needed to know it was coming to be able to do something about it.

A moment later, I saw a chain with a pyramid-like tip flying right at me.

"Astro Guard!" I activated a Full Armor Giant defensive skill. It rendered me unable to move in exchange for multiplying my defense by five.

With this, my total defense was now over 15,000 — the greatest I could reach.

The chain hit my shield with a dreadful amount of power behind it.

"...Whoa!" I exclaimed. My HP had gone down.

My defense was over 15,000, I had a skill that decreased all damage by 20% and another one that took away another 500, yet he had been able to break through all these walls and deal damage to me. It was only natural that the guys positioned at the other places had gotten slaughtered without even getting time to heal.

Thus, the chain that I deflected...

"Gyeeaahhh!"

...went towards and pulverized Ban-blu.

She wasn't the only one, though — besides me, everyone positioned here was attacked by the chains and scattered into a thousand pieces.

"...Sorry," I said. "I can't move, so I couldn't protect you."

With that, the survivors around me disappeared, and I could no longer contact anyone.

Looks like they're all dead and dealing with the death penalty now, I thought. Still immobile, I kept up my Astro Guard stance.

Besides the chains — which were making metallic sounds as they hit and slightly damaged me — the only thing moving was the Over Gladiator, Figaro. I saw him walking up the mountain road when I tried to trace where the chains were coming from.

He had a well-proportioned face, so if — unlike me — he hadn't spent a significant amount of time on character creation and had just gone with the defaults, it was fair to assume that he was handsome in real life, as well.

His apparel was strange, but by using "Identification" — a skill that allowed me to see item names and values — I discovered that everything he was wearing was highly powerful and extremely rare. In fact, some of them were so rare that my Identification level wasn't high enough to identify them.

"The bastard's even wearing some UBM special rewards as if it's no big deal..." I grumbled.

Special rewards for MVPs in UBM battles — Unique Boss Monster — were bound to the MVP and thus couldn't be transferred or dropped. So, despite being damn strong, they were worthless to us.

Though Figaro's face and apparel were deserving of a comment or two, there was something about him that just couldn't be ignored. It was the red chains — several of them — wrapped around both of his arms.

This game had a limit to how many weapons you could wield. The standard amount was either one for both hands or one in one hand and another in the other — like me with my shield. Besides that, normal players could use throwing weapons or items like Gems, but that was the extent of the weapons they could utilize.

However, this Figaro guy was wielding six chains — three on each arm.

And yes, I was completely certain that there were six chains — not just two that seemed separate. They all had the same name — Crimson Dead Keeper — but they weren't connected in any way.

Though Figaro didn't seem to be moving them, all the chains automatically extended and went straight towards me.

Most would think this is a joke, but they'd be wrong, I thought.

According to the Identification results, Crimson Dead Keepers had the skills "Auto Enemy Detect" and "Range Extend." You'd be hard pressed to find a more user-friendly weapon.

From the fact that Identification worked on them, it was obvious that they weren't his Embryo. Which made it all the more obvious that he was actually wielding a total of six weapons.

It was way over the standard wield limit, but I had been aware that the Gladiator job grouping had a skill that allowed the player to wield more weapons. The ultimate maximum was supposed to be a mere three, but since Over Gladiator was a Superior job of that grouping, it wouldn't have been strange for it to have a stronger version of that skill.

Basically, it meant that he'd eliminated all of my clan without using his Embryo and by relying only on his Over Gladiator skills and weapons in hand.

"I'm sure getting blocked a lot today."

Figaro's first words didn't make even a bit of sense to me.

"You have some good defense, but I guess it's normal for a Full Armor Giant," he continued. "Still, it's rare for anyone to be *this* tough. Is your Embryo focused on defense or something?"

I stayed silent. He was stating his impressions, but I had no reason to respond in any capacity. I could try bluffing, but if he had Truth Discernment — a skill that informed the user if another person was lying — he'd see right through me and I'd only end up giving him info...

...such as the fact that my Embryo's power wasn't defensive at all.

"...Hm. Looks like I've taken care of every player killer besides you," he said.

Either by simply feeling it or by seeing that his chains' Auto Enemy Detect weren't picking up anyone but me, he'd concluded that I was the last. And with those words, it became obvious that he'd come here to kill us — the player killers near the capital.

"So, can I assume that you're this PK group's leader?" he asked.

"...What if I said 'yes?'" I replied.

"My only goal here is to secure the means of travel between the duel city and the capital," he explained. "If you promise to leave this mountain pass, I'll gladly let you go."

"...Is that something you say after killing every single one of my clan members?" I asked.

"If I hadn't done that, you wouldn't even be willing to negotiate."

He's not wrong, I thought.

Until he'd eliminated us, we'd all considered him to be just another sucker for easy pickings, so we would've attacked him even if he'd had something to say. After all, we'd had no idea that there was such a huge gap in power between us and a Superior.

However, that made me consider something.

Just how much stronger is he compared to me — a Master with an Embryo in its sixth form? If I can land a perfect hit with my Embryo's ultimate skill... I might be able to kill him. Sure, with him having a Superior job, his level is probably far greater than mine. My level is 500 — the maximum I can reach with low-rank and high-rank jobs — and his can easily be two times higher than that. However, the results of PvP battles aren't decided by level or stats. What matters is how well you can prevent your opponent from using their powers effectively while attacking them with your own. The Superior Killer got his name for a reason. It shouldn't be impossible for me to do it, too.

"All right," I said. "I'll leave this place as soon as I can. We, Mad Castle, won't be hunting any more newbies here."

That wasn't a lie. With players of this caliber now coming after us, our little PK feast in this area was all but done.

We'll back away... right after I kill him, anyway.

"I have a Contract here. Wanna use it?" I reached into my item pouch and took out a piece of parchment.

It was a Contract — a type of item used in agreements between players. Anyone who went against the conditions would receive either a temporary loss of stats, some debuffs, or even the death penalty.

"Well..." Figaro said. "I don't see why not. Let's do it."

"...Okay, I'm done filling it in," I said. "Take a look at it."

Saying that, I began to bring the Contract to Figaro.

Five meters.

Four meters.

Three meters.

Two meters — he was now in range.

A magic circle appeared below my feet and spread around me. It was my Embryo — Atlas.

"Heaven's Weight!" One of Atlas' skills was the increase of weight.

It was able to apply continuous damage to everything in the effective range by increasing the gravity of the surroundings.

The effect was stronger based on distance, reaching its peak at two meters, where the gravity was 500 times greater than usual. At the same time, it applied the "Binding" debuff, rendering Figaro unable to move even a single finger.

The chains automatically tried to attack me, but the overwhelming gravity forced them to the ground, where they could only crawl.

So far, no one had ever been able to break out of this combo between Binding and super gravity.

A standard high-ranking player would have already been crushed to death, but I wasn't naïve enough to believe that the Superior before me would die as easily.

It was time to use Atlas's ultimate attack.

"Astro Guard!"

I used Astro Guard again to multiply my defense by five...

"Emancipated Giant, Atlas!"

...followed by the skill named after Atlas itself.

It converted my defense to offense and multiplied my attack power by ten for ten seconds. My attack power was now over 150,000. A clean hit from that should've been enough to instakill anyone — even a Superior.

And as Figaro was still unable to move, I began barraging him with Atlas' strongest attack.

"Break and die!" I roared.

The ground below me shattered, caved in, and became a large crater. But I didn't give a damn.

For all I knew, he could have multiple resurrection or related accessories. I had to spend each and every one of these ten seconds attacking him.

Suddenly, a sound.

As I continued my barrage, a chain wrapped around my neck. It shocked the words out of me.

I looked down. What I saw was the ground I'd shattered with my barrage, but Figaro was nowhere to be seen.

If he wasn't before me, there was only one place he could be at. By that, I meant "at the other end of the chain tightening around my neck."

It was going upwards, so I looked up and saw Figaro hanging about ten meters up in the air.

"H-How?!" I howled in shock. He'd been affected by five hundred times the normal gravity and had had the Binding debuff — there was no way he could've jumped that high.

"...Ah," I said.

Suddenly, a realization.

I had heard many things about Figaro. Among them was that, for the Over Gladiator, raiding a created dungeon solo was part of his daily life. The very idea of solo raiding was stupid, but any lunatics who attempted it had to make sure they met a certain condition.

It wasn't high stats.

Nor was it the means of healing.

It was all about countermeasures to debuffs.

Paralysis, Sleep, Petrification, and, of course, Instant Death.

When going solo, players didn't have any allies that could help them with such debuffs, so getting one of them would be the equivalent of dying.

Thus, anyone raiding solo would have to have a means of dealing with debuffs. Therefore, it was only obvious that this solo-focused Superior would have been prepared for that.

He had some equipment I couldn't identify. One of them probably nullified all Binding effects.

"No... There's no way!" I shouted.

I'd been about to accept that conclusion, but I simply couldn't. The Binding from my Heaven's Weight was a personal skill from a high-rank Embryo. There was no way it could've been nullified so easily.

Suddenly, another realization.

I thought that he wasn't using his Embryo. But what if I'm wrong? What if his Superior Embryo is already active? What if it's the reason why he was able to nullify my Binding and jump as if the 500 times greater gravity doesn't matter at a—?

Another sound. I instantly looked up at Figaro.

Due to the light behind him, I couldn't make out his expression. However, it gave me chills I couldn't describe.

When he landed, I got a good look at his face, which made the chills turn even worse.

The sound again. His narrow eyes were open wide and shining red. His mouth was in a smile — sharp like a crescent moon and open wide enough to see his throat. The sounds coming from his throat were downright inhuman. It was reminiscent of growls that your average monster would sound — meaningless and thick with bloodlust.

A short scream escaped my mouth. At that moment, he raised both of his chained hands up into the sky.

That motion made the chains wrapped around my neck begin to pull upwards.

My body — more than two meters worth of armored flesh — was separated from the surface and got distanced from the earth.

My ears were overwhelmed by the sound of air grazing my whole body.

Likely by using his chains' Range Extend skill, he made them raise me up at incredible speeds and didn't seem to know where to stop. Figaro was now but a dot on the surface. A moment later, I was higher than the mountain peak, reached the clouds and went beyond.

Soon enough, I no longer had any air around me. I made my lungs work at full capacity, yet nothing was coming in. The word "suffocation" came to mind.

Though *Dendro* allowed the player to reduce all pain to nothing but dull impacts, it didn't do anything about the anguish of oxygen deprivation.

However, there was no need for me to worry about suffocating, because something far scarier happened.

As if it was only obvious, the chains began to get pulled back down to the ground.

The sights I'd seen on my way up now went by me at an even faster speed, making me feel as if someone had rewinded my life.

"HYAAAAAHHHHHH!" A scream of despair escaped my mouth.

It didn't matter that I was in a game. The fall I was experiencing was thick with fear of death.

It didn't matter that there was no pain. The shape of fear living beings feel when faced with imminent death was unrelated to that.

The game's realism conveyed the fear of death all too well.

From sky high and at a ridiculously high speed, I was falling to my death.

Still with a monstrous smile on his face, Figaro was waiting for me on the surface.

Once again, he made that sinister, incomprehensible sound. One of his chains was replaced by another weapon — a chainsaw-like greatsword.

He swung it straight at where I was falling.

A moment later, a twisted, crunching sound ripped from my own body, and I...

[Fatal Damage]
[Party Eliminated]
[Resurrection Period Expired]
[Death Penalty: 24 Hour Login Ban]

Rangyu Restaurant, Kingdom of Altar, Paladin Ray Starling

"...That was one brutal fight." After watching the clip in Marie's crystal ball, I was seriously taken aback. It was paused at the frame where the huge, armored guy — the PK leader — was getting split in half.

According to Marie, the armor guy was an infamous player who had had high defense and a counterattack-like ultimate skill that dealt serious damage.

Due to that description, I found him somewhat relatable and began to feel that his demise — that mangled corpse — was a glimpse of my future if I ever fought Figaro.

"And that's how everyone in Mad Castle met with a sad end," said Marie. "Even if they recover from this, they'll never return to player killing in that area."

Makes sense, considering that stopping the traffic there would make Figaro get involved again, I thought.

"If I ever find myself in the duel city, I'll have to remember to thank Figaro for this," I said.

"Indeed," mumbled Nemesis.

"Hm?" I looked at her.

For some reason, she seemed a bit sulky. Instead of looking at the crystal ball, she was merely eating with Babi, who didn't seem to care about any of this whatsoever.

The amount Nemesis consumed was as great as always, but it almost seemed like she was stress eating.

Why, though? I thought.

"Okay, now let me show you the next one." This time, Marie's crystal displayed a familiar place. It was the first hunting ground I'd ever leveled at — Easter Plains.

Sure enough, there was a group of player killers there. Though they were hiding from players and waiting for their next prey, they weren't hidden from the camera.

A few moments later, another group — and quite a strange one, at that — came from the direction of the capital.

I couldn't tell the exact number, but there were surely more than a hundred of them — all marching towards the player killers.

Each and every single one of the group had an outfit with a crescent moon and a closed eye on it. The design seemed familiar, but I couldn't recall where I'd seen it.

In response to the group's sudden appearance, the player killers became visibly perplexed and only continued hiding.

Soon enough, a single lady walked out of the strange group.

She had black hair that was reminiscent of nightly darkness and reached as far as the back of her knees, which were hidden by her ceremonial kimono. Her beauty made me feel as though I was looking at Princess Kaguya, straight out of the children's tale.

Suddenly, the beauty raised her hand, making the world go through what seemed like a theatrical blackout.

Mere moments ago, it had been daytime and the sun had been shining, but she'd somehow brought forth a "night." It was complete with a blue moon that was downright impossible in reality and perhaps even the game.

A moment later, the player killers who were bathed in the blue moonlight grabbed hold of their throats and began to writhe in pain, which rendered them unable to move properly.

As if they had been waiting for this, the strange group split up and began systematically killing the writhing player killers. With their victims unable to move in any capacity, it seemed less like a battle and more like a tedious job.

However, there was an exception.

A certain player killer — a Beastman type female player with wolf-like ears and tail — could still move even when exposed to the moonlight.

According to Marie, that was one of K&R's two leaders.

Using her claws and fangs, she savagely clawed her way through the enemies surrounding her and closed in on Princess Kaguya.

However, it was all in vain.

The hundreds surrounding her were too much for her to handle, so she ended up dying at the edge of a spear.

The sight made the beauty reminiscent of Princess Kaguya cackle in a discomforting manner.

"That's Tsukuyo Fuso of the Lunar World," Marie explained. "She is the owner of the clan known as The Lunar Society... though I guess the term 'founder' or 'spiritual leader' is more appropriate."

"Spiritual leader?" I raised an eyebrow. It was a strange title, but it reminded me that her job was "High Priestess."

Nevertheless, I found it to be somewhat questionable...

"Um, is this Lunar Society related to the Japanese cult of the same name?" asked Rook.

"...Oh." His words reminded me of where I'd heard that before. "The Lunar Society" was the name of a cult that existed in reality.

"Yes," answered Marie. "The clan 'The Lunar Society' is a part — or, rather, the headquarters — of the cult of the same name."

"...Why are they advancing their religion in a game, of all places?" I asked.

"The Lunar Society's first teaching is 'Escape the shackles of flesh and betake yourself to the true world of souls,'" she explained. "I guess they consider *Dendro* to be that world."

...I'm fully aware of this world's realism, I thought. *Our five senses and the tians we interact with can't be distinguished from the real thing. But... is that really enough reason to take it that far?*

"If their goal is to 'betake themselves to the true world of souls' and they accomplished it by getting here... what are they doing now?" I inquired.

"Oh, yes. Their second teaching is the main one," Marie said. "It goes something like, 'Embrace this free world and celebrate your liberty to your soul's content.'"

...Sounds like the dogma of some dark god, I thought.

"The Lunar Society is quite feared among the players," she continued. "Not only are they more than a thousand strong, they also have roots in reality, so many players are afraid that getting on the cult's bad side might get something done to them in real life."

Well, that's a scary thought, I thought. *If there's the possibility of them abducting me or something, I'd rather not get involved with them, either.*

"By the way, as far as we know, their reason for going after the player killers was the fact that one of their followers was killed by them," Marie added. "It's scary that such a thing can get the entire clan to go after you, isn't it?"

...Would I be wrong to assume that — right next to the war — the cult is another reason why people are leaving the kingdom? I thought.

Next, Marie displayed what had happened in the west.

What I saw first was Lei-Lei — the girl that had participated in the party we'd had on my first day. Just like that time, she was wearing a Chinese dress despite having a northern European face. From what my brother had told me, she was from there in real life, too.

Lei-Lei's fighting style as I saw it in the crystal ball was simple. She didn't bring them up to the sky just to have them fall on a chainsaw, nor did she make them writhe just to have a group come up and impale them.

She simply walked up to the hiding player killers and punched them. That was all. However, the results were downright ridiculous.

Figaro's chains basically turned his opponents into mincemeat, but this was on another level.

The player killers were completely liquefied. They were bursting so easily, it almost made me think that they weren't people, but people-shaped water balloons. The moment Lei-Lei touched them, their flesh simply collapsed, leaving only a blood and entrail-colored liquid and the skin that released it.

Speaking of skin, it was flying around everywhere, decorating just about every surrounding tree. Because they instantly died, it would quickly disappear, but the sight itself wouldn't leave my mind as easily.

I think I can see why she's called the Prodigal of Feasts, I thought. *No proper feast is complete without meat and drink, and she provided both. ...What a grim thought, though.*

Despite seeming like a really jovial character in the party, Lei-Lei had a seriously scary fighting style.

Marie didn't know why Lei-Lei had decided to eliminate the player killers.

With what happened in the south, east, and west now being clear, all that was left was the north — Noz Forest.

It was the place I was the most curious about. After all, I had died there once.

"Now, about the north..." Marie seemed somewhat reluctant.

Just what is she about to show us? I thought.

"Well, I'll just play it, then." Marie controlled the crystal ball and made it show the forest.

It had been filmed during nighttime, when I'd still been raiding the Tomb Labyrinth. Apparently, this was the earliest of the four eliminations.

However, I couldn't see the player killer anywhere.

Sure, the trees and the night's darkness made it hard to see, but there was absolutely no sign of him.

As I continued intently looking at the crystal ball and searching for him, the screen suddenly turned red as the footage ended.

It quickly changed to a recording from another camera, but just like the last one, it quickly got cut off, as well.

The next recording wasn't a clip of the inside of the forest, but an overhead view of the whole area. The camera was probably placed on the capital's outer walls.

Anyway, it showed with great clarity what was happening in the forest.

The forest was being bombarded by artillery shells and set aflame by a rain of incendiary bombs.

Not showing a single person, the clip ended with just that — a flaming forest, making it feel like a scene cut from some war movie.

"Um… what is this?" Rook's question made Marie smile awkwardly.

"Ahaha… This is, uh… the battle between King of Destruction the Unknown and the unidentified player killer widely known as the 'Superior Killer'…" The tone of her explanation made it seem like she had no confidence about what she was saying.

I can see why, I thought. *The clip shows neither the player killer nor the King of Destruction eliminating him. It's nothing but a display of environmental destruction.*

"...If it doesn't show the King of Destruction, how can you be sure that he was the one who did it?" I asked Marie. "Hell, we don't even see the player killer, so it might not be this 'Superior Killer,' either."

"Good point," she replied. "From what we know about him, it's all but confirmed that the PK is the Superior Killer, but we don't have any conclusive proof about the one who attacked him being the King of Destruction. This is only an assumption based on the extent of the destruction displayed here. But you see, the King of Destruction has always been an enigmatic figure that doesn't let anyone know much about him..."

Oh yeah, I thought. *His reason for not participating in the war was that he "didn't want to stand out." Though that's not very convincing when coming from someone who just turned an entire forest to cinders.*

"Oh, but there are rumors that the King's Embryo is a battleship! Take a closer look here!" Marie pointed her finger at a certain spot on the crystal ball.

Beyond the burning forest, shrouded by the darkness of night, there was a large, black silhouette. Its outline was too acute to be the ridgeline of a mountain, and indeed, many would assume it to be a battleship.

"So battleship Embryos exist, huh?" I said, not particularly surprised. My brother's was a tank, so this wasn't outside the realm of expectation.

In fact, I'd been more startled by Tsukuyo Fuso's Embryo. I had a feeling that it was the "night" itself.

"But wait, wouldn't such a large-scale attack harm more than just the Superior Killer?" I asked. *What if it actually killed some tians...?*

"I don't think we have to worry about that," Marie answered. "With all the player killing, almost no one dared to go through there. In fact, I think the King of Destruction only took such a flashy approach because he was certain that no one else would get caught up in it."

"I see." I nodded. Or maybe he'd turned the whole forest to ash simply because he couldn't find anyone. From what I had read on the Internet, no one besides me had even seen the Superior Killer.

Now that I think about it, how did DIN get ahold of information that led them to believe that the player killer was the Superior Killer? I wondered.

"Do you know the reason why the King of Destruction attacked the Superior Killer?" I asked.

"We have no clue whatsoever." Marie raised her hands up in resignation. "Despite being a player that gets strongly involved in many events across all countries, his identity and most of the reasons for his involvement are completely unknown."

"And that's why he's called 'The Unknown,' right?" I asked.

"Yes," she nodded. "We are completely clueless as to what drove him to cause such large-scale destruction…"

…I wonder if something pissed him off, I thought.

"Wait, aren't there too many holes in the information about the north? Isn't this intel a bit too vague?" Rook asked.

I couldn't help but agree with Rook. The price had been 600 lir per area, but the information for Noz Forest seemed worth a lot less than that.

"Oh…?! Now that you mention it…" Marie muttered. "Ah! But wait! There's some extra info that comes with this!"

"Extra info?" I asked.

"Indeed! It's this: the Superior Killer left these flames alive!"

In response to Marie's words...

"Oh?"

...Nemesis — who, up until that point, had been eating with Babi while barely looking at the crystal ball — finally showed some interest.

I could somewhat understand why this was the only piece of info that had gotten a reaction out of her.

In fact, I'd finally realized why Nemesis was behaving the way she was. She was frustrated that the player killers had all been eliminated. She didn't like having the one she'd promised to get revenge on be taken away by someone else. I could relate to that, as well.

However...

"That's great news," said Nemesis.

...he was still alive.

Chapter Six ⟩ The Cat's Tea Party

Noz Forest, Paladin Ray Starling

After Rook and I bought Marie's info and made a plan to meet up later, Nemesis and I went to the place that used to be Noz Forest.

"This is just…" I said.

Beyond the northern gate, there was a great wasteland as far as the eye could see. The forest had simply disappeared, leaving only felled trees reduced to nothing but charcoal.

Noz Forest could no longer be used as a hunting ground, nor was it deserving of the name "forest." In a city-building sim, the wasteland before me would've been a great place for building.

Sadly, *Infinite Dendrogram* was an RPG.

But man, it's hard to believe that a single player can change the map this much, I thought.

I saw bullet holes, explosion marks, and could even smell the lingering stench of gunpowder. I had no clue if the King's Embryo really *was* a battleship, but there was little doubt that — just like my brother's Baldr — it was either heavy weaponry or something greater in the same vein.

Another thing I noted was that — while the other three had targeted the player killers directly — the King of Destruction had, well… destroyed the map. Sure, he'd lived up to his name, but it didn't make it less of a bother. It seemed as ludicrous as removing the whole arm in response to a diseased finger.

"...This is gonna have bad aftereffects — no doubt about it," I said.

"People have already started leaving here at an even faster rate," added Nemesis.

We were talking about the local tians.

Yesterday's bombing had put the entire capital into a state of panic. Thinking that Dryfe's army was launching a surprise attack, the knights had moved out through the northern gate. By that point, however, the bombing had already been over, leaving nothing but a burning Noz Forest.

Though it didn't seem like the flames would spread to the capital, they couldn't have just left them burning as they were, so the knights had spent the entire night putting them out, and were still taking care of the aftermath.

All of this had been told to me by Liliana.

We'd met by accident a short while ago, and she had palpable bags under her eyes. She'd even said, "If you became a Paladin, then come and help us out..." in a slightly whiny manner.

"I know we were underground when the bombing happened and all, but I'm still surprised we didn't notice it," I commented.

"I had other things to worry about back then," said Nemesis. "You, on the other hand, were simply tired and had your senses dulled by fatigue."

Anyway, the event that had reduced Noz Forest — a place the capital's citizens took for granted — to ashes had been enough to make the already-tense populace go into panic mode. Since morning, the amount of people leaving the capital had been increasing by the hour.

Another reason for the increase was the fact that the four PK groups were taken care of. Though the player killers had been primarily targeting Masters, tians were also in danger of getting attacked if they weren't lucky, which had made traffic around the capital grind to a complete halt. Today, the roads were opened again, making the people practically flood out of the city.

Now that I think about it, tians can't differentiate between Masters and other tians, I thought. *Though we Masters use Embryos and are basically immortal, both tians and Masters share the basis of being human. Therefore, to tians, player killers are nothing but murderers. That goes double for the player killers who also go for tians.*

"Man, taking care of this PK business sure came at a cost," I said.

"One of the hunting grounds became unusable, after all," Nemesis agreed. "Also, the horror experience back in the Tomb Labyrinth was all for naught."

Despite all the money we'd spent on it, the advantage we'd gained had lasted for only a single night. Though I *did* feel fortunate to have met Figaro.

"I've gotta say, though..." I spoke. "This 'Superior Killer' guy escaped from an attack that destroyed the entire forest."

From what Marie had told me about the player killer in Noz Forest, the source of DIN's information about him had been Marie herself. Though a bit late, she had gone to gather material about yesterday's calamity right as it was happening. While doing so, she had happened to see the Superior Killer escape from the onslaught that was turning the forest to ash and run off into the distance.

In her own words, "He was using a skill with a concealment effect that hid his identity, but from the features of the Embryo he was using, I couldn't be more sure that it was him!"

Once I asked for those features, she said that it was a handgun-shaped Embryo that shot bullet-like animals. The description matched the one who had killed me.

Apparently, the Superior Killer had been using those bullet-like animals to cancel out all the attacks coming his way. By doing that, he'd been able to safely reach the capital. Despite all he had already done up to that point, the King of Destruction couldn't attack the capital, and had given up on pursuing the Superior Killer.

When all of that was considered, he had been successful where I hadn't — in a battle with the sole goal of retreating from a stronger force.

I was glad to not have the target of my revenge get taken away from me by the King of Destruction, but that notion made me slightly vexed.

"...Let's go back, then," I said. "We have plans with Rook, after all."

"True... hm?" Nemesis said.

As we were about to make our way back to the capital, Nemesis focused on a single point of the landscape as if she'd just noticed something.

"What's wrong?" I asked.

"What do you make of *that*?" Nemesis pointed at something, but I couldn't see anything there.

"What do you see?" I asked.

"There's a heat haze despite it not being hot," she said. "Wait, is that... distorted space?"

Nemesis walked over to where she was pointing... and simply disappeared.

"...Huh?! Nemesis!" I called out, ran over to where she'd vanished, and passed through an invisible curtain.

I described it as a "curtain" simply because — even though there was some sort of resistance — it was extremely weak. Once I'd walked through the invisible curtain...

"…Huh?!"

…I was in a mysterious space that was neither dark nor bright, and didn't even seem to have the concept of up and down.

The space was littered with countless blue, permeable windows and was already occupied by two familiar faces.

Once of them was Nemesis, who looked back at me as I confirmed that she was completely unharmed. "Master, this place is…"

The other person — no, the word "person" didn't apply here.

"…Ohh? Why are you heere?"

The creature skillfully operating the windows was Cheshire — the control AI I'd met when I had begun playing *Infinite Dendrogram*.

A few minutes had passed since we'd found ourselves in the mysterious space beyond the invisible curtain.

Nemesis and I were sitting in chairs and drinking the tea Cheshire had prepared for us.

As we had turned perplexed, Cheshire had said, "I'll explain it all, but just standing around while I do that isn't fun, riight?" and made the tea for us.

At first, this space had had nothing besides the windows — there hadn't even been a floor — but Cheshire had reached into a pocket and taken out chairs and a table as if it was nothing.

It reminded me of that cartoon about a cat robot I had been watching since I was a child. Though, unlike that cat robot, Cheshire had a set of ears.

"So, what is a control AI doing here?" I asked.

"Preliminary arrangements for environmental maintenaance," it answered. "The real work here will be done by control AIs numbers 3 and 5 — the ones responsible for monsters and the environmeent. This space is basically an impromptu operating rooom."

Like a prefab used in construction sites, huh? I thought.

"Though, only we can see and enter these placees," said Cheshire. "But the Embryo girl here seems to be a Maiden-type, and I guess things like this can happen with theem. She basically dragged you in here, didn't she, Raay?"

"What's so different about Maidens?" I asked.

"They're closer to us in some waays," Cheshire answered. "They even keep the *** functionalityy."

Hm?

"What did you say just now?" I was perplexed.

"Oh, sorryy," it apologized. "That's information I can't verbaliize. It's nothing big, though, so don't mind iit."

That answer only left me with more questions, but the AI probably had some developer-set duty of confidentiality it had to protect. We were already behind the scenes, anyway.

I also had other things I wanted to ask, so I decided not to push it.

"So you're gonna fix this area?" I inquired.

Infinite Dendrogram prioritized realism. That was the reason why places such as the Old Orchard could be invaded by bug monsters, but beginners' hunting grounds such as the Noz Forest could be an exception.

However, Cheshire shook its head.

"Noo. We will not directly recreate the now-lost Noz Forest. However, we can arrange some factors that would allow it to take the form of a similar environment. My job is to prepare for thaat."

Cheshire stopped speaking for a moment and took a sip of the black tea before continuing.

Not that it matters, but you'd think a cat wouldn't be able to handle such a hot drink, I thought.

"This is a free world, after aall. We — the control AIs — will never undo the effects a creature's autonomous actions have on this world — be they player, tian or monsteer. The results of freedom are none of our conceern. However, there are some exceptions. After all, we have a control AI meant for punishmeents."

"Punishments?" I asked. "If PK is perfectly fine, then what is actually deserving of that?"

"Hmm… Getting on a country's wanted list, I gueess," Cheshire answered. "You know how this world has laws, right? However, when arrested, players easily can escape jail by simply logging out or killing themseelves. Neither the police nor the knights have any means of preventing thaat. That's why we have a control AI operating a jail for players, nicknamed the 'gaol.' The AI also processes the player's inability to use save points when on a wanted list."

That makes sense, I thought. *If getting arrested or receiving the death penalty were the only demerits to committing crimes, some would just go about repeating them.*

"That's part of the setting, tooo," Cheshire continued. "'A Master who has sinned and cannot return to a save point shall be transferred to the gaol,' and all thaat. That's why you should register on save points in as many countries as you caan."

"…I have absolutely no intention of doing something that'd get me on wanted lists, though," I commented.

"That's good, tooo," said Cheshire. "Well, even if you get on one, you won't be sent to the gaol as long as you don't diee."

…This system sure is lenient on strong criminals, I thought.

"Hmm... If there are control AIs responsible for punishments... what are *you* responsible for, cat?" asked Nemesis.

"I'm the control AI handling choores," Cheshire answered.

Chores? I thought.

"We AIs also have things we're good and bad aat," Cheshire explained. "For example, I'm horrible at management functioons. Especially when it's related to environment managemeent."

"That's not what you're doing right now?" I asked.

"This is just a preliminary arrangemeent," it answered. "A proper environmental simulation would include management of the cloud particles' entropyy."

I was silent. Just thinking about the scale of it gave me a headache.

Though I guess being able to do that is part of being a proper control AI, I thought. *Well, Cheshire said it's not capable of that, though.*

"My primary work is to be the tutorial guiide," it continued. "It's work given to control AIs with unallocated calculation resourcees. I welcome half of the players coming heere."

That sounded like an impressive amount.

"I'm doing the tutorial work right now, in faact. Like soo." Upon saying that, Cheshire split into five.

Five differently-patterned cats spoke while handling the windows around them.

"Like soo," said the first.

"But there's no reason to split in heere," said the second.

"Even if there's five of me, it doesn't affect my work speeed," said the third.

"After all, the calculation volume I use doesn't change at aall," said the fourth.

"In fact, it slightly increases the calculation time and slows me down," said the fifth. And thus, the five became one again.

I was silent again. All this talk about calculations had made me remember that we were in a game server. This might've the first time I'd been presented with a display of cyber technology.

"I get to handle the chores because I'm good at processing the splitting I just shoowed," said Cheshire.

"I see," I nodded. "So, if you take half of the newcomers, the other half is taken by other AIs, right?"

"Yees," it answered. "There's even an AI that doesn't allow you to redo your character's appearance after you set it once."

"…Yeah, I *really* think it should allow that," I said.

That might've been the control AI that my brother had been assigned to.

After an approximately twenty-minute-long chat with Cheshire, we chose to take our leave.

"Not counting the welcoming, it's been so long since I met a person while being in this foorm," said Cheshire. "I'd love to present you with some souveniir… but since I'm part of development, that would be favoritism — a big no-noo."

"No need for that," I said. "The tea and sweets are more than enough. Thanks."

"Indeed," Nemesis agreed. "They were delicious."

…*With how much she ate, a part of me feels like we're already in the "no-no" territory,* I thought.

"Oh, my. Having you say that makes me feel like making them was really worth iit," said Cheshire.

Those cookies were handmade? I thought. *That's unexpected. … Okay, hold on now. How the hell can those cat hands make cookies?*

"You should consider selling them on the market." said Nemesis.

"I'll think about iit," replied Cheshire. "Oh, right. You're heading to Gideon soon, aren't you, Ray?"

I'd talked a bit about that during the tea party.

"Yeah, I am," I said.

"…Take care noow." Cheshire's words seemed ominous.

"Is there something I should know?" I asked.

"There is, buut…" It seemed apprehensive about saying it.

Is it something it can't reveal? I thought.

"I'll just keep it in the safe range, theen: 'The demon's heart lies in its stomach.'"

"Hm?" I raised an eyebrow.

"That's aall," said Cheshire. "Though, it's not like you're guaranteed to meet iit."

Cheshire had given me a riddle… or a clue you'd find in a mystery novel. I couldn't tell.

…Well, guess I'll record it in my memo window, I thought and did exactly that.

"I don't know if we'll ever meet again, but if we do, then until next tiime," Cheshire waved goodbye.

"Yeah, see ya," I reciprocated.

We passed through the exit the cat had created and returned to the previous map. Beyond it was the same wasteland we'd been in before. When I asked Nemesis about it, she said that she could no longer see the entrance to Cheshire's workplace.

I looked at the time and found out that it was a bit past three o'clock in the afternoon. We had planned to meet Rook at four, so we still had enough time.

Nemesis and I made our way to the meeting spot — the facility known only as the Adventurer's Guild.

Infinite Dendrogram had three types of quests a player could accept.

The first type was like the first quest I'd ever gotten — "random event quests."

The second type was like one Rook did for his job — "job quests."

The third type was "guild quests." In other words, the ones received at a facility known as the "Adventurers' Guild."

Due to the word "guild," some could confuse it with job guilds, but the quests were different in nature. The Adventurers' Guild was a service that managed many and varied requests, such as elimination, escorting, collection, or miscellaneous matters. Once registered, anyone could accept quests, regardless of their job or even if they were Masters or tians.

Of course, I was no exception.

My level was decent, so I decided to continue progressing through the game while making some coin from the requests there.

Also, ever since we'd met, Rook and I had been talking about how cool it'd be to party up, so we decided to do that while taking on the same quest.

And so…

"…There are so many requests that I have no idea which one to choose," I muttered.

"True…" Rook agreed.

Inside the Adventurers' Guild, Rook and I were letting our heads lie on a round table as we both eyed a thick book... and honestly, I was tired beyond words.

The books we had were quest catalogs that displayed every request the guild had available.

It was magically enchanted to add new requests and remove taken ones in real-time, making the number of quests being displayed grow and drop without stop. Also, it didn't display quests from a difficulty level the players couldn't take.

To us, it displayed all quests up to difficulty level three, and apparently, access to levels four and higher was based on the amount of completed lower-level quests.

Despite the lack of requests we couldn't see, the catalog was far too thick. It had approximately one thousand pages.

The catalog's thickness, too, had been caused by the King of Destruction and other Superiors. Due to the King destroying Noz Forest, the amount of people wanting to escape the capital had increased. Not to mention that the emancipation of the roads leading to other cities had revitalized the trading routes. As a result, there was a great spike in requests for escorts that could protect those travelers.

The problem *we* were faced with, however, was that...

"...The rewards and difficulties for requests from those going to Gideon are so all over the place that I can't choose," I said.

"True..." Rook agreed.

There were dozens of escort quests where the destination was the city of duels — the place where we could find Figaro. However, there were requests that had different rewards despite having the same difficulty, and vice versa.

Since we couldn't accept any quests without thinking things through, the ones with favorable conditions often got picked by other people and disappeared from the catalog right as we were considering them.

"Also, escort quests aren't even appealing," I said.

"True..." Rook agreed.

The ones who took the escort quests had to protect the requesters for the entire journey. However, Rook and I were players. We had to log out every now and then, and we couldn't do any protection when we weren't in the game.

In the game's setting, we Masters got "sent to another world every now and then," and the tians were fully aware of that. Therefore, we players weren't suited for escort quests, so most of them were taken by tians. Though, there were some exceptions made for Masters of a particularly high level.

"Maybe we should look for quests where we have to kill or deliver something," I suggested. "Though the rewards would be smaller."

"True..." Rook agreed.

"...Rook, that's all you've been saying for a while now," I said.

"Oh, sorry," he said, finally speaking a different word. "Reading this made me remember some things..."

From the fact that he looked like a middle-schooler, I could only assume that he was remembering a time he'd studied for his exams.

"Father's handmade textbook was even thicker than this..." he mumbled as he went through the pages with an empty look in his eyes.

If Rook's face was really the same as it was in reality, he was of Western descent.

I guess the exam struggle is severe all around the world, I thought. *The college entrance exams I had to go through were so damn hard...*

"Hmm..."

"Mmm..."

Nemesis and Babi were intently looking at books, too. However, they weren't quest catalogs.

Nemesis was examining the bounty list, while Babi was staring at the guild's food and drink menu.

"Master," Nemesis spoke up. "It says here that those traveling on the road to Gideon sometimes encounter two boss monsters with bounties on them — King of the Wolf Pack, Lobohta and Great Miasmic Hobgoblin, Gardranda. I hope we meet them."

"I'm not sure if I want to experience something so blatantly dangerous..." I replied.

"Hey, Rook," said Babi. "Don't you think that this Special Pudding a la Mode would be great with Death Sauce? Want to order it?"

"I don't think I want to experience something so blatantly dangerous..." Rook replied.

We shifted our attention away from their... disturbed suggestions and focused on our quest catalogs.

First of all, it was already set in stone that we would accept a quest we could do on the way to Gideon. Rook wanted to go there because the city of duels had a beast market.

On the subject of Rook, though... In our little information exchange, I had found out that — despite being twice the level I was — he had low stats. Though his MP and SP were higher than mine, I had double or more of every other stat.

It was less about me being a Paladin — a high-rank job — and more about Rook's Pimp being a low-stat job. A Pimp's playstyle seemed to be focused on a gamble — you either Charm or die.

At this point, I had absolutely no doubts that it was Rook's vocation. If not "Pimp," the only possible thing he could have been was "Angel."

"Master, get ahold of yourself," said Nemesis. "You're acting as though you're Charmed."

"W-Whoa," I said, and snapped out of it.

Of course, Rook wasn't using his Charm skill on me. He couldn't even if he wanted to, since it only worked on females. However, he was just so handsome that he made the mind drift away every now and then. Even the other adventurers in the guild were throwing glances at our table. Hell, some were downright staring.

Rook wasn't the only reason for that, though — both Nemesis and Babi were exceptionally beautiful, too. With three out of five of us here being so attractive, it was only natural to become the center of attention.

...*Five?* I thought.

"Man, it's been a while since I've visited the Adventurers' Guild. There's quite a large pile of quests today, huh?" Marie — the Journalist who sold us info about the PK incident — was sitting at our table.

...*Okay, just how long have you been here?* I thought. I could've sworn that we'd started with just me, Rook, Nemesis, and Babi. *Do you Journalists have some skill that allows you to sit at tables without getting noticed?*

"Oh? Why are you here, Miss Marie?" asked Rook.

"I had business that involved going to Gideon, so I decided to pick up a quest I could do on the way and noticed you two talking about going to the duel city, too," answered Marie. "I figured that I simply *had* to join. May I come with you?"

Had to join, huh...? I thought.

"...Well, I don't really mind," I said. "What about you, Rook?"

"Same here," he answered. "In fact, having her join us would be reassuring."

"...That's true," I agreed.

It was going to be the first time Rook and I ever traveled to another town. Marie, on the other hand, had been as far as Huang He, so there was no doubt that she was used to long-distance journeys. That alone was enough to make her presence reassuring.

Marie joined us in looking through the quest catalog. "I found one that's named 'Elimination Request — Sauda Phantom Sheep,'" said Rook. "The reward is high, too."

"Oh, that one's no good," said Marie. "Though weak, Sauda Phantom Sheep are extremely hard to find. It would take you three days of searching."

"Elimination Request — Blue Lemmings. This one also has a nice reward," I said. "We'd have to kill a whole fifty of them, though."

"They're weak, mouse-like, easy-to-find monsters that come in flocks," Marie explained. "It should be eas—"

"No mice," said Rook.

"Rook?" I looked at him.

"No mice," he repeated himself.

"O-Okay..."

About ten minutes passed as we continued glaring at the catalog, when suddenly...

"Oh! What would you say to this one?" Marie pointed at a certain page.

Difficulty Level Two, Delivery Request — The Guild in Gideon, City of Duels.

Reward: 30,000 lir.

Please complete a delivery from the capital's Adventurers' Guild to the Guild in Gideon.

There is much to be delivered, so it is recommended that only those with a storage bag accept this quest.

You have three days to complete it.

P.S. If you take the delivery and run, we will send an assassin after you.

"This request is from the guild itself," Marie explained. "We only have to take the delivery to the other guild, so it's nothing complicated. The reward is good, too, so it's a really nice deal overall."

...The P.S. is a bit questionable, but I guess there's no need to worry about it if we play it fair, I thought.

"I'm up for this quest. What about you, Rook?" I asked.

"Yes, it seems agreeable," he answered.

"Then it's decided," said Nemesis.

"Already? I didn't get to eat my pudding yet," Babi complained.

Everyone replied in their own way.

Whatever the case, we had chosen the first quest we would do as a party.

"With that settled, you go on and accept it, Ray." said Marie.

"Hm? But you're the one found it, so shouldn't you be the one to do it?" I asked.

"When several people accept the same quest, the proper procedure is to create a party and have a representative go through the acceptance process," she explained. "That involves the representative writing down his main job."

"Which means...?" I raised an eyebrow.

"The guild's receptionist wouldn't be too keen on giving the quest to a Journalist or a Pimp, right?" Marie elaborated.

She wasn't wrong. The request had come directly from the guild, so there was a chance that they wouldn't give it to anyone who was questionable in terms of ability. However, that would never apply to Paladins such as myself.

...But wait, my level is the lowest out of us three. Won't that be a problem? I thought.

"The first thing that comes up is your label, after all," said Rook. "I also think that you should be the one to do this, Ray."

First Marie, now Rook. They were both fine with it, so there was no reason for me not to do it.

I took the catalog to the guild's receptionist and showed her the page of the request we'd decided upon.

"Understood," she said. "Please give us your card and fill in this form."

I gave her my freshly-made Adventurers' Guild member card and filled in all the fields I had to.

"We have processed your acceptance of this quest," said the receptionist. "Please go to that counter and retrieve the items."

Doing as I was told, I went to take the delivery and placed it into my storage bag.

With that, the preparations were done and we officially had a guild quest — a new step in our *Dendro* career.

Difficulty Level Two, Delivery Request — The Guild in Gideon, City of Duels.

Our destination was obvious.

And so, we began the quest.

Kingdom of Altar, ???

Cheering.

Cheering as far as you could hear.

It represented nothing but delight.

Countless goblins were fiercely expressing their overwhelming joy.

It was all because they had seen some creatures. Though four-limbed — just like the goblins — they were different from them... for they were human.

The goblins hungered. These past few days, no humans had passed through their territory.

Thus, the goblins — with their love for human flesh and the things they hauled — had become hungry beyond words.

They survived by eating other monsters, but compared to the taste of humans and their food, those were simply unsatisfying.

Thus, the goblins were overjoyed.

The human traffic through this area used to be stopped by something at the mountain, and they couldn't be more pleased that it was revived. For, once again, they had access to the food they loved.

The strangely-dressed human that had recently gone through their territory was too scary for them, so they could have only waited for him to pass. However, the humans passing before them now weren't scary at all.

Thus, the humans themselves and the food they carried were nothing but a feast for them.

"Ghgheeeee!"

"Geghyaaaaahhh!"

Letting out their war cries, the goblins began running towards the carriage before them.

"Goblins?! Why are there so many...?!" shouted a human.

"Sir, this is too much for us to handle! Make the horses go as fast as they can!" roared another.

"A-All right!"

"We have to run, too!"

The merchant man increased the carriage's speed as the tian adventurers responsible for guarding him and his goods ran after it, trying not to fall behind.

They were fleet of foot, so it was obvious that the goblins wouldn't catch up.

Thus, the goblins roared. They roared out their cheer and delight.

"What are they doing?! Are they trying to threaten us?!" asked a human.

"Ignore them! Just keep on running away!" howled another.

The goblins weren't threatening them. They might've done that before an enemy, but when faced with food, such acts were meaningless. They were simply calling.

"Ha ha, looks like we escaped... Huh?"

A moment later, the merchant — along with his carriage — was crushed by *something* that fell from the sky.

As the *something* trampled on the corpse — now reduced to fruit-like mush — it faced the nearby adventurers.

"Wh-Wha?!"

"I-Is this actually... the UBM... Gar—"

They weren't even given the time to say anything coherent.

The *something* before them and the goblins that had caught up quickly overwhelmed them all.

"GOOOAAAAAHHHHH!"

And so, after a satiating feast, the *something* and the horde of goblins returned to their den.

All of them were full of excitement for the next time they'd become hungry and have another feast pass their territory.

The area's name was "Nex Plains."

It was south of Sauda Mountain Pass and north of Gideon, city of duels.

…And anyone making their way to Gideon would simply *have* to pass through it.

Chapter Seven ⟩ The Ordeal of Rookies

In Royal Capital Altea, in the front of the Adventurer's guild, Paladin Ray Starling

After we had taken the quest at the adventurer's guild and began getting ready to go to Gideon, Rook spoke up and raised his right hand.

"You can leave the means of travel to me," he said. There was a pale, gem-like object on his hand.

"What's that?" I asked.

"It's a 'Jewel' — an item where you keep your monsters," he answered. "It's the reward I got for my modeling."

Rook began explaining. In the process, he also answered a certain question I'd had while looking at his skills.

Being a Pimp, he had a skill that strengthened his underlings, and seeing that had made me curious about what happened to them outside of battle.

Since we were players, we would return to reality every now and then. Thus, I wondered what his little minions would do while we were away. I was saddened by the very idea of a player who stopped playing after having left some monsters or slaves in a cage or something.

Such problems were solved by Jewels, such as the one Rook had.

Jewels were basically the animal version of the item boxes we always used. It allowed the storage of any underlings you owned, and it was possible to set it so that time inside wouldn't flow at all.

The storage would work even while the player was logged out, and if they didn't log in for two months of real time or half a year of game time, the Jewels would automatically release the creatures inside.

I see, I thought. *Having underlings in such a realistic world would be really difficult without these things.*

Well, there was a need to feed and have them rest outside the Jewel, but that was all part and parcel of being an underling owner.

It was also possible to make the time inside the Jewel go on as normal. Logging out while the underlings were released was an option, too. However, while being outside, the underlings could always get into some sort of trouble, so whether it would be done or not depended entirely on the owner.

"So, you already have a monster in there, huh?" I asked as I pointed at the Jewel.

"Yes," Rook answered. "Mr. Grantzian told me to choose one reward out of a few, but since I had a skill that strengthened monsters, I chose this one."

Pimp was a job that had a low combat ability, but compensated for it with the use of monsters, so that had been the right choice to make.

"Let me show you," said Rook. "'Call' — Marilyn."

Following his words and the unique roar, the Jewel began to shine.

"MMHOOOOOO!"

And, sure enough, a monster named "Marilyn" appeared before us, but…

"…Marilyn?" I raised an eyebrow.

…it was arguable whether the name "Marilyn" was appropriate.

A succinct description of Marilyn would go as such: a triceratops pulling a carriage. Its gigantic body was covered in a blue, solid shell, while its back and shoulders could easily be compared to heavy armor. The very real horns on its head were intimidating enough to make me feel as though they could topple the castle walls.

It was far too obvious that the monster was stronger than us. The thing could even put up a fight against a Demi-Dragon Worm.

Hell, I wouldn't even be surprised if it came out on top, I thought.

"This is Marilyn — a Trihorn Demi-Dragon," Rook introduced the monster. "The dragon carriage came as a bonus."

"Demi-Dragon?" Seriously? I thought. *It actually is on the same tier as the worms, then. That name has some serious power behind it.*

I was momentarily taken aback by the fact that you could get such a thing as a reward, but since the difficulty of the quest had been higher than the one where I'd saved Milianne, it wasn't *that* strange.

"Why 'Marilyn,' though?" I asked.

"It's a girl, so I named her after a famous actress," Rook answered.

I see. It's a girl, huh? I guess it's all fine, then, I thought. … *Marilyn Monroe might or might not be turning in her grave right now.*

"Wow, what a sight!" Marie commented. "Though, something this strong might exceed your Minion Capacity."

"Minion Capacity?" Rook and I asked simultaneously.

"Oh, let me explain it, then." Marie reached into her item box, took out a sketchbook-like item, and began her explanation while drawing something on it.

A sketchbook? I thought. *Why does she even have something like that? Is it because she's a Journalist?*

"First of all, in *Infinite Dendrogram*, the maximum number of people you can fit in a party is six." Marie finished drawing and showed us the result — little chibi versions of me, Rook and herself. All the detail on them made the drawings seem strangely high-quality.

"In our case, three of those slots are already taken," she said. "Now, the other three slots can be taken by tamed monsters or Guardian-type Embryos." Marie added chibi versions of Babi and Marilyn.

"You say they 'can' be taken... Does that mean it's possible to make the monsters fight without doing that?" asked Rook.

"Yes," she answered. "It's possible to not count them as party members and instead treat them as an extension of the owner's power. That's where Minion Capacity comes in."

Underneath Rook's picture, Marie drew a small tree diagram that led to Babi and Marilyn.

"With this method, they won't use party slots, but there is a limit to it," she said. "Minion Capacity is basically the name for that limit."

"I see," I nodded.

"Open your status screen and look at the additional entries."

I did as she'd said and took a look at the auxiliary screen. Sure enough, I saw an entry that said "Minion Capacity 0/50."

"Is this it?" I asked.

"Yes, monsters that fit the Capacity can be used as part of your own power," she explained. "The amount of the Capacity taken depends entirely on the individual monster. For example, one level 1 Little Goblin would take 1 point." That meant that I could control a total of fifty level 1 Little Goblins. A nice number, but questionable overall. I could just picture them all getting blown away by a single area attack.

"My Capacity is 500, so I can own five hundred of them," said Rook.

That's ten times more than mine, I thought.

"Pimp is a job with a high Capacity," Marie said. "Though, Ray, since your job is in the knight grouping, you will have to use mounts, so I think that your Capacity is above the high-rank class average."

Mounts, huh? I thought. *I should get one of those someday.*

"Anyway, I see how it works now…" I said.

If it was impossible to call your monsters without using party slots, jobs such as Tamer and Pimp — both of which had low base fighting ability — would have a hard time getting into parties. With the use of Capacity instead, they could count their monsters as part of their own power, making them no worse — if not better — than any other job.

"What happens if you exceed the Capacity?" I asked.

"You get a limit on your abilities and stop gaining XP," she answered.

That's quite a huge demerit, I thought.

"Miss Marilyn here is too much for your Capacity, Rook," said Marie. "Demi-Dragons are strong and have a cost that represents that."

If I had to choose between fighting 500 Little Goblins or one Demi-Dragon Worm, I'd pick the former without a moment's hesitation, I thought. *That's just how much stronger the latter option is.*

"With that in mind, let's place Marilyn in the party," Marie suggested. "There aren't many of us, so we have some free slots, after all."

"Hey, I have a question! What's my cost?" asked Babi.

"An Embryo's cost is always 0," she answered. "If it weren't, then Masters who evolved Guardian-type Embryos wouldn't be able to draw out their full potential."

That was true.

"Well, that sure took a while to explain. Now, let's return to the matter at hand," Marie continued. "By riding Marilyn's dragon carriage, we could reach Gideon in about one whole day."

"Then I guess we'll have to give up on doing it now and depart tomorrow morning, instead," I said. "Do you two have any plans?"

I was referring to real-life stuff. Our journey to Gideon would take us a total of three days, which meant that we'd have to dedicate an entire real-life day to this.

"Not really," said Rook. "I'll be free the whole time."

"Same here," said Marie. "I'm jobless right now."

...I'm having trouble figuring out if I should laugh at that or not, I thought.

The next day, we were riding Marilyn's dragon carriage on the road to Gideon.

The road was wide enough to let two Marilyns ride side-by-side without any problems. Her size had made me wonder if she would block the road, but my worries seemed to have been completely unfounded.

Marilyn's walking speed was greater than I'd expected, too. She could pull the dragon carriage uphill without even the slightest drop in speed, which reminded me of four-wheel drive off-road cars.

Looks like our journey to Gideon will be smooth, I thought.

Although we had to take care of the occasional monster attack, so it wasn't like we could get there without stopping. However, since we were going through a newbies' hunting ground, the monsters never attacked us in large groups. The most we'd had to fend off at once was three.

In fact, Rook, Babi, and I had just defeated such a group. Marie, meanwhile, stayed sitting in the dragon carriage and cheering for us while sipping on some tea. There were things to be said about this setup. Still, she wasn't doing nothing without reason. Honestly, it was my own fault for not asking her about it beforehand.

"Journalist" wasn't a battle job in any sense of the term. However, Journalists had a characteristic skill called "The Pen is Mightier than the Sword," which increased the XP gain of the entire party in exchange for rendering the Journalist unable to fight. The skill couldn't be turned off, either. With that in mind, it was safe to conclude that Journalists were like a decoration that were of absolutely no use in battle.

Sure, I appreciated the bonus XP. And yes, we were going through a newbies' hunting ground, so the enemies weren't something we couldn't handle ourselves. She was also more knowledgeable than us. The advice she gave was useful, and her monster info was accurate.

Still, I can't help but feel that... well, whatever, I thought.

"The skill is called 'The Pen is Mightier than the Sword,' so I was expecting it to be an attack with a pen," said Nemesis.

"That saying's meaning isn't physical," I said.

Though I wouldn't be surprised if this world had a pen that was stronger than a sword, I thought.

All the same, the journey was going smoothly. Due to the XP bonus, both Rook and I had already gotten some levels. I was now level 16, while Rook was level 27.

The battles were coming and going in a satisfying manner, and it didn't look like we'd have any trouble with the monsters of this level range.

Speaking of "no trouble," the mountain pass before us had once been blocked by a bear-like monster. Just from appearance alone, it had seemed like the boss monster of this area. However, before we could even begin our fight with it, Marilyn — seemingly angry at it for blocking her way — had defeated the bear as if it wasn't a big deal at all.

Rook had retrieved the drops, which had come in a "box," so yes, it had been an actual boss monster. A boss's loot was always a welcome thing. However, as a rule of thumb, boss monsters were always the most powerful creatures an area could offer.

And it sure didn't seem like that when Marilyn handled him, I thought.

Another thing to note was that most boss monsters were multiple-of-a-kind and took part in the ecosystem, but according to Marie, there were some monsters that were unlike any other. They were called UBMs — Unique Boss Monsters.

All of them — without exception — were equipped with special abilities, and some were even powerful enough to eliminate high-rank parties without much difficulty. However, since they were one-of-a-kind, even encountering them was rare.

Once out of the wavy Sauda Mountain Pass, we entered an area of nothing but wide plains. The area was named "Nex Fields," and the road leading through it was supposed to take us to Gideon.

As we all were thinking about just how smooth of a journey this was, something entered our vision.

On the road ahead, there were several carriages which looked like they belonged to peddlers. They were all under attack by a throng of goblins that easily numbered more than a hundred.

The goblins in this horde had a significantly better physique than the Little Goblins Rook and I had fought back on Easter Plains.

While the standard Little Goblin was about half my size, the ones here reached approximately 80%. Not only that, but they also wielded swords and bows, and were clad in proper armor. Some of them were even riding some small monsters resembling carnivorous dinosaurs. The names above them — Goblin Warrior, Goblin Archer, and Goblin Rider — made it all the more obvious that they were superior to the ones we were familiar with.

And a proper throng of them was attacking the peddler carriages.

I could see some tian-looking people try to fend them off, but alas, the numbers were against them.

"...That sure is a lot of goblins. And it seems like every single one of them is stronger than the monsters in the Mountain Pass. What shall we do?" Marie evaluated the enemy, asking whether we should join the battle or not.

I began to ponder. We were rookies, and calling us strong would be nothing but a mistake. Marie was a veteran, yes, but she couldn't participate in any battles, not to mention the fact that the opposing force would greatly outnumber us even if she could.

We clearly had a low chance of victory. The safest option would be to turn around, retreat to the Mountain Pass, wait for the goblin horde to go away, and return on the path to Gideon then.

However, that would mean leaving the people there for dead. And that... would leave a bad taste in my mouth.

"Rook, Marie," I spoke up. "We might get the death penalty and fail the quest because of it, but..."

...if you guys don't mind that, then...

"Let's do it," Rook said before I could finish. Then he freed Marilyn from the dragon carriage...

"Run them over."

...and set her on the goblins.

"MMHOOOOOOO!" she roared and burst into a dash.

Keeping her three horns at the forefront, Marilyn charged into the goblin throng with all she had. Once they noticed the presence of something other than the carriages — their prey — it was already too late. Nearly fourteen goblins got pulverized by Marilyn's horns.

"Let's go, Ray," said Rook. "Marilyn might be strong, but that's still too much for her alone."

"...Yeah!" I agreed.

"I see." Nemesis seemed to realize something. "Just like my unexpectedly fiery Master, this Rook fellow seems to have a dangerous side to him, too."

"Mrrgh!" grumbled Babi. "No fair, Marilyn! I was with him first, so I'm supposed to do the most!"

Rook, Babi, and I all jumped through the space opened by Marilyn and began fighting the goblins around us.

"Hghaah!" I tightened my grip on Nemesis — who was already in her greatsword form — and swung her at the Goblin Warrior before me with all I had. The blade sank into the top of the Warrior's shoulder, but the armor he wore made it stop after going only about ten centimeters.

"Ghghee!" The wound wasn't fatal, so the Warrior still tried to swing his weapon at me.

"Then how about… this?!" I raised my greatsword upwards — lifting the Warrior along with it — and quickly swung it down to the ground. The momentum added to my attack made the Warrior — and his armor — split in half.

Thanks to the levels I'd gained recently, such feats weren't particularly hard for me.

But it takes a while to do it, I thought. *So next time, I'll be aiming straight for the neck.*

"Heh heh heh, what an aggressive battle," chortled Nemesis. "It's to my liking."

Well, someone seems to be having fun, I thought. *I find it a bit strange that she can't handle zombies, but she's just fine with all this gore here.*

"Behind you!" she warned me.

"…Whoa!" I turned around, swung my greatsword sideways and decapitated the Warrior that had tried to attack me from behind.

Sadly for him, having Nemesis at my side basically let me see from every direction. Being surrounded wasn't a big problem for me.

"What are you people?!" one of the escorts fighting to protect the carriages exclaimed.

I chose to make our explanation succinct.

"We're Masters heading to Gideon," I said. "We're here to help. That Demi-Dragon is with us, so don't attack it."

"I see! We will make sure not to harm it, then! Thank you for your help!" Convinced, he began telling his comrades about us.

With that, it was now established who was on whose side. Of course, since the only enemies were goblins and their mounts, simply telling them about Marilyn was more than enough. However, we were still seriously outnumbered.

Surrounded by goblins, Marilyn couldn't get enough speed to kill them as quickly as she had at the start. The carriage escorts were doing their best, but it still wasn't enough to make up for the difference in numbers.

Suddenly, I realized something. Rook and Babi weren't with us.

I looked around and found them both standing in one place.

That was all they were doing. Despite all the chaos around them, they were just *standing* there, back-to-back.

However, they soon began to move.

"Male..."

"Lilim..."

Rook extended his right hand... while Babi — her left...

"...Temptation!"

...and — while simultaneously saying that word — they motioned their hands as if beckoning something.

The next moment, a particularly fierce female Goblin Warrior decapitated the goblin next to her.

Another one — a Goblin Archer who seemed to have a commanding role — suddenly crushed the head of the mount he was riding on.

"Ghgheee?! Sis! W-What did you dooo?!"

"Captaain?!"

Screams, confusion, and — most important of all — chaos began to spread throughout the goblin army. The number of victims was increasing by the second. One after the other, goblins lost their minds and began attacking their own.

The Charmed goblins were attacking those who weren't, while those who weren't Charmed were hesitant about fighting back and could only get Charmed themselves or simply die.

The damage done to the horde increased exponentially, and when all the goblins were either dead or Charmed…

"Lilim Draaain!"

…Babi started draining the life out of every single Charmed goblin.

The process made some of them come back to their senses, but just like before, they either got killed by the Charmed goblins or simply got Charmed again.

"Thank you for the meeaal!"

Considering just how hellish the situation was for the victims, the nonchalance in her voice was quite inappropriate. Nonetheless, those words were what marked the end of the battle.

The throng of goblins had been completely annihilated. Excluding those that had been defeated by me or the carriage escorts, all the goblin corpses had been either killed by their own or sucked dry to the point of making them look like mummies.

"In contrast to our counterattacks — which are effective against single bosses like those damn centipedes — their abilities are frighteningly good at exterminating large groups of vermin," commented Nemesis.

She was right. Our strengths and theirs were strikingly different in nature. By using Charm, Rook and Babi had created scattered allies within the enemy ranks. That had rendered the enemies unable to focus their attacks, and had destroyed any semblance of cooperation they had.

As they had been trying to recover from that, the effects of Charm had spread and gotten even more of them on Rook's side.

Cue repeating downwards spiral. It was a nightmare scenario in any group-based battle.

"I'm glad he is not our enemy," said Nemesis.

I couldn't agree more.

The tian escorts and even peddlers in the carriages were shocked stiff at what Rook and Babi had just done. That was only natural.

We were fully aware that they weren't bad guys, but there was no arguing that what they had just done had been downright villainous.

Charm was scary — end of discussion. It reminded me of why I was afraid of Rocbouquet.

"This was the first time I've used it in battle, and I'm very glad it was useful," said Rook.

"It wasn't very tasty, but I'm sooo stuffed right now!" declared Babi.

The fact that they are a Master with a low-rank job and his first form Embryo makes me dread imagining how they'll be in the future, I thought.

"Ah! Rook, Rook! I have a new skill! I reached my second form!" Babi squealed.

"Really?!" he exclaimed.

And that was exactly when I heard them say that.

Although her appearance didn't change, this battle — or rather, "extermination"— had caused Babi to evolve. That wasn't unexpected, considering just how many goblins there had been.

I looked at Rook's basic stats and saw that he, too, was quite a bit over level 30 now. I, however, was level 20.

"Congratulations," I said to Rook.

"Thank you!" he replied. "So, Babi, what kind of skill did you get?"

"Umm… It's called 'Drain Learning!'"

Rook took a look at his Embryo window and examined the new skill. He let me have a gander, too, so I read its description.

It said "Gives a low (1%) chance to learn a random skill from the monster being drained."

"…Learning, eh?" I said to myself. It was much like the blue magic from that famous RPG series. Basically, it allowed the user to learn and utilize the skills of enemy monsters.

In Babi's case, the chance of that happening was a mere 1%. However, if my calculations were correct, that meant that she had a greater than 60% chance to get a new skill after draining a hundred times. Since there was no limit to the amount of skills one could have, it had the potential to be an extremely useful ability.

…I have a feeling she's gonna be really formidable in the future, I thought.

Suddenly, Nemesis sounded a groan that seemed really troubled. "Mmrgh…"

"What's wrong, Nemesis?" I asked.

"I feel like you and I didn't do much compared to them, and I find that a bit troubling," she answered.

"…Come on, now. No one cares about that," I said.

Well, it was true that we hadn't gotten to be particularly valuable players since we'd defeated that one Demi-Dragon Worm. We'd even died once. Then again, if all we ever faced were beasts such as the Superior Killer or Figaro, we would be dying all the time.

That's why it's all too bad when we don't get to show off, I thought.

And so, though it was likely unrelated to Nemesis' worries and my sentiments...

"GOOOAAAAAHHHHH!"

...something screamed and landed on the goblin corpse-littered battlefield.

No — the word "landed" wasn't appropriate, for it made the action seem soft. Something large — a demon — *crashed down* on the battlefield.

The demon's feet cracked open the ground — making it tremble — and yet the monster itself was unharmed.

In awe, I looked up at its daunting appearance.

It was monstrous in every sense of the word. I lacked the words to describe it. Most of it was brown and black in color. The horn on its head — combined with a stature that surpassed five meters in height — made it appear exactly the way I expected a demon to look. However, it had a feature that was wholly unnatural and nothing short of discomforting.

It had large mouths on its head and both of its shoulders. All of them were leaking a dark purple smoke, the very sight of which made a cold chill go down my spine.

Last but not least, the words "Great Miasmic Hobgoblin, Gardranda" were hanging above it.

The intimidating presence of this "Gardranda" was enough to affect our reaction speed. Before we could even realize, it raised its right leg, crushed one of the escorts... and followed it up with a punch from its huge fist — directed straight at me.

"Counter... Absorption!"

Nemesis spawned the barrier of light just in time to stop Gardranda's fist from hitting me directly, which greatly lowered its damage.

Since she'd had experience in suddenly activating that skill, Nemesis was quick to react. That was about the only good thing about the current situation.

"This one has more power than those centipedes…!" she exclaimed.

"So it's actually above the Demi-Dragon Worms, huh?" I asked.

"Great Miasmic Hobgoblin, Gardranda." This monster had both a title and a name.

I've never seen a monster with this kind of presentation before… I thought. *Wait, wasn't his name on the bounty list Nemesis was reading yesterday?*

"Ray! Rook! Be careful!" Marie — who was standing outside the battle — suddenly shouted to us. "That's a Unique Boss Monster!"

Her warning made me remember a certain bit of information I'd seen on the wiki.

UBM.

Just as it said in the name, it was a term that referred to boss monsters who were unique — unlike any other creatures in this world.

Standard boss monsters, such as the Demi-Dragon Worms, often came in groups. But UBMs were different. There was only one of each UBM in the entire world. No current UBMs have ever existed before, and no past UBMs would ever come again. All of them — without exception — were really powerful and even came equipped with their own unique abilities. In a way, they were like the "Masters" of the monster faction.

Thus, they were several tiers stronger than any bosses of the same level.

"Why would such a monster appear here...?" I couldn't help but ask. Considering the power of the goblins surrounding us, Gardranda was simply far too powerful to be here.

Wait... the goblins? I thought.

"I see how it is..." said Nemesis. "This demon is like the ringleader of the goblins. It came out because its subordinates were annihilated."

In other words, it had come here because we'd enraged it. However, there was something else on my mind.

I shifted my gaze and fell silent. My vision was fixed on a single corpse. It belonged to the carriage escort who'd been attacked at the same time I had. It was the same one I'd spoken to not too long ago.

His corpse — the body flattened by the demon — seemed somewhat inauthentic.

Obviously, I only felt that way because my experience with destroyed corpses didn't go beyond fiction. However, the extent of this world's realism was great enough to replicate the weight...

...the *gravity* of a lost life.

I had fought undead before and had caught glimpses of players vanishing into the dusk-veiled forestry as they were massacred by the Superior Killer. In fact, some of the escorts here had died at the hands of goblins before we'd joined the battle.

However, the one that had gotten pulverized by Gardranda was the first person that had died right before my eyes.

I was at a loss for words. I didn't know his name, nor was I aware of what kind of person he had been. I even had trouble remembering his face.

But... I'd been talking to him just a short while ago.

He was beyond helping now. This world wouldn't allow him to come back. He was simply *dead*.

"This'll leave a bad taste in my mouth…" I said with a palpable anger in my tone, and looked up at the demon's sizable frame.

I saw veins popping out and pulsating on its head. No — it wasn't just the head. That was happening on the skin around its shoulder-mouths, as well.

"It's releasing some sort of breath!" shouted Marie. "Back away from it!" I couldn't tell if her warning come too late or if *it* happened too fast.

With great intensity, Gardranda's three mouths simultaneously sprayed out a dark purple smoke.

"…Huh?!" I exclaimed.

It was somewhat reminiscent of insecticide. The sprays that instantly killed the irritating, buzzing pests we were all so familiar with. I had used such sprays myself, of course. However, I'd never once expected to have someone use something like that on *me*.

The poisonous breath was launched in three directions — at me, at Rook and Babi, and at Marilyn and the escorts — and it quickly covered us all.

The dark purple miasma didn't do any damage at first. However, it soon made me go dizzy and forced me to drop to my knees.

I looked at the status window, where I saw that I was under the effects of three debuffs — Poison, Intoxication, and Weakness.

Poison made my health gradually decrease, Intoxication made it hard for me to even stand up, while Weakness cut my stats to less than half their original value, making it so that even my gear felt heavy to me.

I shifted my gaze and saw that the escorts and peddlers were on the ground, as well.

Rook, however, was above us. Babi had raised him up before the miasma could reach him.

"Mh-mhoooooo...!"

I heard the familiar roar, but it was far weaker than before. Its source was Marilyn. She, too, was under the effects of the miasma's debuffs. And yet, she mustered all she had, pushed her feet on the ground, and charged towards Gardranda.

It was the very same charge that could trample fourteen goblins at once and even instantly pulverize lower level bosses, and yet...

"GOAAAAAHHHHHH!"

...Gardranda stopped it.

The demon extended its log-like arms and grabbed on to the outer two of Marilyn's three horns. Though it was pushed a few meters back, Gardranda was able to stop Marilyn's — a Demi-Dragon's — charge.

Then, the demon added a bit more power...

"GeeeeYYAAAAHHHH!"

...and threw Marilyn into the air.

Drawing an arc through the air, the several-tons beast flew about ten meters before hitting the ground with an unpleasantly strong sound.

"Marilyn!" Rook seemed slightly panicked.

"Mh, mhoo, mo..." Marilyn released a weak sound.

With the damage from the fall and all the debuffs weighing down on her, it was obvious that she was at her limit.

"Recall!" Rook's words made her return to the Jewel. Time stopped for the animals within it, so Marilyn was safe for now.

"Mrrgh! It's not workiiing!" Babi had been trying to use Temptation on Gardranda for a while now, but since the demon's level, MP, and SP were so high, Charm simply had no effect.

"Suitability, huh?" I whispered to myself. Rook and Babi weren't cut out for boss battles.

If there was anyone here who *was*, however…

"Master!" In response to Nemesis's shout, I shifted my attention back to Gardranda.

As I knelt there — barely mobile due to all the debuffs — the demon swung its right hand at me as if crushing a fly.

"Don't underestimate me!" I forced my heavy body to move, swung Nemesis into Gardranda's palm…

"Vengeance is Mine!"

…and activated the skill the very moment the sword landed.

The damage from the nullified Gardranda's punch mixed with the HP I'd lost to Poison, got doubled, and made the demon's right hand burst.

The attack tore the palm apart and made three of the fingers fly straight off.

"GUUUOOOAAHHHHH?!" Gardranda screamed in agony.

But the damage I'd done was low. Since the damage I'd accumulated from Gardranda at that point hadn't been particularly great, Vengeance is Mine hadn't done that much damage, either. Also, the attack on the palm had used up all the damage I'd accumulated by then. To use another Vengeance is Mine, I'd have to accumulate damage all over again.

"Ghh!" Following the attack, I swung Nemesis once again and launched a standard attack. However, it was a few tiers weaker than it usually was, and had none of its usual brilliance.

The reason for that was obvious. The debuffs were still affecting my body.

The Great Miasmic Hobgoblin, Gardranda had both the physical power to let it throw something as heavy as Marilyn and the ability to weaken its opponents in three different ways.

The gradual HP reduction from Poison wasn't much of a problem as long as I made sure to observe the HP bar. However, Intoxication paralyzed the semicircular canals and thus negatively affected my ability to control my body, while Weakness cut my stats by more than 50% and turned the most basic fighting into a struggle.

"This is bad…" I muttered. *Damn it, my chances were low even without these debuffs.*

Suddenly, Marie called to me from behind. "Ray!"

I turned around, expecting her to warn me about something, and instead got a glass bottle to hit me right on the face and shatter.

"Khah…!" I exclaimed.

"Master?!" Nemesis was confused, as well. As the impact made me throw my head backwards, I got showered by the bottle's shards and contents.

My pain settings were set to "off," so it didn't hurt at all, but I couldn't help but wonder what had brought this about.

Marie had the stance of a pitcher who had just thrown a ball, so it was pretty obvious that she had been the one who'd thrown it.

As I was about to yell at her for messing about during a battle, I noticed something.

"…I'm healed, and the debuffs are gone," I muttered. My HP was at 100%, and the three status effects were no longer on my status window.

What is this? I asked in my head.

"It's the Elixir I'd prepared just in case! With this, you should be immune to disease-based debuffs for the next 180 seconds! However, I don't have a spare, so use it well!" Marie explained.

Elixir? So that's what was in the bottle. Apparently, it's quite a powerful drug. However, with this…

"Looks like we're at our best again," I said.

"Indeed," agreed Nemesis. "With no debuffs hindering us, this Gardranda is the equivalent of one of those damn centipedes — except with hair."

With my current HP and defense, I could bear the demon's attacks, and if I could bear them — I had a chance of winning.

"For the poison, for Marilyn, and for those who died... you'll get what's coming to you, you demon bastard!" I brandished Nemesis and charged towards Gardranda.

The Elixir's effects would last for another 154 seconds. That was the amount of time I had before I returned to being vulnerable to Gardranda's miasma and got the three debuffs again. Thus, I had to settle it before that time expired.

"Rrraaaghhh!" I held the greatsword aloft and swung it at Gardranda's knees. It cut through his skin and spilt some blood, but the wound wasn't deep in the slightest. Though it bit through the skin and sunk into the muscle, it wasn't even close to reaching the bone.

Even when I was at my best, my standard attacks weren't good enough to do any proper damage to him.

My STR wasn't particularly great, and though Nemesis might've been a great weapon when I'd been level 1, she was among the weaker ones now that I was level 20. If I tried to beat it with just my standard attacks, not even 1,500 seconds would be enough, let alone 150.

However...

"GUUOOOAAAHHHHH!" Gardranda retaliated with a kick, and I chose to let it hit me.

"Ghh...!" I got blasted away about seven meters, but was able to make a smooth landing.

Though it sent me flying, the attack didn't hurt me all that much.

The damage it did was about 600. That was approximately a quarter of my total HP.

I was level 20. With the bonus HP I'd gotten for leveling up while being a Paladin, the bonus from my Embryo, and the skill "HP Increase," my total HP had reached 2500.

One of my skills — Paladin's Aegis — reduced all incoming damage, and my equipment was far better than it had been when I'd fought the Demi-Dragon Worm. Thus, a creature that hit a little bit harder than them could never kill me in one hit. And if I couldn't die in one hit, I had the means to earn victory.

"First Heal!" I ran while casting my healing spell on myself and complemented it with a use of one of my Heal Potions. With that, my HP was almost back to full.

"Rrraaghh!"

Then I simply repeated what I'd done before. *Attack. Get hit. Heal.*

I merely had to repeat this for those 150 seconds. That was my only chance at winning.

One repetition took about twenty seconds and got me 600 damage, which became 660 when I considered the damage nullified by Paladin's Aegis. I could do it a total of seven times and gather 4620 damage. Vengeance is Mine would double that amount and damage for 9240.

Can you survive getting that hit on your head, you damn demon? I thought.

"That is our only optio— Master!"

As I calculated the remaining time and the damage I could gather, Nemesis called out to me. Being familiar with her tones, I instantly knew that it was a warning.

"Look above!" she shouted.

I quickly did as she told me. In the sky, hazy with Gardranda's miasma…

"KIIIAAAAAAAA!"

…I saw a large, crimson bird of prey as it dove towards me at high speed and readied its talons.

"Whoa!" I hastily jumped to the side, making the crimson gust go by me.

Seemingly annoyed due to failing to grab me, the bird of prey flapped its wings once and suddenly rose back up into the sky.

Before it completely got away, I caught a glimpse of the name displayed above it: "Crimson Roc Bird — Mount Owner: Great Miasmic Hobgoblin, Gardranda."

"A… a mount…?!" I stuttered.

The description made me realize something. When Gardranda had come here, he'd simply fallen from the sky. However, the demon had no means of flying or jumping particularly high, and these flat plains didn't have any places that would give it the necessary height to make such an entrance. Thus, there was only one reasonable explanation: Gardranda had been brought here by something that could fly. And that something had been hanging above us ever since we'd started this battle.

"…This is bad," I muttered. I was no longer able to focus on Gardranda.

The bird's speed and physique made it obvious that it was quite a powerful monster. If I had to guess, I'd assume that it was just as strong — if not stronger — than the Demi-Dragon Worms. It could even grab me with its talons and drop me from a great height, rendering me completely unable to fight back.

This bird was a dangerous enemy, indeed.

However, if I kept focusing on trying to avoid it, the Elixir's effects would wear off, and I'd no longer have any means of achieving victory.

"What do I do…?" I asked myself.

"Ray!" Before I could figure out how to handle the new enemy…

"We'll take care of the Roc Bird!" Rook shouted.

"I can fly, so leave it to me!" Babi called out to me.

"You just focus on Gardranda, Ray!" added Rook.

"But…!"

Rook and Babi couldn't do anything against a monster *that* powerful. It was probably immune to their Charm skills. Before I could tell that to them, Rook spoke up.

"We'll buy time until you defeat Gardranda!" he shouted.

"Yeah! So don't worry about us!" added Babi.

Holding Rook, Babi rose up and flew towards the Roc Bird. I silently watched them.

"Master," Nemesis spoke to me. "You are not thinking of letting their conviction go to waste, are you?"

"…Like hell," I replied. I brandished Nemesis and once again ran towards Gardranda.

The reason why I could continue fighting was because Marie had used her Elixir on me. The reason why I could focus on the fight was because Rook and Babi were holding back the Roc Bird. Nemesis and I weren't alone in this battle.

It wasn't like the time we'd been killed by the Superior Killer. I… no, *we* were fighting as a party.

"57 seconds left," I said. "By lowering our focus on healing, we can do this three, preferably four times."

"Let it be done, then!" Nemesis expressed her enthusiasm.

We ran, attacked Gardranda, got hit back, stood up, and ran again. It was to not waste the opportunity our comrades had given us... and to uplift our chances of victory. I didn't care how tattered I would become doing this.

Soon enough, we only had 10 seconds left.

"Nemesiiiis!" I shouted.

"Accumulated damage: 4973! We can do this!" she cried. "Master!"

Everything slotted into place when Gardranda hit us for the final time. I had less than half of my total HP, but I could still move. All that was left was to hit the demon with Vengeance is Mine.

I dashed towards Gardranda with the sole purpose of landing this lethal hit.

7 seconds left.

6 seconds. 5 seconds. 4 seconds.

"Guuuhhh— GHHAAAAAAAAGHHHH!"

We had only a few more steps to take until the demon was within our range.

That was the moment when the mouth on the head opened wide and released a crimson-red flame.

It wasn't the miasma this time.

This breath was meant purely to damage anyone it touched.

All this time, Gardranda had been hiding this trump card from us, and there was no way I could survive a direct hit from those flames.

However...

"Take... it... *all*!" I shouted. "Counter Absorption!"

The barrier of light summoned by Nemesis stopped the purgatorial fire and absorbed the damage it did.

"Vengeance is… Mine!"

The attack carrying the doubled weight of the damage from Gardranda's hits *and* fire completely pulverized the demon's head and ended its life…

…or so it seemed.

The loss of its head made Gardranda turn silent. However, its body continued moving around and attacking me as though it was only natural.

"Huh?!" I exclaimed.

Despite losing its head — and brain — Gardranda swung its left arm at me, making it obvious that it simply didn't care for the damage I'd done. And I — fresh out of my means of defense and tired due to having just used my most intense attack yet — was unable to evade the demon's arm.

"…Gh!" It hit me head-on, sent me flying, and had me slipping on the ground for about ten meters after landing.

However — likely because Gardranda had lost its head — the damage it'd done wasn't as great as before, and it didn't kill me.

"First… Heal…" I stumbled to my feet while casting healing magic on myself.

However, the time was up. 180 seconds had passed since I'd been put under the effects of Elixir, and the effects were now gone.

The air around me was still thick with Gardranda's miasma, so I was instantly put under the effects of all three debuffs.

"Damn it…" I couldn't even fight properly in this state, yet the demon was still perfectly fine.

At least he can't see without his hea— my thought was cut short.

"Just how much of a monster *are* you?" I yelled, not expecting an answer. On both of Gardranda's shoulders — right above the mouths — appeared a gory orb — obviously an eye.

It didn't seem like the shoulder-eyes worked yet, but it was clear that they'd soon gain vision and let the demon see and kill me without much trouble.

"Why is this happening?! We clearly destroyed it!" shouted Nemesis in confusion. Our Vengeance is Mine attack had created an explosion with Gardranda's head at its center.

Naturally, the head was gone without a trace, and even its chest had a hole carved out of it in a semicircular shape.

It looks like we even got its heart, and yet...

"...Heart?" I felt something off about my words, that word in particular.

Suddenly, it came back to me.

I controlled my hands — shaking due to Intoxication — went to my menu, and opened my memo window.

There, I found the memo saying, "The demon's heart lies in its stomach. — Cheshire"

"...So that's what that meant," I muttered.

"Master?" Nemesis sounded confused.

Cheshire's words fit the situation perfectly.

The cat had probably known that I'd be facing Gardranda the moment I'd said that I was heading to Gideon. Cheshire had given me those words just in case I got into a situation such as this one.

Gardranda's heart — the core that governed all of its life functions — was in neither the head nor the chest, but the stomach. Thus, Gardranda wouldn't die until said "heart" was crushed.

To this demon, the head was nothing but another means of attacking. Even if I destroyed the remaining "faces" on the shoulders,

Gardranda would continue to move as long as the core in its stomach was intact.

My previous attack should've been aimed at the stomach instead of the head.

But even if I figured that out, I'm all out of power to—

"...Like hell," I muttered.

"Out of power?" Who gives a damn? I thought fiercely.

Rook and Babi were still holding back the Roc Bird. Therefore, I — who had been entrusted with the role of defeating Gardranda — had no business giving up while they continued to struggle.

"Not yet..." I said, gritting my teeth.

I couldn't give up. Even if I couldn't move or if my stats were brought down to the gutter, giving up simply wasn't an option. I had to bear through it all for as long as I could and land another hit on Gardranda's stomach.

It wasn't a matter of whether I "could" or "couldn't." My friends had given me this role. They'd entrusted it to me. Thus, I would to do it even if it meant breaking through my limits.

I would grab hold of the chance of victory.

"If I can't do that much, I can't even dream of getting my revenge against the Superior Killer!" I said fiercely. Despite being on the verge of defeat, I gathered my resolve.

"Master!" Nemesis shouted.

"Nemesis, the odds are against us, but it's not over yet," I said to her. "You don't mind continuing this, right?"

"That goes without saying," she replied. "However, that's not what I want to say."

What?

"What do you make of this?" she asked.

On the corner of the windows I had opened, there was an unfamiliar red window.

[Master's life endangerment: confirmed]

[Master's intent to live: confirmed]

[Embryo Type: Maiden, "Maiden of Vengeance, Nemesis," accumulated XP — green]

[*** execution available]

[Preparing *** activation]

[If you wish to cancel, please do so within the next 20 seconds]

[Do you wish to cancel? Y/N]

What is this? I thought dumbly.

"Nemesis?" I addressed her, hoping for an explanation.

"I know nothing of it, either," she said.

"What *is* this…?"

The window was red, making it seem much like a warning.

From the text, it was obvious that it was related to Nemesis. However, the most important part of it seemed to be corrupted — no, my head couldn't even process it as proper language.

What, exactly, did it mean?

I silently watched as the countdown's timer continued to go down. When it hit 10 seconds, I began to worry, and reached towards the window with the intention to stop it…

"CUUAAAAGGHHHHHH!"

…but before I could complete the motion, Gardranda's shoulder-eyes became able to see, and the demon charged at me while roaring from its shoulder-mouths.

"Why *now*, of all times…?!" I shouted.

The timer on the red window before me was going down as Gardranda got closer to me by the second.

I was left with no choice but to ignore the window and face the demon.

However, with Weakness reducing my stats and Intoxication making it hard for me to move, brandishing Nemesis was about all I could do.

I have to use my defense and healing to create another opportunity to use Vengeance is Mine, and...

[Countdown Complete]

[Acknowledged intent to initiate the emergency evolution process via *** protocol]

[Examining the 172 patterns made available by the accumulated XP and calculating the optimal solution to the current situation]

[Target Embryo: "Maiden of Vengeance, Nemesis." Initiating emergency evolution via ***]

[To reduce load, the interval until the next evolution will be extended]

Right after I saw that message, Nemesis lost her physical integrity and was reduced to floating particles.

"Eh...?" I gasped.

That was the exact same phenomenon that had always happened whenever Nemesis transformed from her human form to her greatsword form. This time, however, she neither returned to her humanoid shape, nor did she become a sword again. Instead, the particles whirled around my surroundings.

"CAAAAAAGGHHHHH!"

As I became unable to process the situation, Gardranda only continued to get closer to me.

[*** complete]

Not giving me a moment to understand anything, the window output displayed a new line.

[Form 2: "The Flag Halberd"]

Nemesis's particles whirled around me and began to gather in my hand.

After having turned to floating grains of light, Nemesis returned to me in a completely different form than before.

"Jump, Master!" It was her voice.

I hastily listened to what she said, kicked my feet off the ground… and left Gardranda a long distance away from me.

"Huh?!" a voice of surprise escaped my lips. Before I realized it, I had jumped a whole twenty meters.

The surprise was aimed at both my unbelievable jumping power and the fact that…

…Nemesis wasn't human.

Nor was she a greatsword.

She was a spear.

Though, since she had an axe popping out from one end of her grip, the word "halberd" was more apt.

The part opposite of the axe blade was leaving a trail of black light, making the whole of her look somewhat like a battle flag.

I looked at the equipment window and saw the name "The Flag Halberd."

"Nemesis... what happened to you?" I couldn't help but ask.

"I'm not sure I'm able to answer that question," she replied. "I happened to become like this before I could even realize it."

I guess she was unconscious while she was turned into particles, I thought.

"However, there is one thing I'm certain of," she continued.

"And that is?" I asked.

"I've evolved into my second form," Nemesis revealed. "The power inside me is greater than ever."

Evolution.

That was the primary feature of every Embryo — the function that gave them powers from infinite patterns.

The red window had also said something about "emergency evolution."

Is that how it normally goes? I asked myself. *It didn't seem that way when Rook's Babi evolved, though...*

"...Well, this ain't the best time to think about this, anyway," I muttered. I had to focus on only one thing right now.

"COOAAAGHHH!"

After having lost sight of me once, Gardranda noticed me again and roared with both of its shoulder-mouths.

"By the way, Nemesis," I said.

"What is it, Master?" Nemesis replied.

"You said that your power is 'greater than ever'... to what extent, though?"

I could almost see her put up an intrepid smile.

"Enough to make it possible for us to defeat that damn demon," she answered.

"Perfect," I smiled. The possibility was there.

The fact that she'd only said that it was "possible" made me remember the first time we'd met. However, that was all I really needed. If the possibility of us winning was there...

...then, for the sake of Rook, Babi, Marie, and the tians in danger of dying...

...we only had to bet on that possibility and give it all we had.

"Let's do this, Gardranda," I said.

Since Gardranda's appearance after we'd annihilated the goblins, the demon had possessed the upper hand, it had even been able to corner us after getting its head smashed. But now, we had a new way of achieving victory.

I know how you work, I thought. *I'll end it soon.*

I brandished The Flag Halberd above my head and roared at the headless demon. "This... is the final round!"

After spinning the halberd above my head, I charged at Gardranda.

Though Weakness was supposed to have lowered my stats, I was running much faster than I could have run while in my normal state. And though Intoxication was supposed to be making my vision turn dim, I felt like I could perceive far more than I ever could.

Gardranda attacked me with a swing from its right arm — the one with fewer fingers on the hand — but I was able to smoothly evade it and sink the halberd's axe into the demon's wrist as I did so.

My attack bit through the skin, sunk into the meat, and cleared its bone. I cleanly cut the demon's hand off, causing crimson blood to burst from the wound.

"We're doing well," I said. It was obvious that her evolution had improved Nemesis's stats and bonuses, but the difference between this and her previous form was just too great.

Yeah, I think we can handle this... Oh, wait... I thought, and remembered something.

I was still under the effects of Poison.

If I'm not careful, my HP might decrease a whole lot, and... Huh?

"...we're doing *way* too well," I muttered.

Though Poison was supposed to be gradually lowering my HP, it was actually going up instead.

The increase in my physical ability, the clarity in my sensations, and the continuous HP regeneration. It was as though the debuffs had been reversed.

"I see, so this is your..." I said slowly.

"Indeed," said Nemesis. "This is my new skill: 'Like a Flag Flying the Reversal.'"

Nemesis opened a window that showed the skill's name and described what it did.

Basically, it reversed the effects of debuffs received from an opponent.

Instead of dealing continuous damage, Poison healed me.

Instead of lowering my stats, Weakness increased them.

Instead of paralyzing my senses, Intoxication made them clearer.

"Like a Flag Flying the Reversal" was a buff skill that reversed all and any afflictions that affected me.

"It's quite ideal for this situation," said Nemesis. "It honestly seems a bit overly-convenient."

"...You're not wrong there," I said. "However..."

According to the message on that red window, out of the possibilities available to her, Nemesis had been equipped with the "optimal solution." However, that message had merely described what happened.

For some reason or another, I was convinced that *I* was the one who'd summoned this result. Regardless, this skill made it possible for me to find a way out of this situation... It was much like the first time Nemesis and I had met.

Thus...

"For now... I'm betting it all on this possibility!" I shouted.

"Then we are of the same mind!" she called back.

Nemesis and I released a battle cry as I made my way through Gardranda's arm attacks and continued chopping away at the demon.

The three debuffs it had given me had originally been simply the worst. However, now they were making me stronger and closing the power gap between me and Gardranda.

I was effectively buffed with HP recovery, perception, and physical strengthening, while the demon had lost its head and practically had its miasma's ability completely negated. Our power balance was now equal — no, in fact, it had been reversed.

"CUUUOAAAGGGHHH!"

Seemingly upset at this turn-around, Gardranda began randomly releasing miasma in every direction.

However, to me and Nemesis, those fumes were nothing but a smokescreen.

"Rraagh!"

As Gardranda continued to release the miasma, I pierced into its stomach. The Flag Halberd dug through the demon's meat and touched the weak spot — the core — within it.

"CEEEAAAAGHH...!" Gardranda roared out in anguish. That was proof enough that the stomach was where I had to aim.

However...

"It's regenerating!" Nemesis shouted.

The wound I had just given it disappeared with a dark purple smoke.

"Hah," chuckled Nemesis. "It appears that only the weak spot is protected by regeneration."

"That means it'd take us forever to defeat it if we relied only on weak attacks," I said.

"It's not like we can keep fighting for particularly long, anyway," she said.

I knew exactly what Nemesis meant by that. Due to the effects of Like a Flag Flying the Reversal, my HP was continuously regenerating. However, my SP only continued to decrease. That was the cost of keeping the skill active.

Compared to my HP, my SP wasn't particularly high. It wouldn't last for long. Thus, I had to figure out what I had to do to win.

Upon considering the regenerating core, the limited amount of time and our abilities...

...there was only one answer.

"I have to stop evading and simply let him hit me," I said.

"Nothing else would work," agreed Nemesis.

I would accumulate the damage the demon did to me and hit it with another Vengeance is Mine. This time, however, it would go straight to the weak spot in the stomach.

"There is something to keep in mind, though," said Nemesis.

"What is it?" I asked.

"This form doesn't allow the use of Counter Absorption and Vengeance is Mine," she answered.

"We're already out of Absorption uses, anyway," I said.

"No," she said, refuting that statement. "My evolution increased its stock to three, so there's one more use left. However, just as

Reversal can only be used by The Flag Halberd, those two can only be used when I'm in my greatsword form."

Basically, to use Vengeance is Mine, I had to change The Flag Halberd into the greatsword. That meant losing the effects of Like a Flag Flying the Reversal.

To be able to land a clean, lethal hit while under the effects of the debuffs... I have to kill its mobility! I thought.

"Nemesis, let's go for the legs!" I shouted.

"Understood!"

I swung The Flag Halberd and repeatedly damaged Gardranda's ankles.

The demon retaliated with swings from its arms, but I simply let them hit me.

Naturally, I got damaged, but the reversed Poison quickly healed me back to full health.

Things were going much like they had when I'd been under the effects of the Elixir. Except — thanks to the continuous regeneration — I could attack, get hit, and heal much more smoothly than before.

"...3250... 3784."

As I listened to Nemesis speak the amount of damage I had gathered, I looked at the edge of my status window and checked on my SP.

53... 52... The amount of time I could keep the Reversal active was already below one minute.

"...4265, Master!" she called.

All right, I'm betting it all on this!

"Hhaaaagh!"

I dashed through the miasma — which was nothing but a smokescreen to me — dove right next to where Gardranda was standing, gathered my resolve, and horizontally swung The Flag Halberd at the demon's legs.

Both of its tendons had been severely damaged by my attacks up to that point, so with that deadly swing, the ax-head split both of them apart.

"CUEEEEEEGHHH!!" Gardranda screamed and fell to its knees, making the ground tremble.

"Do it now, Nemesis!" I shouted.

"Form Shift — Black Blade!" she called. Her command made The Flag Halberd lose its integrity and scatter into particles of light, which soon gathered once more to create the familiar black greatsword.

At that very moment, I was put under the effects of the three debuffs. However, it didn't matter anymore. I only had to land my final attack.

As my legs were shaking due to Intoxication, I dashed towards the demon. Gardranda was still kneeling, and when I raised my sword and readied myself to strike...

...I noticed something.

The dark purple miasma smokescreen was hindering my vision. However, it did nothing to hide the fact that both of the demon's shoulders were emitting a bright red light.

"CHHHHGHAAAAHH!"

Deadly flames.

They weren't limited to the head I'd destroyed — Gardranda could release them from its shoulder-mouths, too.

However, I refused to stop.

"Counter Absorption!" Nemesis spawned the third barrier of light — the one she'd gained from evolving. It stopped the flames and absorbed the damage they were meant to do.

Though it was unnecessary, that made the damage I'd accumulated reach the greatest amount ever.

I couldn't be more certain that I had it in the bag.

"Now, Master!" she called.

Once I passed the flames, the barrier of light dispersed.

Finally, I began to swing my sword at Gardranda's stomach...

"CHHHGHAAAAHH!"

...and was suddenly faced with the demon's left shoulder-mouth, ready to spit more fire.

"What...?!" I gasped.

"Huh...?!" Nemesis exclaimed, as we realized that Gardranda had actually learned something from the battle up till now. The demon had used the lethal flames from both its shoulder-mouths separately...

...just for the sake of getting past Nemesis's Counter Absorption.

All the miasma it had previously released hadn't been meaningless, either — it was a preparatory action meant to render us unable to see that the demon had separated the flame bursts.

"Master!" shouted Nemesis.

I was already swinging the sword.

The blade was slicing through the air for the sole purpose of striking Gardranda's stomach with Vengeance is Mine. Even with the debuffs, I could land the hit in a mere three seconds. However, the demonic flames would reach me faster.

As if on the verge of death, I began seeing the world in slow-motion.

The left shoulder-mouth opened wide and was about to bathe me in flame. "Gyaghghghghghgh!"

But before it could do so, something resembling a bullet broke through the miasmic veil and hit Gardranda's left shoulder.

The familiar object exploded and the demon's left shoulder — when caught in the burst — blew up before it could release its fires.

The moment the heat waves caressed my cheeks...

"Vengeance is Mine!"

...Nemesis and I shouted the name of the skill, landed the hit on Gardranda's stomach, and pulverized its core.

Gardranda's body got split in half and fell to the ground with a loud thud before getting reduced to shining particles and vanishing like any other monster.

With the demon's disappearance, the lingering miasma began to fade, as well.

The dense fog vanished into the sunlight as if it was only natural.

[UBM, "Great Miasmic Hobgoblin, Gardranda," was defeated]

[Selecting MVP]

[Ray Starling was selected as MVP]

[Ray Starling is presented with an MVP special reward — "Miasmaflame Bracers, Gardranda"]

The disappearance of the miasma and the system message made it clear that the battle was over.

I read the message while lying on the ground.

"It appears that... we've won," said Nemesis.

"Not yet!" I rejected that notion. Rook was still up high, fighting the Crimson Roc Bird.

I had to go help him...

"But Master! You still have the debuffs..."

I looked at my status summary and, sure enough, the three status effects were there. Poison was draining my health, while my MP and SP were at a perfect 0. However, the battle wasn't over yet.

I didn't mean just the Roc Bird, either. There was also the attack that had hit Gardranda before I'd destroyed it.

That was obviously the…

"Ray! Are you okay?!"

I turned to the source of the voice and saw Marie — who I hadn't seen since she gave me the Elixir — running up to me.

She was probably approaching me because the miasma was no longer there.

"Your status screen looks horrible," she said. "Give me a second."

Saying that, Marie reached for her inventory and took out a few medicine bottles. Unlike my inventory — which was bag-shaped — or Cheshire's — which was pocket-shaped — her inventory had the appearance of a wristband.

Some of the bottles she took out were HP potions, just like the ones I'd used. There were also some that had the labels "MP" and "SP."

"Here's some first aid for you," said Marie. "It would be great if I could also remove your debuffs, but I don't have anything that could treat Intoxication or Weakness… And I've already used up all the Antidotes I had…"

With those words, Marie looked at the people at the carriages, who had also been affected by the miasma.

Everyone — including the escorts — was down on the ground due to Intoxication and Weakness, but none of them had died of Poison.

From her words, it was safe to assume that Marie was the one who'd helped them.

"I had quite a lot of Antidotes, too," she said. "But there's a total of twelve people there, and treating them all required all I could give.

Walking around and making people drink medicine made me feel like I'd switched my job to Pharmacist," she laughed.

Apparently, Marie had been doing her best to protect the people — the tians at the carriages — from dying.

"Heh..." I smirked a little bit.

"What? Why the smile?" she asked.

Whoa, did I really make it that apparent? I thought.

"Well, it's just that... you're pretty kind, aren't you?" I asked.

"I don't think that kindness has anything to do with that," Marie responded. "I just... wouldn't like it."

"Wouldn't like what?" I asked.

"When killed, we players only get the death penalty, so that's all okay, but tians don't come back to life, right?" she explained. "I simply don't like the idea of them being lost forever."

"...I know what you mean," I said. It was probably akin to the bad taste in my mouth I'd feel whenever tian deaths were involved.

Though she basically just said that player killing is okay, and as someone who was killed recently, I... wait...

"Marie, it just came back to me," I spoke up. "When looking around this place... did you happen to see the Superior Killer?"

"Oh! Yes yes! I almost forgot!" Realizing something, Marie put her hands together. "I saw him! The same man I saw in Noz Forest — the Superior Killer — fired at Gardranda's left shoulder! ...He left right after that, though."

So that thing was actually the Superior Killer's Embryo...

But why had he only shot the left shoulder? If his goal had been to kill Gardranda — a UBM — he'd surely have fired the same way he did when he killed me. With the way he'd gone about it, I could even assume that he'd helped me.

"One more thing about him…" Marie continued. "From the direction he disappeared into, I think it's fair to say that he's heading to Gideon."

"I see…" I said. If that was the case, I could expect to meet him again.

"Oh, are you healed?" asked Marie.

"Yeah," I replied. My stats had replenished while we were talking. Though my HP was still going down due to the Poison, my MP and SP were at max.

Nemesis changed into The Flag Halberd. However, unlike before, the skill Like a Flag Flying the Reversal didn't activate. It was probably because I'd defeated Gardranda — the source of the debuffs.

"Well, whatever," I said. "I can do just fine without the Reversal."

"Indeed," Nemesis agreed. "…By the way, Master."

"What?" I raised an eyebrow.

Nemesis raised the halberd's spearhead upwards…

"How, exactly, are you planning on joining an aerial battle?"

…and asked something that I'd completely failed to consider.

"…"

"…"

"…"

We all turned silent as I realized that there was nothing I could do.

Clearly, I didn't think this through, I thought. There was literally no way for me to assist them.

"Umm… how about hurling some rocks?" asked Marie.

"There's no way I can throw that high…" I said.

They were so high up that even the Roc Bird — with all its great wingspan — looked like a small point in the sky.

And Rook and Babi aren't visible at all... Oh! I thought and noticed something.

"They're coming down," said Marie.

The Roc Bird began to look bigger as it began losing altitude. However, something seemed wrong.

Instead of diving down at high speed — as it had when it'd attacked me — it was descending in a strangely gentle manner.

When the Roc Bird in my sight was large enough for me to make out its details, I finally realized what was up.

Rook — who was supposed to be fighting it — was riding it, instead.

The Roc Bird gently landed on the ground and let Rook dismount.

"Ray! Marie! Are you all right?!" he ran up to us.

"Yeah, we're fine, but... how about you? And where's Babi?" I asked.

"The battle exhausted her, so I had her return to me," Rook answered while showing the crest on his left hand.

"I see." I nodded and shifted my gaze to the bird. "And this is...?"

"Audrey!" he replied with enthusiasm.

"CAAAW!"

Audrey? I thought. *Oh, I think I know what that refers to.*

"So, does the fact that you've given it a name mean that..."

"Yes!" Rook said before I could finish the question. "I Charmed and successfully tamed her!"

Well, it was true that Rook's Male Temptation skill had a low chance of taming female monsters.

...So this thing's a girl, too, huh? I thought.

"Hey, wait..." I said. "I'm quite sure this bird is Gardranda's mount."

"The Charm skill didn't have an effect on her at first, but it suddenly started to work when the miasma cleared," he explained.

That was basically the moment when I'd defeated Gardranda.

So, with the demon's death, Audrey had no longer been a mount, making the difficulty in Charming and taming her drop significantly.

I looked and saw Audrey rubbing her wings on Rook's back...

Is that some sort of courtship behavior? I thought. Whatever the case, she seemed to be quite attached to him.

I also felt that the name "Audrey" fit her far better than "Marilyn" fit the Trihorn. *Though, for all I know, Audrey Hepburn might also be turning in her grave right now.*

"The miasma was too thick for me to see what was going on, so I was pretty worried about you guys," said Rook.

"Well, as you can see, we won," I stated. "It's all thanks to you guys."

"And me, of course!" Nemesis interjected.

"I know that much," I said. "Thank you, Nemesis."

"...Y-You're welcome," she muttered. "I-It's fine as long as you're aware."

Hm? I thought. *What a strange response.*

"So everything's taken care of now," said Marie.

"Seems like it," I agreed.

I still had the Superior Killer on my mind, but if he wasn't here anymore, worrying about him was meaningless. Thus, I left that matter for later.

Using my healing magic and Marie's potions to restore my HP, we waited for the debuffs to go away. Because the cause of them — the miasma — was gone, the debuffs on me and the carriage people disappeared within ten minutes.

Their leader — a merchant named Alejandro — was beside himself with gratitude. When the people got teary-eyed and thanked us with words like "Without you, my whole family would've died," "You're lifesavers," or "We can't thank you enough," Rook and I both became a bit bashful.

They, too, were heading towards Gideon, so we offered join them. Personally, since they'd lost a number of escorts in the previous battle and the ones that had survived were not in the best of shape, I was kinda worried about them.

Alejandro instantly — and with great joy — agreed to have us tag along.

After we'd raised up the overturned carriages, I saw the survivors take something out of the pockets of the deceased. Upon further inspection, I realized that they were box-shaped inventories.

A moment later, the survivors stored the remains of the deceased into those boxes. Each and every dead person got stored into their own inventory.

I asked Marie about it, and she said that it was how traveling tians treated their dead — by putting them into those "coffins."

With monsters terrorizing the roads, tians took the danger of death as a given. If some lost their lives while others survived, the dead would be put into those "coffins" so that they could be sent to their homes and families without decaying. That was why they all carried inventories where they could store themselves.

It made me more aware of how tians — who were always in danger of dying — perceived life and death.

"...Coffins, huh," I whispered. I'd never cared much for any NPCs who'd died in other games, but it was different here.

It gave me a lump in my throat.

Even if I knew this was a game, I didn't think I could ever get used to seeing people die here. That might've been because *Infinite Dendrogram* was simply far too realistic.

Or perhaps...

"I... I'll just leave this for later." I stopped that train of thought and returned to helping prepare the carriages.

Half a day had passed since we'd gotten back on the road again. Marilyn's dragon carriage was gently shaking me when I suddenly began to feel extremely sleepy. It was probably caused by me pushing my limits during the battle against Gardranda.

"Why not take a nap? I'll wake you up if something happens," offered Marie, and I gladly accepted. Logging out would've resulted in me being left behind, so I took a nap while logged in, just like I did at the inn.

Sitting down, I placed my back against the carriage's cargo and closed my eyes.

Not even five minutes had passed before I felt someone sit next to and lie against me.

Wondering who it was, I opened my eyes and saw Nemesis sleeping with her head placed against my upper arm. Apparently, I wasn't the only one who was tired enough for a nap.

"Man, you sure are quick to fall asleep... Nemesis," I said. Then I tried to follow her example and closed my eyes again.

However, probably due to having opened my eyes once, I couldn't fall asleep, and instead began to think about things. Specifically, I remembered the many and various things that had happened since I'd started *Infinite Dendrogram*.

Despite the fact that only three days had passed in real time, they'd felt extremely dense.

The most vivid memory I'd had so far was the battle against Gardranda. In terms of danger, it might've even surpassed my encounter with the Superior Killer.

Not only that, but — probably because Nemesis and I had told each other how we felt about it — the regret I had been haunted with after getting PK'd had faded, and it wasn't nearly as strong as before.

At the current moment, the dominant feeling in me was the vague pain I felt after seeing the bodies of the tians killed by Gardranda and the goblins.

They were nothing but characters inside *Infinite Dendrogram* — a game. And yet, my heart was grieving for them as it would grieve for those who'd died in reality.

A part of me felt that such sentiments were wrong. I didn't know what to say to that idea. Before I realized it, I'd opened my eyes and looked at Nemesis.

She was my Embryo, my partner... and an existence that was limited to the game known as *Infinite Dendrogram*. However, the longer I looked at her sleeping face, the more I felt like I was looking at a living, breathing girl.

She's alive, I thought to myself. *I just can't think otherwise.*

"'AI with intelligence equal to that of a person,' huh?" I murmured. My brother had said that tians — the inhabitants of this world — were recognized as such. "But..." The drowsiness that I'd thought was gone came over me again and slowly overwhelmed my brain.

As my consciousness became more and more vague, I once again began to run my mind through the things I'd thought at the party on my first day.

Liliana and Milianne — tians.

Demi-Dragon Worms and Gardranda — monsters.

And…

"Nemesis…"

…Embryos like her.

They all felt… so *alive* to me.

"Is this really…"

…just a game?

Before I could voice those words, my consciousness was finally lost to the realm of slumber.

Undisclosed Location

["Polaris Bear, Polar Star" was defeated]

[Final level: 83]

[MVP: "God Hunter" Carl Lourlou, level 263 (total level: 763)]

[Embryo: "Indestructible and Everlasting, Nemean Lion"

[MVP special reward: Ancient Legendary item, "Ultimate Suit Series, Polar Star"]

["Ore Dragon King, Dragnium" was defeated]

[Final level: 64]

[MVP: "Giga Professor" Mr. Franklin, level 198 (total level: 698)]

[Embryo: "Magic Beast Factory, Pandemonium"]

[MVP special reward: Ancient Legendary item, "Ore Dragon King's Complete Remains, Dragnium"]

["Navalport Strikefish, Portorpedo" was defeated]

[Final level: 42]

[MVP: "Great Admiral" Koukin Shoyu, level 229 (total level: 729)]

[Embryo: "Great Flame Brewer, Abura-sumashi"]

[MVP special reward: Epic item, "Come-and-Go Torpedo, Portorpedo"]

["Fox-eyed Charcoal, Enryou" was defeated]

[Final level: 56]

[MVP: "The Glaive" Aono Hokugenin, level 335 (total level: 835)]

[Embryo: N/A]

[MVP special reward: Legendary item, "Incinerating Fox-eye, Enryou"]

["Great Miasmic Hobgoblin, Gardranda" was defeated]

[Final level: 24]

[MVP: "Paladin" Ray Starling, level 20 (total level: 20)]

[Embryo: "Maiden of Vengeance, Nemesis"]

[MVP special reward: Legendary item, "Miasmaflame Bracers, Gardranda"]

"Hm?" Surrounded by darkness, still recording and doing its preset activities, *it* suddenly tilted its head.

Considering that it always did nothing but work without as much as saying a single word, that was a rare occurrence.

"How curious," it said. "To defeat an UBM that's above you in level... that is quite rare."

Its confusion was only natural. UBMs were exceptional creatures far beyond the norm. They all had multiple times the power of any boss monster at the same level. Even high-rank Masters had a hard time fighting them.

Thus, it was extremely rare for a UBM to be defeated by someone of a lower level.

Thinking that this defeat had been the result of a large number of low-level players and that the person had only been selected as an MVP by accident, it opened the battle log. However, the reality was far beyond its expectations.

The person — Ray — had defeated the UBM all by himself.

"Hoh?"

That person was equipped with abilities that were optimal for giant-killing. The mid-battle evolution caused by *** had given him a new ability that was simply perfect for the situation. That person was equipped with an indomitable will.

There were many reasons for his victory, but there was one that particularly stood out.

"He realized it right after destroying the first head," it said. "That is far too early."

The creature it acknowledged as an UBM — "Great Miasmic Hobgoblin, Gardranda" — was a gathering of traps.

First, there was the head that flagrantly released miasma and flames.

The player would think that to be its weak point and destroy it, but that would cause it to create two new faces on the shoulders.

All of those visages were traps.

Getting rid of them would not only fail to destroy Gardranda — it would cause it to be strengthened even further.

Even if all its heads were destroyed, it would go through more transformations and become even more powerful than before.

It was completely indestructible as long as the core within its stomach was intact.

Due to that, *it* had expected Gardranda to grow into a particularly powerful UBM. In fact, it wouldn't have been surprised if the demon had reached level 100 — the apex of UBMs and the greatest level available to monsters — and broken through it to join the ranks of the exceptions known as SUBMs — Superior Unique Boss Monsters.

However, in reality, this low-rank Master had been able to miraculously defeat Gardranda and stop its growth process.

"Well, there's no use in overthinking it," it said. "Such cases aren't unheard of. I will keep this in mind in my future work."

It finished analyzing the battle and closed the battle log window.

However, its thoughts suddenly escaped through its mouth as words.

"Whatever the case, this is reason to be joyous. It's all meaningless if only the current Superiors grow stronger. If no new powers emerge, we will never have a hundred Superiors... and never reach Infinity."

After nodding at its own words, it took another glance at Ray's log and continued talking.

"Now... I wonder if he will make good use of Gardranda."

Imagining the future, it formed a faint smile.

"Whether you do or not... just grow stronger while having fun. To you people, this world — from start to finish — is nothing but a game."

And so, control AI No. 4, Jabberwock — the one tasked with handling UBMs — returned to its busy, busy job.

Afterword

Bear: "Time for the afterword!"

Cat: "Thank you very much for buying the first voluume!"

Bear: "As you all can surely tell by the words next to our speech, this afterword will be presented by yours truly — his bearliness Shu Starling…"

Cat: "…and the only *Dendro* cat so far, Control AI no. 13 — Cheshiire! Just so you all know, at first, the author was thinking of acting proper and greeting his dear readers directlyy…"

Bear: "…but changed his mind and figured that *Dendro* is best represented by its mascot duo!"

Bear: "Now, bear with us as we tell you how it got published."

Cat: "Good ideaa. It happened about 11 months ago. The author looked into his inbox on *Shōsetsuka ni Narō* and found a message from a sender whose name was in red… The red name caused him to quake with fear, but he somehow got himself to read the subject line. It said **'Publishing Offer.'** It was actually an offer from Hobby Japan's editor, K!"

Bear: "Naturally, the author was surprised, fur he never expected to get contacted by a publisher whose releases he'd read in his school years."

Cat: "The author replied with a cautiously optimistic message, soon after which he had to go to a preparatory meeting…"

Bear: "…where he received an explanation and quickly sealed the publication deal with a contract."

Cat: "However, there was a problem after that… Well, 'problem' might not be the right word."

Bear: "Basically, Editor K raised his expectations and standards so high that the author's heart couldn't bear it."

Cat:

"'The illustrations will be done by Taiki,' said the editor.

'The one who does *those* designs? I'm so happy!' replied the author.

'A month before it releases, we're putting *Dendro* leaflets in *HJ Bunko*,' said the editor.

'Wow! That's so much advertising!' replied the author.

'It's also getting a dedicated site and a preview video,' said the editor.

'Y-You're going *that* far?!' replied the author.

'I'll also get fifty artists to draw something in support of *Dendro*,' said the editor, and at this point, the author could only shake uncontrollably."

Bear: "All of this is completely true."

Cat: "The author will be at ease if the work sells well enough to meet Editor K's expectations. I earnestly hope that this afterword is read by many people, and that means the book is selliing."

Bear: "Last, but not least, put your paws together for the author's words of gratitude!"

Hello there.

I would like to give my thanks to everyone who bought *Infinite Dendrogram* Volume 1, everyone who supported my work on *Shōsetsuka ni Narō*, my sister — who checked on every part before

I uploaded it — and, of course, Hobby Japan and their editor, K, for picking my work for publication.

I will keep on writing *Infinite Dendrogram* and do my best to live up to your expectations, so I would be thankful if you continued to support me.

Regards, Sakon Kaidou.

Cat: "Now that that's over, let us meet again in volume twoo!"

Bear: "This afterword was brought to you by Brother Bear…"

Cat: "…and Cheshiire!"

Bear: "The second volume is planned to be released in the coming months, so grin and bear it until then!"

J-Novel Club Lineup

Ebook Releases Series List

Amagi Brilliant Park
An Archdemon's Dilemma: How to Love Your Elf Bride
Ao Oni
Arifureta Zero
Arifureta: From Commonplace to World's Strongest
Bluesteel Blasphemer
Brave Chronicle: The Ruinmaker
Clockwork Planet
Demon King Daimaou
Der Werwolf: The Annals of Veight
ECHO
From Truant to Anime Screenwriter: My Path to "Anohana" and "The Anthem of the Heart"
Gear Drive
Grimgar of Fantasy and Ash
How a Realist Hero Rebuilt the Kingdom
How NOT to Summon a Demon Lord
I Saved Too Many Girls and Caused the Apocalypse
If It's for My Daughter, I'd Even Defeat a Demon Lord
In Another World With My Smartphone
Infinite Dendrogram
Infinite Stratos
Invaders of the Rokujouma!?
JK Haru is a Sex Worker in Another World
Kokoro Connect
Last and First Idol
Lazy Dungeon Master
Me, a Genius? I Was Reborn into Another World and I Think They've Got the Wrong Idea!
Mixed Bathing in Another Dimension
My Big Sister Lives in a Fantasy World
My Little Sister Can Read Kanji
My Next Life as a Villainess: All Routes Lead to Doom!
Occultic;Nine
Outbreak Company
Paying to Win in a VRMMO
Seirei Gensouki: Spirit Chronicles
Sorcerous Stabber Orphen: The Wayward Journey
The Faraway Paladin
The Magic in this Other World is Too Far Behind!
The Master of Ragnarok & Blesser of Einherjar
The Unwanted Undead Adventurer
Walking My Second Path in Life
Yume Nikki: I Am Not in Your Dream